SECRETS EXPOSED

by

Madeleine Passmore

Grosvenor House
Publishing Limited

This book is published by
Grosvenor House Publishing Ltd
Link House
140 The Broadway, Tolworth, Surrey, KT6 7HT.
www.grosvenorhousepublishing.co.uk

This book is a work of fiction. Any resemblance to
people or events, past or present, is purely coincidental.

A CIP record for this book
is available from the British Library

ISBN 978-1-80381-318-9
eBook ISBN 978-1-80381-319-6

FAMILY TREES

Elizabeth's family tree

~~MILLICENT~~ = ARTHUR ------------ EDITH m DAVID -------------- MICHAEL m LOUISA

ROBERTA   **ELIZABETH** m WILLIAM   CHRISTINE JESSICA STEPHEN

DUNCAN   CHLOE   FABIAN

Margaret's family tree

~~CONSTANCE~~ m CHARLES m SUSAN m ~~ARNOLD~~ m ~~ANNIE~~

~~HUGH~~ m **MARGARET** m PETER   ANGELA m VINCE   RONALD m COLETTE

XAVIER MARCUS FAYE   OLIVIA (daughter) TIMOTHY   LUKE

Peter's family tree

(SISTER)----STELLA m RUFUS   ~~VERNON~~ m ~~FRANCES~~ m ~~SIDNEY~~

MIRANDA PETER m LAVENDER   VERONICA m AARON m ESME   RUTH m ERIC

(?)   MARGARET m **PETER**   PHOEBE

MARCUS   FAYE

Hugh's family tree

AGATHA m JULIUS

HUGH m MARGARET SEBASTIAN m ROZINA   SONIA m WOLFE

XAVIER

GUINEVERE (3 daughters) ATHENA

BETTINA   TOBIAS   RALPH

PROLOGUE

His hand felt along the wall, in its habitual action, to turn on the light. He shut the door automatically and then was startled to see someone sitting at his desk.

"You gave me a fright," he said, smiling. "What are you doing here, sitting in the dark?"

"You might well ask," came the angry reply. "Your dirty little secret is out! How could you? How could you lie to Mother, to us all?" The accuser slumped down in the chair. His father went over to him and put his hand on his shoulder. It was shaken off and the accuser stood up, confronting his father.

"I ask again, how could you? All these years..." He trailed off, unable to speak anymore. His father was shocked; he had no idea what his son meant.

"What is this all about? What has happened?" he asked.

"She's gone," said his son, "she's gone, she's left me and it's all your fault." He pointed his finger at his father's chest. They were the same height, so looked directly into each other's eyes. His father could see the pain in his son's eyes.

"Who has left?" He thought quickly. "You mean Jessie has left?" He knew they were in love with each other.

His son nodded.

"And it's all your fault."

"Sit down and tell me what has happened." He sat in the vacated chair and indicated another chair to the side of his desk. His son remained standing.

"No, I don't want to sit down." His son stared down at him accusingly.

"Start at the beginning," he said. "Please," he added. "Where has Jessie gone?" He had left his daughter asleep that morning when he went to work. What on earth could have happened during the day? He had not returned home until now. His wife had met him at the office with fresh clothes. He changed, and they had gone straight out to dinner with some friends. They had just arrived home.

"I don't know where to start," said his son forlornly, walking around the room. "I suppose it started about five months ago, when Jessie got her passport, so she could visit Chrissie in America." His father nodded. Jessie was going to see her sister in America in the summer. He had arranged a new passport for her. "Someone at university said something about the passport and how when they sent for theirs, the birth certificate went astray for ages. This set us thinking; we had never seen our birth certificates. You kept them hidden in your safe." He nodded to a door in the wall behind the desk. "Jessie was suddenly very curious. So she arranged her trip to London; she arranged to have a copy. They said they would send her one." He paused. "It came this morning!"

He looked intently at his father, who was gazing at the high ornate ceiling. He watched his father's hand go to his forehead. He groaned and slumped into his chair, just as son had done earlier.

"Yes," his son accused, shouting. "Now we know. Your lies are exposed. How could you? Deceiving us into believing that you and Mother had adopted Jessie. How could you deceive Mother like this?" He stopped shouting for a moment. "Aren't you going to say anything? How do I know I am your son? You could have adopted me. At least we know you told the truth about Chrissie, as she has found her family. But what about us?" He paused again.

His father got up and opened the safe behind him. He got out his son's birth certificate and showed it to him. His son looked down and saw his name, Stephen Harrison, and looked across at his parents' names, Michael and Louisa Harrison. He looked up at his father.

"So, I am your son," he said quietly but then shouted again. "But what about Jessie? Your name was on her certificate as her father." His father nodded and stared at him helplessly.

"So?" demanded Stephen.

His father just shrugged. What could he say? The secret was not his alone. He could not expose it without hurting so many people.

CHAPTER 1

She woke up on what was supposed to be the best day of her life. She stared at her three-quarter-length cream lace wedding dress hanging on the wardrobe. There was a knock on the door, and it opened immediately. Elizabeth came in, carrying the traditional bottle of champagne and two champagne flutes.

"Happy wedding day, Maggie," she said as she popped the cork. They watched it fly across the room, and Elizabeth poured some into the glasses.

Margaret took the offered crystal glass, sipped the contents then placed it on the nearby table.

"This is becoming a habit," she said.

"Let's make this the last time," said Elizabeth. "I don't want to marry anyone except Bill."

Margaret laughed. She looked so mournful.

"Don't worry," she replied. "No one else will have you."

"Well," started Elizabeth indignantly, and then she threw a pillow at Margaret. Margaret grabbed another pillow and fought back. They were in the middle of a pitch battle when Margaret's father, Charles, appeared.

"Really, you two are acting as if you are six again, not nearly 26." He laughed at their indignant expressions. He was so relieved to see Margaret happy again. He kissed both girls and left them to their fight. They resumed but not with the same intensity and soon stopped.

Elizabeth drained her glass and filled it up again.

"To you and Peter. I hope you will be as happy as me and Bill."

Elizabeth raised her glass to Margaret and took a sip. Margaret's eyes filled with tears.

"I hope so, too."

1

Elizabeth hugged Margaret and got off the king-size bed.

"I'm going to get ready now. See you later." She waved as she left the room.

Margaret reflected on the differences between her first wedding to Lord Hugh and her wedding now to Peter. Her first wedding had been a flurry of activity at her mother's ancestral home, Cranford Manor. There had been so many people and so much to do. Today was quieter. She enjoyed the tranquility of her parents' home, The Firs. She laid back in her bath and shut her eyes. The only thing she wanted to be the same was to have her mother there. She had needed Peter's support last year when the first anniversaries of the deaths of her first husband and her mother came round. The second anniversary, earlier this year, had not been any easier.

She heard a knock on her bedroom door. It opened.

"Lady Margaret?"

"Yes, Emma," replied Margaret, coming from the bathroom wrapped in a towel; another she used to rub her auburn hair dry.

"Doris Burrows is here."

"Thank you, Emma."

Margaret dried herself off and put on her underwear and dressing gown. She went downstairs.

The drawing room had been turned into a mini beauty parlour. Doris had set up her equipment and was already doing Elizabeth's hair. Emma came in with the tea tray and poured everyone a cup. Lady Agatha was waiting to have her hair done; Margaret sat on the sofa beside her.

"As I said last night, I appreciate you coming. I know it must be hard for you." Lady Agatha found she couldn't answer. She and Hugh's father Julius had discussed Margaret and Peter. When Margaret returned from Devon in the spring last year, they could see that she and Peter had sorted out their differences. It had been lovely to see Margaret smiling again instead of moping around the house. They liked Peter and knew he would be discreet regarding Hugh. Hugh had liked Peter and they trusted him. They were pleased that Peter loved Xavier, Hugh's son. They loved Margaret

2

and would always be grateful to her for returning Hugh to them. They had fallen out over his way of life. They both admitted that they had been worried about Hugh's future. Neither had openly spoke of Hugh's sexuality but finally admitted that Hugh had his own needs. Margaret gave him respectability and she gave them Xavier.

"Where's Irene?" asked Elizabeth. "I thought that she was going to help." Doris Burrows had opened her own salon, but she had closed it that morning to be available for Margaret and her old friend Elizabeth. She hoped to use some pictures of the wedding to advertise her business. She had recently employed Irene Grayson to help her.

"She is still upset after the attack. The bruises maybe fading, but the mental scars are taking longer." Elizabeth nodded understandingly. Irene had been violently assaulted on her way home from a party at Taw Lodge Hotel a couple of weeks previously.

"Have they arrested anyone yet?"

"No, but Irene says she would know him if they did arrest him."

Doris finished Elizabeth's hair, and as Elizabeth got up, she asked how Doris was getting to the wedding. Doris replied that her fiancé was picking her up, then she indicated to Margaret it was her turn.

At last everyone was ready to leave for Bishop's Tawton Church. The convoy of cars left The Firs and drove the six miles to the church. As they entered the church, everyone turned to watch the wedding party come down the aisle. First, Charles and Margaret, followed by Elizabeth, matron of honour, and Xavier, page boy.

Peter was waiting at the altar for her. He heard the music start up when she arrived. He let out a breath he did not realise that he had been holding while waiting for Margaret to arrive. He slowly turned to greet Margaret as she arrived, and they shyly smiled at each other. The service was not long. The wedding breakfast was at Taw Lodge Hotel. Though it was not a big wedding, the small church was packed with friends and family.

They seemed to be photographed forever outside the picturesque church. At last they could stop smiling and then laughed at each other as they both felt their sore mouths. Before leaving they went over to Margaret's mother Constance's grave and stood quietly for a few minutes, then Margaret took a rose from her bouquet and put it on her mother's grave. They walked down the path to the waiting car. They were covered in confetti when they climbed into the wedding car to take them to the hotel.

They were directed to the grounds before going into the hotel to have some more of the endless photographs. The photographer wanted to take them before the afternoon light faded. They walked down the path to the gazebo. Though the day had been dry, the lawns were still wet from the rain of the previous days. Margaret obediently smiled some more and looked at the dying sun shining its last embers of light on the underside of the gritty clouds, turning them salmon pink. She shivered. Peter took her short white fur cape from Elizabeth and put it around her shoulders.

"I think we should go in now," he said.

They were each handed a glass of champagne as they entered the ballroom. Peter gratefully drank a big gulp, but Margaret only had a sip. They toasted each other then put the glasses down to get ready to greet their guests. Peter first, then Margaret next to Charles, then Elizabeth's parents, Edith and David, and Elizabeth and Xavier.

Though they had not invited a large number of guests, the line seemed never ending. Xavier soon got fed up and ran off to play with Elizabeth's son, Duncan.

The food was served and speeches made. Charles hinted at more grandchildren in his speech, and Margaret and Elizabeth deliberately did not look at each other. He stopped as one of the guests, Elizabeth's aunt Louisa, was choking. She quickly left the room, her husband Michael following her. Peter had to cut his speech short as he was overcome with emotion. This totally enthralled their guests. David had been thrilled when Peter asked him to be best man. It was unconventional, they both agreed, but Peter really wanted David involved in the ceremony. After he had been evacuated from London, David and Edith had become his parents.

After the wedding breakfast, some guests drifted off home, but some stayed, making the most of the pleasant surroundings and chatting to friends and family. Elizabeth took Duncan and Chloe, who had just turned one, home. She would be returning without the children.

Margaret and Peter wandered around speaking to their guests. As they walked through the ballroom, they saw William talking to the new chef. William introduced them.

"Peter, Maggie, this is Benjamin Lyon."

"I hope you enjoyed the meal."

"Yes, we did, very much. You surpassed our expectations. When Bill showed us the menu, it wasn't quite what we expected," said Peter.

"My early years were spent in India, with all their different flavours. When I returned to England, all the food seemed tasteless. When I joined up in '44, I chose a regiment that was due to go to India, but I posted further east, so this gave me more new ideas. I like to experiment."

"Keep experimenting," replied Peter. "You could easily get a job in London. You will lose him soon, Bill."

"I have just come from London, Sir. I was at the Dorchester but wanted to try something different. I...we...my sister and I wanted to get away from the grime of London."

"You have certainly picked the right part of the country. It is well away from London here." They were interrupted by Elizabeth and Edith returning. Elizabeth went with Margaret to help her change. They carefully stowed her bridal dress and toiletries in Peter's car. Margaret still looked stunning in her fitted knee-length cream travelling dress. The front was plain, but the back had a dozen buttons and a bow for decoration. Elizabeth had changed as well from her calf-length pale green dress, with a full skirt, to a gold halter neck frock but still wore her diamond necklace, given to her by Constance.

Charles came up to them with his neighbour, Susan, and her daughter, Angela. They greeted each other. Angela looked enviously at Elizabeth's jewellery. Elizabeth glared back at her, then Angela shrugged and turned away. Elizabeth saw William looking at her adoringly. She returned his smile and absently fingered the jewellery she was wearing.

Constance had given her a 14-carat white gold and blue topaz and diamond necklace, earrings, bracelet and ring. She had been shocked when Edith brought out the velvet-covered boxes last year. Edith had sat her down and explained that Constance had wanted her to have the set as a thank you for looking after Margaret. Elizabeth was puzzled, then a previous conversation came to mind. Elizabeth put her hand to her mouth.

"No," she said.

"Yes," said Edith. "Constance knew and was very grateful to you that there wasn't a scandal."

"But..." Elizabeth did not know what to say. She thought they had been so clever.

"She only mentioned it a couple of years ago. She had always had her suspicions but could not say anything. But she said she wanted to know before she passed away. I couldn't give her much information, but she was so grateful to you. She wanted to give you a more valuable set, but we decided that would arouse too much curiosity. We felt this set would be ideal."

"What about Uncle Charles? Won't he wonder where they've gone? And Maggie?"

Edith shook her head.

"Constance had spoken to him – about the jewels, not about the... you know. He was happy for you to have them."

Elizabeth had not worn them before now, but it felt right to wear them for Margaret's wedding.

The guests that were left were getting into the party spirit in the bar. Everyone had congregated there, and they were interrupted by William's niece having a hiccupping fit. They were very loud, so she was taken outside. Margaret looked at Peter, and they both started laughing. Peter was to blame for this. Margaret was thankful to him for not letting their 'hiccup' ruin their relationship.

Peter had arranged to stay at Royston House, Hugh's estate, in Sussex for his birthday last year. Margaret and Peter had only seen each other briefly at the anniversaries of Hugh's and Constance's deaths; neither felt it right to advertise their relationship at that time. Peter had worked hard to get his building plans moving and they were ahead of schedule. His new garage was nearly ready, so he felt he could take a few days off. He arrived late on the Wednesday. He and Margaret planned to spend a couple of days in London. They left Royston House on the Saturday morning, arriving just in time for a late lunch at Brunswick House, Hugh's family house in London. They went to a show Saturday night and continued exploring London together, returning to Royston House on the Tuesday. On the Sunday evening, Hugh's brother-in-law Wolfe joined them, staying at Brunswick House. Margaret had Hugh's old room and Wolfe had the room next to that. Margaret took the precaution of locking the door. She had seen the way he looked at her when Hugh first introduced them, and with Peter on the floor below, she wasn't taking any chances. Wolfe was staying in London to finalise the details of his exhibition, which was opening on Tuesday. He gave them tickets for the preview on the Monday evening.

While in London, they were sitting in Regent's Park when Peter decided it was time to address what had happened at The Firs, which had nearly destroyed their relationship. He felt Margaret would not create a scene in public view.

He took Margaret's hand and looked at it.

"You hold my happiness in the palm of your hand." He felt Margaret stiffen beside him. He continued. "I could not bear it if you left me again." He gently put both hands around Margaret's hand so that she could not run away. "We have a problem that needs resolving, because I don't want it left to fester and drive us apart. It was a total misunderstanding between us. Based on our previous experience, we need to address the situation, but the time is not right yet. Until the time is right, we need to find a way we can cope without feeling upset or embarrassed. Do you agree?"

He finally glanced up at Margaret, and she nodded imperceptibly. Not able to speak.

"We need to have a name to refer to the incident, one that we are comfortable with and that will help to relieve the tension.

We can't keep saying 'The Situation'. We need something mundane to help… trivialise… that's the wrong word, the situation. But you understand what I am trying to say."

Margaret nodded again and swallowed. She tried to speak but couldn't. A ball came in their direction, so Peter picked it up and threw it back to the boy who came over for it.

"Thanks, Mister," he said, running off.

Margaret started laughing at the surrealness of the situation. She couldn't stop, and Peter joined her. Finally, Margaret calmed down but was left with hiccups.

"That is what we will call the situation. A hiccup. Please continue to laugh." Peter put his arm around her and began to kiss her neck.

"Stop… (hic)… please… (hic)… stop."

"I'm trying to get rid of your hiccups."

"You won't do it like that!"

"Maybe not, but I like trying. Anyway, it is a prelude to getting rid of our big hiccup." Margaret was thinking. She agreed they needed to do something. Peter continued to kiss her.

"You can stop now. My hiccups have gone," she told him.

"Yes, and so will our big hiccup. I promise you I will do everything to make it so enjoyable for you that afterwards you will want to keep hiccupping." Margaret shivered with excitement. She did not understand what he said, but she could sense the anticipation.

On the Monday evening they went with Wolfe to his exhibition, just off Kings Road. They were offered a drink and Wolfe left them to look around. They found his paintings.

"He really is very good," said Peter, impressed. He had only seen a couple of his paintings before, but here they looked stunning. He mainly did portraits and had painted a collection of his daughters and Hugh's sister, Sonia. They were displayed all along one wall, his family in the centre.

"Yes, he is," said a silky voice. They turned to see who was speaking. "Hello, I'm Fleur Fitzgerald." She bent forward to air kiss them both. "You must be Margaret and Peter. I have heard so much about you."

"We saw your paintings earlier. They are very... modern," said Peter.

"Thank you. Wolfe is good, isn't he? He has even made Sonia look beautiful. Of course, his best picture is not on display, his nude painting of me!" She swiftly turned and went to greet more people, leaving Peter and Margaret open-mouthed. They watched her swaggering around the room. They left shortly afterwards, returning to Brunswick House.

Next morning, they were greeted by the butler, Withers, who informed them there was a guest for breakfast. They went into the dining room to find Wolfe and Fleur having breakfast.

"Hello, again," said Fleur.

"Good morning," they replied, slightly stunned.

Breakfast was mainly eaten in silence, only broken by Fleur's voice. Peter and Margaret finished as soon as they could, loaded the car and left.

"We were meant to believe that Fleur stayed the night, but I happened to hear her arrive, as I was awake. She demanded to see Wolfe and stay for breakfast."

Margaret was relieved. She didn't like Sonia much but did not want Wolfe to be unfaithful even though she knew he had a roving eye.

Peter said a reluctant goodbye on the Wednesday but was determined to pick up the pace with the new house. His garage was nearly finished, so he would have time to dedicate to the house.

The wedding party was in full swing. Peter could suddenly wait no longer; he wanted Margaret alone. He put down his glass.

"It's time to leave, Maggie." Margaret looked at him and felt a thrill run down her back. They went around to everyone saying goodbye. It seemed to take forever. They finally got to the car.

"Where are you staying tonight?" someone asked.

"Somewhere you can't find them!" someone else shouted back.

"Do you know where you are going, Maggie?" asked Elizabeth.

Margaret shook her head. She was unable to speak, tense with anticipation about the night ahead.

"Peter?" continued Elizabeth.

"Not too far," he replied. "But far enough." And with that, he accelerated up the drive. He saw everyone watching as he turned left and drove off through the village.

CHAPTER 2

Margaret woke up, momentarily wondering where she was. She turned to see her husband smiling at her. Her heart leapt at how handsome he looked, with his blond tousled hair and smouldering blue eyes.

"Hello, you look so beautiful," he said. He had dreamt for a long time of this moment, being there when she awoke. "How did you sleep?"

"Wonderfully. I did not know... I was very tired."

Peter laughed. He kissed her and threw back the bedcovers.

"I will be the maid, as I told the staff not to come in until later. I will bring you breakfast in bed." He got his dressing gown and wrapped it around him.

"No, just tea will be fine," replied Margaret, her heart beating at the ease of the way he covered his nakedness. She blushed as she realised she was naked too. She quickly pulled the covers up to her chin. Peter laughed again and left the room.

Margaret sat up, still holding the covers. She looked round for her silk nightdress and spotted it in the middle of the floor. She quickly got out of bed and put it on. She made her way to the ensuite bathroom. As she returned to the bed, she saw something on the floor, sticking out from under the bed. She bent down and picked it up. She carefully looked at it and recalled the previous night. While Peter was in the bathroom, she was sitting up in bed looking around the room when she spied something on Peter's bedside table. She leant over to get it. She studied it and gave a gasp as she realised what it was. She recalled a conversation that she and her sisters-in-law Sonia and Rozina had had a few months ago. She had not understood at the time, but now she did.

Lady Agatha had invited Sonia and Rozina over for tea. Sonia and Rozina were discussing their pregnancies. Rozina wanted another baby. Since Sebastian had been nominated to stand at the next election for the Conservatives and they had moved to the bigger house in Horsham, Rozina had become more approachable. She was enjoying being a politician's wife. She had been invited to join several committees and become a governor to the school. When Lady Agatha had left room, Rozina turned to Sonia, smiling, and said. "I hope to catch you up soon, but Sebastian is reluctant."

Sonia smiled back.

"We just can't help it."

"You must use something to stop the babies. Seb insists on it. He doesn't want lots of babies." Rozina held up her hands.

"I know. We do, most of the time. But sometimes the... mood just takes over and it's too late."

Margaret was unsure exactly what they were saying, but now all became clear.

Peter returned with the tray of tea. He put it down on the side table and started pouring. As he brought Margaret her tea, he saw what she was holding.

"This stops us having babies," Margaret said, "but I want to have your baby." She looked up at him. He sat on the bed next to her.

"I want you to have my baby, too," he replied. "But not just yet. I want us to enjoy our honeymoon without worrying about your health. You are looking forward to our honeymoon, aren't you?"

"Oh, yes, very much. I have never been skiing before." Peter planned to take Margaret to the French Alps in February.

"I thought we would wait until we returned before having a baby." Margaret nodded in agreement. She turned the packet over in her hands.

"I don't know what to do," she said quietly, almost to herself. Peter gently took it from her. He opened the packet and gave the condom to Margaret. Margaret looked at it, still puzzled.

"Where does it go?"

Peter looked at her, his dressing gown open.

"Where do you think, love?" he whispered. Margaret glanced at him.

"Oh," she said. "There?" She pointed.

"Yes." He could hardly speak. Margaret started to put it on. Peter could bear it no longer. As gently as he could, he pushed her back onto the bed. Margaret pulled him to her.

An hour later, Peter came out of the bathroom, buttoning his shirt. He smiled at Margaret but was immediately concerned as tears were running down her cheeks. He rushed over to her.

"I'm sorry, Maggie. I didn't mean to hurt you."

Margaret shook her head.

"You didn't." Her heart was pounding. He looked so handsome in his crisp white shirt.

"Why are you crying?"

She shook her head again.

"Please tell me. Please don't keep me wondering."

Margaret sighed.

"We have been married less than 24 hours and we have made love twice." She blushed. Peter smiled and hugged her. "It was months before Hugh made love to me. I don't think he loved me at all."

Peter stiffened beside her, confused.

"But... I saw the sheet from your bed on your wedding night."

Now it was Margaret's turn to be confused. Then she smiled.

"Oh, no, that was all pretence. It seemed so important at the time because of what I had heard." She saw Peter's puzzled expression. "Hugh made a small cut on his finger and smeared the sheet." Peter shook his head.

"I don't believe it."

Margaret pushed him, and he stood up. She threw back the bedclothes to reveal a small blood stain on their sheet.

"I'm so sorry," he said again. "I should have been more careful."

"No, it's not what you think. My leg, look at my leg." She held out her leg. He saw the cut was bleeding slightly. A few days previous she had fallen over. They had been walking over the fields and she tripped as she climbed over a stile. It had been funny, and Xavier could not stop laughing as Mummy had her feet in the air. She had torn her slacks and cut her leg.

Peter was relieved he had not hurt her. He remembered the agony he went through thinking of Margaret and Hugh together. He had been in the kitchen, chatting to the maids to take his mind off them, when the sheet came in. He could not stand everyone poring over it, so he left. Now he realised he had been upset over nothing. He paused, then said, with effort,

"Hugh did love you, Maggie. He just showed it differently. Please don't think he didn't." He knew Hugh loved Margaret, and he hated to see Margaret upset. He thought how strange it sounded that he was going into battle on Hugh's behalf but wanted to reassure Margaret. Then he thought back to a conversation he had had at Hugh's graveside earlier this year. He had taken Margaret and Xavier to the graveyard on the second anniversary of Hugh's death. While he stood at the graveside alone – Margaret and Xavier had gone into the church – a man came alongside him.

"I hope you and Margaret will be very happy. You will make her much happier than Hugh did."

Peter turned to look at the older man, Howard.

"Thank you, I think," he said. "And thank you for your discretion."

"You don't have to worry about me. I am leaving for Italy next week, as we planned." He saw Peter looking puzzled. Howard sighed. "Hugh wanted to be with me. He did not want to hurt Margaret more than necessary. After Xavier was born, he started to sort his affairs out. I purchased a house in Italy for us both. Hugh was going to start staying there for short periods, gradually getting longer and eventually moving there permanently, then he would divorce Margaret. We both hoped that she would turn to you, as we could see how you felt about each other." Peter was startled. "Please don't be distressed or offended. We really did not want to upset anyone, but we could be apart no longer. Then fate intervened, and neither of us had him." They stood silently for a few minutes until they heard Margaret and Xavier returning. The pale, aged Howard noiselessly slipped away.

Peter stopped daydreaming and looked down at Margaret, who smiled up at him.

"Thank you."

"Right. Now, do you want breakfast in bed?"

"No, I will eat downstairs."

Peter picked up the tea tray and left the room. Margaret put on her matching silk negligee and recalled how Peter had taken it off the night before. She looked at her wedding suit hanging in the dressing room, with its pale coffee walls and soft mint green décor, as she walked through to the ensuite decorated in forest green with chrome accessories. She thought back to the previous evening when they arrived. They went straight up to the bedroom. Peter undid her buttons on the back of the suit. He slipped his hands inside and kissed her neck. She reluctantly pushed him away, saying she had to get changed, grabbed her case and rushed off to the bathroom. She was shaking with emotion; she had not felt like this before. Finally she changed into her ivory nightdress and matching negligee. When she returned to the bedroom, Peter was in bed but sprung out when she came into the room. She took off her negligee and draped it over the armchair. Peter had slowly slipped her thin nightdress straps over her shoulders and carried her to the bed. Margaret trembled at the memory; she was so happy. She quickly left their room and walked along the landing to the sweeping stairs, eager to be with Peter again.

Peter had laid breakfast in their new kitchen. He had designed an area in the kitchen to have informal meals. He had loved eating in Edith's kitchen; it felt homely. He had tried to do the same to their new house.

"Are you happy eating in the kitchen?" he asked, suddenly concerned that Margaret would want breakfast in the dining room.

"Oh, yes," she reassured him. "This is lovely." She also remembered the times she had eaten in Edith's kitchen during the war and thought it was a great idea to have a special eating area, somewhere informal to eat with Xavier, and more children.

She drank her tea and sighed. She smiled at Peter.

"Thank you for bringing me here. This is so much better than going to a hotel, with other people around."

Peter was relieved. He had been worried about bringing Margaret back to their house rather than going to a hotel. He had designed it for her. When they had parted after their 'hiccup', he was ready to throw his plans in the bin. He was distraught and did not know what to do. It was the darkest day of his life, closely followed by the day his mother had been killed. Elizabeth had been there for him then, too. She pulled him out of his dejected mood and persuaded him to keep going with his plans, and Margaret would be back. He had depended on her and spent hours with her until Margaret was ready to resume their relationship.

He had insisted on carrying Margaret over the threshold.

Suddenly, the door of the kitchen, leading to the scullery and beyond to the garage and outside, opened.

Peter and Margaret burst out laughing. In the doorway stood a startled Barbara Bancroft, holding an iron about her head. She slowly lowered her arm.

"I thought you were burglars. I wasn't expecting to see anyone. You didn't tell me you would be here," she said accusingly.

"No," said Peter, "it was a secret. Sorry to have startled you."

Barbara smiled at them.

"It was a lovely wedding yesterday." They had made a beautiful couple, she thought. "Well, I better get started on lunch. Look at the mess you've made of my kitchen."

"I'm going to have a bath," announced Margaret.

"Do you need help?" asked Peter innocently.

Margaret blushed. Peter and Barbara laughed. Margaret pretended to flounce out of the room. Peter had employed Barbara as a cook. He knew that Margaret was undomesticated, but he didn't care. It wasn't her fault. During the war, she had been sent to stay with Elizabeth's parents, David and Edith. She helped with some chores, but when the war was over, she stayed at Cranley Manor, Cheshire, and Cranley House, London, with their multitude of staff. When Margaret's parents bought The Firs, there was a staff of only two or three people, and at Royston House there were about six or seven. Peter knew that Margaret wanted to run the house; he was happy to help but would be working in his garage. The solution was to employ a cook, Barbara Bancroft, and a daily maid, Sally Cope, to help her.

They also had Ivy, Xavier's nanny. Peter hoped she would help with their children as well.

* * * * * * * *

It was a lovely early summer day as all their family and friends gathered around the font of the small church. Peter looked so proud holding his son. Margaret could not believe how lucky she was. Why had it taken her so long to see?

Peter slowly gave his precious bundle to the vicar. The vicar carried out the service, and Peter only slightly winced as the vicar named his son.

They had had a big discussion about names. Peter wanted to name his son Charles after Margaret's father, but Margaret did not want this. When she went to school in Bishop's Tawton with Elizabeth, there was a boy in class called Charles and everyone referred to him as 'a right old Charlie'. Margaret suggested her father's second name. Peter was interested; he suddenly realised he didn't know his father-in-law's middle name. They agreed their son would be called Marcus. Margaret wanted to name him after Peter's father as well, but he refused point blank. Margaret persisted; she wanted to make sure her son felt part of a family. Xavier had his family name, and she wanted Marcus to have family names. At last Peter told her what she wanted to know, and she insisted on calling their son Marcus Samuel.

After the service, Margaret and Peter took their son to Constance's grave.

"I don't know where my mother was buried," Peter suddenly announced. Margaret was startled. She didn't know what to say. She recalled how her mother had told Edith about Peter's mother's funeral. Only her and Charles had turned up. Constance had paid for the funeral. Margaret had not realised that no one had told Peter. She wondered if her mother had put the information in his tin box. Her mother had said that Peter was clutching the tin box when they found him half buried under the debris. He would not let it go until he got to hospital. It was now sitting at the back of the wardrobe. She needed to look in the box. She squeezed Peter's arm reassuringly. Her heart went out to him, and she mentally cringed as she remembered how horrible she had been to him. She was so sorry for the way she treated him.

Margaret and Peter welcomed everyone to their house for lunch. Margaret's heart always flipped as they drove up the drive. She finally understood why her mother had loved The Firs so much. It was hers. Margaret loved her house, especially as Peter had designed it and built it for her. She knew originally it was going to be a bungalow, but circumstances, and guidance from Elizabeth, made Peter build this house. Constance had left Peter a large sum of money and he had bought the big field next to his garage. He rebuilt his garage on the original plot, which had included a small cottage. He moved the entrance to the garage back about 20 feet from the road and named the short wide drive from the road to the garage gate after her mother – Constance Drive. Peter said he wanted a permanent memorial to the woman who rescued him and saved his life. The name plaque was unveiled on the second anniversary of her death. It was then that Peter proposed to Margaret. She had immediately said yes, so long as it wasn't a long engagement. They arranged their wedding for the end of October.

The land that was purchased next to the garage was a large field that gently sloped away from the main road. Access to the field was from the busy South Molton road, but the rest of the farmer's land was accessed further down the lane that passed Peter's garage. Peter's garage was on the corner of the land to Venn and the road to South Molton. The entrance to the garage was now just down the lane, if you continued down the lane and then turned left at the end. The farmer lived about a mile that way, but due to the height of the field above the road, this field did not have a gate or that lane, so the farmer was happy to sell to Peter.

The red brick house was set at the top of a slope, the drive circular in design. The large entrance porch, in the centre of the circle, led to a spacious peach-painted and oak hallway. The kitchen and laundry room to the left, making an 'L' shape, lead outside with a gate through to the double garage. Opposite the front door, slightly to the left, was a formal dining room, with doors to the back of the house, out onto a veranda and the tiered garden. Then on the left side, a large lounge with doors outside as well. These were open today. To the left of the front door was the large sweeping oak staircase, and in the right corner was a door leading to Peter's study and a downstairs cloakroom, with an outside door for easy access to the repair garage through a gate in the hedge. Up the stairs was Margaret and Peter's room, over the lounge, with a dressing room and bathroom. There were four other bedrooms and three further bathrooms on that floor. Then up a smaller staircase to the large open loft room, two bedrooms and a small bathroom. Peter had called the house Veronica Cottage, after his mother, though 'Cottage' did not describe how big the house was.

Margaret wandered through the lounge to the veranda, greeting everyone. She had just come down from the nursery where Marcus was now asleep. She was stopped by Susan, who was now engaged to her father. She was still not comfortable with the idea but was glad to see her father happy again. The drawn and gaunt look had gone from his face and body. She was glad to see Peter approaching.

"Here you are. I missed you."

"I was just helping Ivy put Marcus down."

They heard crying come from the lawn below the veranda. They watched as Elizabeth disentangled the boys. Xavier and Duncan did not want to be separated; they were still trying to fight. But Elizabeth, with Charles's help, managed to keep them apart. Peter put his arms around Margaret.

"Thank you."

"What for?" she asked.

"This." He waved his arm around. "Our families, friends, little Marcus. This is more than I ever dreamt of."

* * * * * * * *

"I am so sorry," said Benjamin. He had spilled sauce down Edith's arm and over her grey silk dress. "Let me help you."

He quickly put a napkin over the stain. He led Edith out of the dining room and across the reception area to the door marked 'private'. He opened it for her and followed her in. He opened the first door on the right, one of the old bedrooms reserved for staff, also used as a storage room, now not used for guests since the new extension and refurbishment.

"Take your dress off," he ordered, throwing his chef's hat onto the bed. "I will get some water and towels." He disappeared into the bathroom. He came out with a damp towel and a bathrobe he had placed there earlier. He turned his back as Edith carefully started to remove her dirty dress. As the bedroom door slowly opened, he suddenly moved next to Edith, and a woman entered. She had a camera in her hand. She was poised to take a photo of a half-undressed Edith and Benjamin.

CHAPTER 3

Suddenly she dropped the camera.

"I can't. I can't do it," she said and burst into tears.

Benjamin went over to her and put his arms around her.

"It's alright. Don't worry. I feel bad as well."

"Does that mean I don't have to take the picture?"

"Yes, honey." He gave her a big hug. "I don't want to either. It means we don't get any money, but money's not everything."

"Will someone tell me what is going on?" demanded Edith in the bathrobe, holding her stained dress, her blue eyes flashing angrily at each of them.

Benjamin and Roberta stared at her. Roberta burst into tears again.

"We won't do it," he said reassuringly to Roberta, "but we will have to say goodbye to your jewels and probably end up in a police cell." He pointed to the necklace around Edith's neck.

Roberta started to cry even more.

"What are you talking about? What about my jewels? They were given to me by my best friend."

Benjamin glared at her.

"Then Elizabeth's jewels must be Bobbie's," he said.

"No, they are not," she said firmly. "I think, perhaps, I should call the police."

"Oh, Mrs Harrison, please don't," begged Roberta. "We just wanted..." She trailed off, not sure what to say. Edith looked at her white tear-stained face.

"Let me get dressed. I need to return to the wedding. We will talk as soon as the opportunity arises and you can tell me all about it," she spoke gently to Roberta and patted her hand. Roberta nodded and she and Benjamin left the room.

Edith went into the bathroom and carefully washed away the sauce. She noticed that there was not as much as she thought. She dried her grey silk dress as best she could and pinned her cream rose corsage to cover it. She adjusted her blonde hair, getting more and more grey, she noticed, and fingered the silver and amethyst necklace. She thought about her best friend who had given it to her. It was her widower that was getting married, and she suddenly realised that the bride had also married the widower of her first best friend about 35 years ago. She shivered, then splashed cold water on her face and returned to the wedding,

As she walked into the dining room, she saw Benjamin serving the food. He looked at her, so she inclined her head in acknowledgement and walked down the gently sloping open corridor to the new lounge. There she found her family.

"You've been gone some time, love," said David, her husband.

"Yes, I spilt sauce on my dress, but it is all sorted now," she said firmly. David looked at her knowingly. There was something amiss. He was about to question her more when his attention was taken by their grandson. It was about an hour later before he could question her further. They were standing on the veranda that went round the hotel, overlooking the River Taw, alone for once. Edith sipped her champagne.

"Tell me what happened." Edith did not pretend not to know what he was talking about; she had been anxious to talk to him. She quickly explained the situation. David wanted to call the police, but Edith stopped him.

"Let's hear their explanation first," she said. "I feel there is more to this than a simple robbery gone wrong."

David inclined his head to show agreement. "But I don't like it," he declared.

Guests started to leave. It was supposed to be a small wedding, but it had grown bigger than both bride and groom wanted. Finally the bride and groom left for their honeymoon in London.

Edith saw that Benjamin was alone, clearing the buffet. She grabbed David and they went to confront him. They sat at an empty table in the corner.

"Right, I need an explanation," demanded David.

"Ben, what on earth were you and Roberta thinking?" asked Edith more gently.

Benjamin looked at them.

"I don't know where to begin," he said. Edith and David looked at him expectantly. "I suppose it all began with Bobbie."

"Your sister," said Edith. "But what has that got to do with us?"

"She is your niece, and you stole her money," he blurted out.

Edith and David looked at each other.

"Are you saying that Roberta is Michael's daughter? I don't believe it. He would never be unfaithful to Louisa." David was aghast, springing to his brother's defence.

"No, not Michael," he added quickly. He looked at Edith. "She is your brother's daughter."

"Arthur? But Arthur is dead." Edith was horrified. She looked at David.

"I know," Benjamin continued. "But before he died, he and my mother... fell in love."

"But... but my brother died in 1936."

"I know," said Benjamin again. "Bobbie was born in 1936."

"But..." said Edith again. She was at a loss.

"The joke's gone far enough, Ben. Let's put a stop to this right now," said David angrily. "I'm going to get the police." He hated seeing Edith upset.

"It is not a joke. Arthur wrote to you just before he died, saying that he and Mother would be getting married as soon as possible and that they were expecting a baby. I know that you are scandalised that they were having a baby without being married, but it does happen." He finished defiantly, raising his voice.

"We can't talk about this here," said David. He noticed that they were getting glances from the few remaining guests, including his daughter.

"Come over tomorrow afternoon," said Edith. "We can sort this out then."

* * * * * * * *

There was a loud knock on the wooden front door. *Right on time*, thought David as he went to open it. He silently invited his guests in.

"Come in, Roberta, dear." Edith was more welcoming. She was looking at Roberta's scared, white face. Benjamin and Roberta sat on the edge of the sofa.

"I have some tea ready. I will just go and get it." While she went to the kitchen to get the tea, the others sat in tense silence. To everyone's relief, Edith was soon back. She poured the tea and offered home-made biscuits. David could wait no longer.

"Right, let's hear it. Let's get this farce over and done with. Persuade me not to call the police. Blackmail and assault is a serious business," he said crossly. He was angry that Edith had been subjected to it.

Edith looked at him and smiled. She turned to Roberta.

"Roberta, start at the beginning. When were you born?"

"I was born in July 1936," she said. "My mother, and Ben's mother, was Millicent Lyon. She was married to Ben's father but fell in love with my father as soon as she saw him. She was not happy with Ben's father." She smiled an apology to Benjamin.

"Don't worry. Just tell your story," he reassured her.

"My father, Arthur, died before I was born. Before they could get married."

"But your mother was already married. To Ben's father," interrupted David.

"This is where I come in," said Benjamin. "I remember some things. I was 10 when Mother met Mr Huxtable. I only met him a couple of times. I know my parents weren't happy; there were lots of rows. It came to a head just before Christmas '35. They decided to part company. My father was to bring me back to England. He booked us onto a ship. At the time I knew nothing about Mother's relationship with Mr Huxtable or about Bobbie. I wasn't too happy about leaving India, but I had no choice. While we were in Egypt, the ship docked at Alexandria and Dad took me to the local market. He bought something to eat. He tried to get me to eat it, but I didn't like the look of it. Anyway, as we sailed across the Mediterranean, he got sick. We called at Gibraltar and got a doctor for him, but he just got worse. He died as we crossed the Bay of Biscay. My grandparents were there to greet us. Christmas was not a happy time. They were discussing telling Mother. Father had indicated in his last letter to them that the marriage was over. They were distraught at the thought of the scandal and blamed Mother for everything. I said I would write to her."

Roberta picked up the tale.

"I am very sketchy about that time. Obviously it was before I was born. Mother did not say much about it, but as I got older, I got more curious. What she did tell me was that Ben's father agreed to divorce her when he got back to England. He was happy to return; he had had enough of Delhi. As soon as he arrived, he would start proceedings on the grounds of desertion, as she stayed in India. There were mixed emotions when she got Ben's letter. She was happy that she and Father could get married quickly, without waiting for the divorce, but sad that Ben's father had died. She did not want Ben to grow up without a father. She wrote to Ben's grandparents asking for the death certificate and to send Ben back to her. They declined on both counts."

She took a deep breath.

"This is when things got bad. My father was on his way to the British Embassy to see his friend, who was going to be his best man and was a lawyer, to get his advice. But as he crossed the road to enter the embassy, he was attacked and robbed. His friend, who had been waiting at the gate, saw everything, but there was nothing to be done. He was dead." She stopped, crying. Ben tried to comfort her. David coughed.

"This is all well and good, but we still have no proof you are who you say you are."

"After Father died, Mother contacted Father's friend asking for help. While he was sympathetic, he could not do anything. He sorted out Father's affairs and left Mother with nothing."

"It all went to you," Ben said accusingly to Edith. "Mother was left destitute." He sat back, glaring at Edith.

"As I said before, where is the proof?" David sighed. "Let's start with your birth certificate." He was greeted with a flood of tears from Roberta.

"I can show you," said Ben. He passed it Edith. "But it won't be any use. It doesn't have Arthur's name on it. It doesn't have any name on it."

"Mother tried to get Father's name on it." Roberta sobbed. "But as he had died, they wouldn't let her. In desperation she tried to get Ben's father put on it. but he was dead too." David was looking sceptical, but Edith was sympathetic.

"You said Arthur had a friend at the consulate. Had he told him about you and your mother?" Roberta nodded.

"But he couldn't do anything. He had to follow Father's instructions in his will. He tried his best and employed Mother to look after the house until it was sold and gave her the proceeds of some of the furniture so that Mother could go into a decent hospital when her time came to give birth. Please don't blame him for that," begged Roberta.

"We don't," said Edith reassuringly. "What was the name of this person? If he could vouch for you, it would help."

"Sir Dominic Hales, but he is dead now." David nodded. He recognised the name from the will; both he and Dominic were executors.

"You are named Roberta, after Arthur," said Edith. Roberta started crying again. Edith was looking at the birth certificate. She hated to see the blank space where Arthur's name should be.

"This doesn't prove anything. It is all circumstantial," said David.

"Arthur wrote to you before he died, telling you about Mother and Roberta. You deliberately ignored it and took the money anyway," Benjamin said angrily, losing patience.

"Don't talk to us like that." retorted David.

"Wait a minute," said Edith. "I'm trying to think. Now you say about a letter. I have been thinking back. We received the telegram from the London solicitors a few days after Arthur's death. It was a shock. Then we had more formal documents. We went to London to complete the procedure at the end of the year. I put everything in a box. About a week after we received the telegram, a letter did come, but I couldn't bear to open it. I just put it aside and left it."

She stood up and went over to the bureau. She opened the bottom drawer and brought out an old box. "I haven't opened this in years." She put it on her lap and took off the lid. On top were the documents from the London solicitors. Underneath was a wad of letters. "I kept all of Arthur's letters. If it arrived, it will be in with these." She went through them one by one, everyone watching intently. She checked to make sure they were opened. About halfway down she discovered one that was unopened. She looked at David. She put all the other papers on the floor and sat with it in her hand. She looked at Benjamin and Roberta. She made to open it.

"Wait, love," said David. "Let me think." Everyone waited expectantly. "If we open this, while we have all seen it, depending on what it contains, if left in the possession of one of the parties, the other party may claim that it was altered while left in their possession. Do you understand what I am trying to say?" Everyone nodded. "I suggest we get a solicitor to open it and keep it, then there can be no doubt as to what it says." Everyone signalled their agreement. "Also I suggest, Ben, you and I both sign the back, across the opening so that we both know it hasn't been opened in the meantime." Benjamin nodded; that had been at the front of his mind. David rose and got a pen.

"I have a couple of photos to show you," said Roberta, opening her handbag. She took them out and handed them to Edith. "My parents weren't together very long, so only had a couple of photos taken together, after Ben and his father left." Edith took the photos. Her brother looked just the same as when he had come over for their parents' funeral in 1930. She smiled at his big bushy moustache; he had been so proud of it. Then she looked at the woman standing beside him. She looked very much like Roberta; there was no doubt that was her mother. The other photo was of them sitting on a veranda of a typical colonial bungalow.

"They were taken at my father's house by Sir Dominic," explained Roberta.

"It is a shame that Sir Dominic is dead," said David as he and Benjamin rejoined the ladies. "He could go a long way in vouching for you."

Roberta was looking at David, thinking.

"I don't actually know he died. Mother received sporadic correspondence from him when he returned to England after the war. I just assumed he had died, as Mother hadn't heard from him for a couple of years before she died. He was old when she returned to England, nearly 60 I think." David and Edith exchanged wry glances.

"In that case he would only be in his early seventies now, not old at all," David said pointedly. "Do you still have an address for him?"

"You mean he might still be alive?" said Roberta excitedly. Then despondently, "I don't think so. I got rid of a lot of Mother's things. I couldn't bring them all back to England after her death. But I will look through the few papers and things I have."

"Very well," said David. "We can ask the solicitor to trace him as well. I will ring them tomorrow and make an appointment for us all to see him."

"Can I ask who it is?" said Benjamin. "Is it one of your close friends?" He gave David a knowing look. David sighed.

"Would you like to choose one?" he asked.

Benjamin thought for a moment. He didn't know any.

"We will use your solicitor, but I may want a second opinion in the future."

"Mr Bond, Godfrey Bond, of Bryant Solicitors and Partners."

* * * * * * * *

Mr Bond looked around at the faces watching him intently. He had never had to do anything like this before. He was just as tense as they were.

"Here goes," he said. He picked up his chrome paperknife, embossed with his name, and carefully and skilfully slit open the envelope. He cautiously pulled out the letter. A couple of photographs fell out onto the desk. He picked them up and looked at them. Then he handed them to David, who gave them to Edith. They were the same ones they had seen a couple of days previously. Edith looked at Roberta and handed them to her. Mr Bond opened the letter and began to read aloud in his dry voice.

My Dearest Edith,

I cannot wait to tell you. Since my last letter the most exciting thing has happened to me. I have met the most wonderful woman. I would not have believed I could fall in love again, but I have. And what is even more wonderful is she returns my love. But dearest Edith, please do not be shocked, but continue to wish me happiness. She is married. Unhappily, of course. Though, there is good news, lots of it. Her husband is returning to England and from there will grant a divorce so that we can marry. There is a desperate heartbreak for my love in all of this. Her husband insisted on taking their son with him. This is breaking her heart. She reassures me, but I know she feels it deeply.

We have had some photographs taken and I am sending some to you. Please wish me all the best.

I had to break off before but am now continuing my letter. My darling Millie has given me some more wonderful news. Please, again, I beg of you, do not be shocked, but she is with child. It is now imperative we marry. She should be receiving the divorce documents from her husband soon.

I had to break off again. We now have news that her husband died on the way back to England. He and Benjamin took a ship back to England and he died during the voyage. This means we are free to marry.

Edith, dear sister, I have not been this happy since you know when, but this time I am bursting with joy at the thought of fatherhood. I never expected to become a father. I thought I was too old at 46. I still do, but Millie assures me age is no barrier to being a good father. And I intend to be the best. With Millie by my side, so much younger than me, only 30, I feel a spring in my step.

I will write to you soon about the wedding. I was wondering if you and David might visit for the festivities, but we both want the marriage to take place as soon as possible. Maybe you could visit later in the year.

Darling Edith, please be happy for me.

Your Loving Brother

Arthur

Mr Bond stopped reading, put the letter down and looked at his audience. Both the women had tears running down their faces. Despite Mr Bond's monotonous voice, the sentiment of the letter had touched them.

CHAPTER 4

David and Benjamin just sat in their chairs, stunned. Mr Bond continued talking.

"The date of the letter is 1 November 1935, then crossed out and changed to 1 December 1935, then crossed through again and changed to 1 January 1936. I see from the file that Mr Huxtable died 2 January 1936." He peered over his glasses. No one said anything. He sighed and broke the silence himself.

"I am satisfied that you are who you say you are, Miss Lyon. You have provided both your birth certificate and passport. Mr Lyon, while I believe you are who you say you are, I do need a bit more proof than just your birth certificate. Do you have a passport?"

Benjamin shook his head.

"I came back on my father's passport and have not needed one since. I do have my Army Service ID at my grandparents' house."

"Thank you. If I could have that as soon as convenient. Edith and David, I have known you for over 30 years. Now to the letter, Edith, you can confirm that this is Mr Huxtable's writing."

Edith nodded. Benjamin spoke, angrily.

"Of course it is. Do we have to continue this? It clearly states that he is Roberta's father."

"No, Mr Lyon, it does not."

"Do you think we forged it, 28 years ago, and hoped that Mrs Harrison wouldn't open it? Or that we wrote it recently and broke into their house and hid it in a box we didn't know existed."

"No, Mr Lyon, I do not, but I must make sure everything is in order for the courts. For all of you. We cannot overturn the will unless there is fraud involved."

"There is," persisted Benjamin. "They stole my sister's inheritance." Mr Bond sighed.

"Mr Lyon, that is what we are trying to determine. I have to make sure it was a deliberate act by Edith, then we have to prove that Miss Lyon is indeed Mr Huxtable's daughter, then we can go to court to get her inheritance. If we don't, there maybe other legal implications."

"Or she could just hand over the jewels she bought."

"I keep telling you they are my jewels."

"Please can we keep to the point," Mr Bond interjected. "As I was saying about this letter. Edith, if you could bring another letter from your brother so that we can compare the handwriting. Now why did you not open the letter at the time?"

"It was too upsetting. I had just heard about his death, and I couldn't bear to open it. I was going to later, but I forgot about it."

"Very convenient."

"Mr Lyon!" Mr Bond was getting exasperated.

"I can see this is an old letter. Now to the photographs, you can confirm that this is your brother?" Edith nodded. "Do you have other photographs?"

"Yes, we had a photograph taken when he came over for our parents' funeral."

"Good. Now the lady in the photo; Mr Huxtable refers to her as Millie. Unfortunately he does not include a surname, and he does not actually state she is his... fiancée, but it is implied as he uses the word 'us'. I can see a likeness between you, Miss Lyon, and the lady, but it does not prove she is your mother. She could be your aunt or cousin. Do you have any photographs of your mother?"

Roberta shook her head.

"We were never in a position to get photographs taken. Wait, I think I may have one of us when I was a baby."

"Not ideal, but bring it to me anyway. What I need is someone who knew you or your mother."

"They are all in India. I may be able to give you a list."

"What about Sir Dominic?" asked Edith. "He came back to England and knew you, your mother and Arthur." Then to Mr Bond, "But Roberta thinks he may have died."

"Do you have his address?" asked Mr Bond.

They all shook their heads.

"He was at the British Consulate in Delhi. Maybe they will have his address," suggested Roberta.

"I will contact them," said Mr Bond. "I think that is all we can do at the moment. I will get in touch to arrange another meeting as soon as I have news."

* * * * * * *

They were called back to Mr Bond's office 10 days later. He got straight to point.

"I have checked all documents etc. and everything seems to be in order. I have Sir Dominic's address; he is still alive and living in Bath. He has agreed to come down in two days. If he confirms what you have told me, then we will go to court. I assume you will not be challenging the claim, Edith." She shook her head. "What I will need is an account of the assets disposed of and what you still have. Is that a problem?" She shook her head again.

"Most of the money is unspent. It was set aside for Elizabeth. I only bought the hotel, for her."

"You only bought her the hotel!" responded Benjamin. "I have been working at my sister's hotel." He started laughing.

"No, that hotel is William's. I bought her The Coaching Inn in Wiltshire." Benjamin sat back and stared at her. He hadn't been serious when he mentioned the hotel. He was sure, despite Edith's protests, that they had spent the money on jewels. His mind was now racing. Shortly after arriving at Taw Lodge Hotel, he had fallen in love. He was taking his break in the staff room when she walked in. He had no idea who she was and tried to think of something to say. All he could think of when she sat down with her cup of tea was to mention the weather.

"Mild for the time of year," he said. He now cringed when he thought about it. But she just smiled at him.

33

"Winters are usually mild down here," she responded, "but we can still get snow." She was right, he thought, when he remembered the snow that winter,1962–63, one of the worst in history. After that they sporadically met in the staff room. It was the following summer when he finally managed to speak to her with more than just small talk. He had not seen her for a couple of weeks and when they did meet, he was horrified. She saw his expression and quickly moved her hair to cover her face. He was so appalled he forgot all his inhibitions and went over to her. He gently moved her hair back and looked at her fading bruises.

"What on earth has happened to you?"

"I fell down the stairs."

Benjamin led her to the sofa.

"Tell me exactly what happened."

"I told you. I fell down the stairs."

"I don't believe you." He sat holding one hand in his; his other gently moved back the hair. "What really happened?"

"Larry..." she started to say, "found me." She finished lamely. He dared to give her a hug, and tears spilled from her eyes. After that, whenever he saw her, he looked at her face and arms for bruises. He hated what he saw, but she always denied it.

It was Christmas when the barriers finally came down and she admitted that her husband hit her.

He started to give her a kiss every time they met. He begged her to leave him, but she wouldn't. He spent the summer trying to persuade her, and at last she began to relent. After a particularly rough beating, when she saw the effect on her daughters, she agreed that she couldn't stay, but she had nowhere to go. She could stay at the hotel, but Larry would find her – and at all the other places. Benjamin had racked his brains and finally put a plan into action. He had come to North Devon for a particular purpose and now was the time to bring it to a close. There was a wedding coming up and he arranged to carry out the plan then with his sister, and he also got Marilyn to agree to go away with him on the Monday. After her husband had left for work, he went to pick up her and her daughters and take them to his grandparents' house. But his plan hadn't worked, and Marilyn had second thoughts, not about leaving her husband but going away with him. She saw him at the hotel on the Sunday and explained that while she loved him and wanted to be with him, she was not going to run away.

"But you can't stay with Larry," he declared.

"No," she said. "Tomorrow morning I am going to pack all his things and kick him out. I have told Bill and Beth and have their support. They will help if I need anything." Benjamin was pleased to hear she was not going to stay with Larry but wished it wasn't William and Elizabeth she had turned to.

"You are right," he said. "We don't need to run away. We can stand together." He hadn't known where they could go. They needed to get away, as Larry was still causing trouble. Though since he had been thrown out, he had not laid a finger on Marilyn, he still went round shouting and making a nuisance of himself. The idea of another plan was now forming in his mind.

* * * * * * * *

Two days later, they were all, again, sitting in Mr Bond's office, waiting for the arrival of Sir Dominic. There was a knock on the door. Roberta, who was nearest, got up to open it. Sir Dominic walked in. He looked at Roberta, holding the door open.

"Bobbie, my dearest. You are so grown up. How are you? How is your mother?" He reached forward and gave her hug. Roberta remembered how he had dwarfed her last time she saw him. He seemed so much smaller now.

"I'm well, Uncle Dominic. My mother... Mother passed away a few years ago."

"I am so sorry, Bobbie, she was a fine woman. If I hadn't already been married, I would have married her myself."

"How is Lady Amanda?"

"Not so good. She wanted to come but was not well enough."

Mr Bond gave a quiet cough.

Sir Dominic and Roberta broke off their conversation and Roberta guided him to a spare chair. She introduced everyone.

"I think from your entrance we can infer that you recognise Miss Lyon." Sir Dominic nodded. "Do you recognise Mr Lyon?"

Sir Dominic shook his head.

"Sorry, Mr Lyon. I think I only met you once, just after Arthur introduced me to Millie. You would not have been very old."

"I do remember you," he said with a smile. How could he forget those big bushy eyebrows? They were jet black then, now grey. He kept dreaming about them for weeks; they came alive like giant caterpillars.

"Can you confirm this is Mrs Lyon?" asked Mr Bond, holding out a photograph.

"Yes, I took the photograph." He looked accusingly at Edith.

"Why did you not help Millie and Bobbie? I know Arthur wrote to you telling you all about them. I tried to help them after Arthur's death, but my hands were tied."

"I didn't know about them." Edith sobbed. "I was so upset at Arthur's death I didn't open the letter. If I had known, I would have most certainly done what I could to help." David took Edith's hand.

There was an awkward silence, broken by Mr Bond.

"I think that confirms everything. Sir Dominic, I will need an affidavit from you confirming you identified Miss and Mrs Lyon." Sir Dominic nodded. "I have all the paperwork ready."

They all walked slowly out of his office.

"How long are you staying, Sir Dominic? You are not driving back straight away, are you?" asked Edith. She wanted to hear more about her brother.

"No, I didn't drive. I came by train. I was going back later today."

"Before you leave, could we take you to lunch?" Sir Dominic nodded; he was feeling hungry. They all piled into David's old Humber. Peter had tried to persuade David to get a new car, but David refused, saying he was too old to get used to another car now. Sir Dominic sat in the front while Edith, Benjamin and Roberta sat in the back. David drove carefully to the Taw Lodge Hotel. They settled down at a table in the dining room. Benjamin excused himself; he had to go back to work in the kitchen and promised them an excellent lunch.

Elizabeth joined them. She was introduced to Sir Dominic and sat beside her cousin.

"So, I officially have a new cousin," she said happily.

"Yes," said Roberta cautiously, "it seems so."

Elizabeth beamed at her.

"I am so pleased. Why did it take you so long to get in touch? Why didn't your mother contest the will?"

Roberta shrugged her shoulders.

"I don't know. I suppose she was too upset, and perhaps she didn't realise she had a claim. I really don't know."

"Why didn't she come back to England?"

"I think she wanted to stay with Father. I buried her with him."

"I'm sorry. I didn't mean to upset you."

"No, you didn't. I know you have a lot of questions. So do I. But it is too late to get answers now."

"What did your mother do? I mean, how did you live? Sorry, I'm prying." Roberta smiled at her.

"I will answer as best I can. After Father's house was sold, and Mother had to leave the hospital, Sir Dominic got her a position as housekeeper for an owner of a tea company in Delhi. Then the war came. She did some translation work for the troops that were there, as she spoke fluent Hindi and understood some other Indian languages. After the war she taught English privately, but then Sir Dominic came back to England. She decided I needed a formal education; she had been teaching me at home. She took a job teaching English in a good school and was paid a pittance because she asked if I could sit in on lessons. We also lived at the school. When I was 16, she made me do a secretarial course. I got a job in a typing pool. I moved to the Personnel Department, which was more money, and because I could speak both English and Hindi. Then Mother got sick. She left the school and went back to teaching privately. We moved into a small flat. Mother got sicker and died in 1958. I was in contact with Ben but not on a regular basis. He told me to come back to England. I didn't know what else to do. He met me off the plane; it was the first time we had seen each other. He looked after me in London and got me a job at the hotel where he worked. Then we decided to track you down. I had got rid of most of Mother's things. I couldn't carry them on the plane. I knew Father had a sister and I tried to think what Mother had said. I knew you lived in Devon and Father's name was Huxtable. Then we set about trying to find you."

"But Devon is so big. It must have been like looking for a needle in a haystack."

"Luckily Mother had spoken about the sea, how Father liked to fish from a boat. So that narrowed it down a bit. Then I remembered Mother mentioning that Father helped his parents take their produce to a pannier market."

Elizabeth nodded.

"Mother's parents worked on a farm, and they took the produce to the pannier market every Friday."

Roberta continued.

"So, we found out all the places near a coast that had a market. Luckily, we decided to start at the top of Devon. We stayed in Bideford first, then Ben got a job in Ilfracombe. I remembered one conversation with Sir Dominic before he left. When we were talking about Father, he mentioned that his sister was married, and it took days of racking my brain to remember her married name. I knew it began with H, same as Father's name, then suddenly I heard someone talking about some Harrises and it came to me, also that your father worked in a bank, like my father. So we wrote down all the banks in the area and decided to visit. We finished the ones in Ilfracombe and moved to Barnstaple. We rented a flat and I got my job in the cinema as an usherette. We started visiting the banks again, and eventually we found the one your father had worked in. It was more difficult now he was retired. We spoke to lots of people at each bank; everyone knew your father.

"We were told he lived in Bishop's Tawton but not where. We didn't want him to know about us, so we didn't like to ask too many questions. On my day off, I visited Bishop's Tawton and as I was walking past the Taw Lodge Hotel, I saw the notice about a vacancy for a chef. I told Ben, and he got the job. It was easy then to find out about your father. We worked out a plan and waited for an opportunity, hence the incident with your mother. I am so sorry about that. We... I just hadn't realised how horrible that would be."

"Never mind, no real harm done. And it served its purpose. I have found my cousin." They smiled at each other. "And now you can get what you are entitled to."

"Even if it means losing your hotel."

Elizabeth looked sad for a moment, took a deep breath and said,

"Yes, even if it means losing the hotel. It means so much to me, so many memories, but it should not have been mine in the first place."

Roberta had felt her warmness and now saw her sadness. She needed to talk to Ben. She had plans.

CHAPTER 5

"Peter!" came the screaming panic-stricken shout from the dining room. She pushed back her chair and ran out into the hall. "Peter," she shouted again.

She yanked open the door of his office, but it was empty. She turned round.

"Where is Peter?" she demanded.

"He must be at the garage," said Mrs Bancroft, who had rushed out of the kitchen, closely followed by Sally. She was horrified to see Margaret so agitated.

"Go and get him, Sally," Margaret ordered. Sally rushed out of the side door, down the garden path and through the gate in the hedge. This was a shortcut to the garage next door, to save having to go down the drive to the road, along the road towards Barnstaple, left up the lane to Venn Village and down the drive. She ran into the office.

"Sir, the missus... Ma'am needs you," she said, puffing, out of breath. Peter looked up, astonished, but immediately started back towards the house.

Jeremy came out of the service bay. He had heard Sally's voice. Usually, she made any excuse to talk to him. He had decided to ask her out next time he saw her, but she just gave him a smile and a wave and rushed off back to the house, following after Peter.

Peter rushed into the hall, and then into the lounge. Margaret and Mrs Bancroft were there.

"I'm so glad you are here, sir. I will go and make some tea."

Peter went immediately to Margaret's side. Her green eyes were wide with fear, her face more pale than usual.

"What on earth is the matter?"

"This." She waved a letter at him. "They want to take him away. Don't let them. Don't let them take him away." She burst into tears. Peter put his arm around her and in the other hand took the letter Margaret held out. It was from Eton College; they were confirming that they had a place for Xavier to start in September.

"Don't let them take my baby away. He is too young to go to them. I couldn't bear it."

Mrs Bancroft came in with the tea. Peter signalled his thanks. Peter sat Margaret down on the large cream sofa, placed to get the best view of the garden and hills beyond through the French doors. He poured them their tea and sat down beside her.

"How did this arrive?"

"It came in the post this morning."

"How did they know to send it here?"

"They didn't. It went to Royston House first."

"Where is the envelope?"

"I left it in the dining room." Peter went next door and retrieved it. He saw the envelope had been re-addressed in the neat handwriting of Lady Agatha, Margaret's previous mother-in-law. It was agreed she would forward any correspondence to them in Devon. He returned to Margaret.

"I will ring Eton College and tell them that Xavier will not be starting in September. But, Maggie," he took her hands, "you do know that he will have to go there eventually." Margaret nodded.

"But not yet. He is only a baby."

"He is six, not a baby, six and a half in September. But I agree he is far too young."

"Why did they send this letter?" Margaret suddenly asked. "How did they know about him?"

"I think Hugh may have had something to do with this," said Peter slowly. He remembered a conversation he had had a few years ago.

"But Hugh died five years ago. How could he?"

"He must have contacted them before he died."

"But Xavier was only one. Why would he have contacted Eton College? He didn't know he was going to be killed."

Peter sighed. He didn't know what to tell her. He didn't want to tell her that Hugh was going to leave her for his lover.

"I will ring the college and deal with this now. Drink your tea. Don't worry; no one is going to take Xavier away from us."

Peter left the lounge and went into his office. He dialled the number and asked to speak to the letter signatory. He spoke to his secretary, and she said he was busy but would call back in the next half hour. Peter was glad that he and Margaret had decided that he should adopt Xavier; it gave him full powers to discuss his future. Xavier's paternal grandfather, Lord Julius, was at first doubtful, but Lady Agatha was on his side; she knew that Peter had Xavier's interests at heart. When her son Lord Hugh had died, Lady Agatha saw with her own eyes that Peter had acted swiftly to stop any gossip. Peter had destroyed all the incriminating photos that her son had that might have brought about a scandal if some people had got hold of them.

Peter returned to Margaret.

"Xavier will continue to go to my old school as we planned until he is 11, then he must go to Eton," he said firmly. Margaret nodded unhappily. Peter continued. "We have plenty of time to sort things out. He will not be going for another five years." Peter heard the telephone ringing and went to answer it.

"Thank you, Sally, I will take this call in my office." Sally curtsied and went back to the kitchen. Peter sighed. He wished she wouldn't do that.

All the time Peter was gone, Margaret hardly dared breathe. At last he returned. She looked at him expectantly. He looked at her worried face, it pained him to see her so upset.

"It is agreed that Xavier will start in September 1970." Initially they were reluctant to talk to him, but as soon as he explained, they readily agreed to his suggestion. "When we go to Sussex for Ralph's christening – why we have to go, I don't know – we will take a trip to Eton so that you can look round and meet some people. It will ease your mind."

"Thank you, Peter. What would I do without you? Sorry I over-reacted, but it was a shock. First the envelope with Hugh's name on it and then the contents." She smiled up at him. He bent down and kissed her. They were interrupted by the clock chiming the hour.

"I must go back to work," said Peter, disentangling himself from her. "I will be back for lunch." He blew her a kiss, and he left the lounge.

****

They pulled up outside the front door of Royston House in the late afternoon. Immediately there was a mass of people, all greeting each other. Finally, they organised themselves. Ivy took Xavier and Marcus off to the nursery, with the footmen, Clive and Phil, bringing their luggage. Clive was dispatched to the nursery and Phil took Peter and Margaret's luggage to their room. Even though the Peter's Zephyr had a large boot, it was not enough room for all the cases and boxes, apparently. Some had to be put on the roof and some inside the car.

Lady Agatha and Lord Julius were thrilled to see them. Peter and Margaret had come for the christening of their third grandson. While Peter had been happy to visit Lady Agatha and Lord Julius, he grumbled about going to the christening.

The christening was being held in Horsham where Sebastian and Rozina now lived. Sebastian was Hugh's younger brother; he was the Conservative MP for the area. It was his son that was being christened; he also had another son and daughter, Tobias and Bettina.

They had gathered outside the church waiting for Sebastian and Rozina. A large crowd had congregated to watch them. At last they arrived. Sebastian got out the car and waved to them. Rozina accepted a small posy of flowers from a girl; she loved this. This is what she was expecting when she married Sebastian. He had promised her that she would be Countess of Royston one day, but then his stupid brother got married and had a son, so that was that. Now they had changed direction and her husband had been elected as a Member of Parliament, she was patron to several charities and on more committees.

Suddenly there was a shout.

"Don't let that German near the son of our MP."

And then another.

"We don't want Germans here. Keep Britain for the British."

Sebastian appeared to look puzzled. He stepped forward. Someone took a picture.

"What do you mean?" he demanded.

"Send Herr Leinberger home."

"Choose a British godfather, keep England pure."

"No, he is my brother-in-law."

"No matter, send him home."

A chant started, "Send him home."

Sebastian tried to plead with them. Someone touched his arm.

"What iz thiz? I will go," said a man in a thick German accent. "What do they say? I do not understand."

"They are ignorant proletariats. Don't they know that the war is over? The cessation of hostilities has begun."

"I do not understand what you are saying. They want me to go." Sebastian shrugged. "Then I will go."

Peter was watching the scene with a mixture of trepidation and puzzlement. Friedrick Leinberger saw him watching. He grabbed Peter and pulled him forward.

"This man. He is an England. Him. I will go." And with that Friedrick disappeared. His sister called after him, but he ignored her.

Sebastian held his hand up for silence. There was some shushing, then quiet.

"I will bow to the will of the people. I will forgo Friedrick as a godparent and choose Peter instead." There was some loud cheering and more clicking of cameras.

Sebastian ceremoniously led the party inside the church. Everyone was stunned and shocked. When they came out of the church, most people had dispersed, but some were left. They cheered. There was a small family reception at Sebastian and Rozina's house.

Most people were outside, taking advantage of the early spring sunshine. Peter wanted to find Sebastian. Something didn't feel right. He walked round the corner of the house, then quickly retreated. He slowly peered round, then ducked back but remained there to listen. Sebastian and Friedrick were in deep conversation; now he knew something was up. Suddenly someone pushed passed him. It was the man that started the trouble. He went up to Sebastian and Friedrick and held out his hand. Sebastian gave him some notes.

Peter returned to the party, distracted. What was going on? Suddenly he realised what had been bothering him. Something had been niggling at the back of his mind. Friedrick had just spoken in perfect English, with a definite accent but not the thick accent he used earlier.

Peter was relieved when they could leave.

* * * * * * * *

Margaret was enjoying her ride on Savannah; she was toying with the idea of taking her back to Devon with her but decided to leave her at Royston House. Savannah would miss Bedford, Lord Julius's horse, and also Margaret would not be able to ride as much as she wanted due to Savannah's accident five years ago. She would get a new horse for her and a pony for Xavier.

She was content with her visit to Eton College earlier in the week. It had been agreed that Xavier would start in September 1970 and be a weekly boarder, spending weekends at Royston House and holidays in Devon. Margaret and Peter would try to visit every other weekend.

Peter came down to breakfast on the Saturday. They were due to leave the Sunday and had been there just over a week. He was the first in the breakfast room and the papers had been laid out on the side table. He picked up the *West Sussex County Times*, scanned the headlines, then turned the page.

He nearly choked on his bacon. He was staring at a large picture of the christening. The reporter had taken a picture of Sebastian and Friedrick arguing with the crowd in the causeway to St Mary's Church. Behind them were Rozina with Ralph, holding Tobias's hand, walking ahead. Looking back were Margaret with Xavier, Peter with Marcus, Lord Julius and Lady Agatha, Sonia, and Sebastian's sister holding her youngest

45

daughter, Guinevere. Just off the picture, half of her husband, Wolfe. Their other girls running about in the far background, heading towards the church. He started to read the narrative. He was so engrossed he did not hear Lady Agatha come into the room.

It began with the headline, *England for the English!*

At the christening of local MP Mr Sebastian Browne's second son last Sunday, there was a riotous scene. Mr Browne had chosen his wife's half-brother, Herr Friedrick Leinberger, as godfather. The crowd did not like it that Herr Leinberger was German. Mr Browne stepped up to confront the crowd. He said he would bow to their wishes, but the war was over. They needed to rebuild their lives and put it behind them and that he would work tirelessly on their behalf. There was loud cheering at this. Mr Browne would like to point out that his wife is Dutch and when her father died, her mother then married Friedrick's father, also that Friedrick was not old enough to have fought in the war. Mr Browne confirmed that his sister-in-law's second husband would become godfather. His sister-in-law was widowed when Mr Browne's brother was killed in a car accident. Lady Margaret, is granddaughter to the 10th Duke of Cranley, and cousin to the current duke. The infamous Lady Margaret, whose partying made all the headlines before she married Lord Hugh, is now married to Peter Eastman, whose parents were killed in the bombings of London during the war.

There was a smaller picture of Sebastian being cheered by the crowd. *What is he standing on?* wondered Peter. Sebastian was several inches shorter than Peter, who was 6ft 3in. Sebastian could clearly be seen towering over the crowd.

Peter slowly put the paper down and looked up. He met the eyes of Lady Agatha.

"Your son has surpassed himself this time," he said angrily, thrusting the paper at her.

"Just a moment, don't speak to her like that," admonished Lord Julius, coming into the room. Lady Agatha held up her finger to her mouth to quieten him while she read the article. She passed it to Lord Julius when she had finished.

"I'm so sorry," she said. "We had no idea."

"I know," responded Peter. "I am not blaming you. I am glad I am Xavier's legal guardian. I will protect him."

Lord Julius stormed out of the room, declaring he would have words with Sebastian.

"I would like to take that page out of the paper. I don't want Maggie to see it." Lady Agatha nodded. They finished breakfast in silence. Lord Julius finally returned.

"He apologised and said it was nothing to do with him. He regrets any hurt this has caused and has offered to respond. I told him not to bother. Least said soonest mended." And he helped himself to a large breakfast.

Peter did not believe Sebastian. He remembered seeing him huddled in the corner with Friedrick and giving money to the third man. He pocketed the newspaper article and asked if he could use the phone. He went into Lord Julius's study and rang Charles, Margaret's father. He quickly explained the situation and that he wanted to distance himself from Sebastian for all their sakes. Charles agreed, but said he felt sorry for Sebastian's parents. Peter did not move after he had replaced the receiver. He sat contemplating Sebastian; he knew he had been right not to trust him. He was glad he had sorted out Hugh's belongings and destroyed all the scandalous material that Sebastian would have enjoyed destroying his brother's reputation with. He had liked Hugh, even though he had married Margaret despite his sexual predilection. Peter clenched his fist when he thought about the article. How could he rake up Margaret's past like that? It was all unfounded and circumstantial. Margaret did not drink, even though she always appeared with a drink in her hand, since an incident that happened when she was 16 after she had too much to drink. She had been hounded by a photographer whose advances had been rebuffed. He made a point of getting the worst photographs of Margaret and making sure they were published. Hugh had made him stop. Peter would always be grateful to him for that.

Some other statements in the article did not ring true, either. Over the years he had heard bits and pieces of information.

He took the article out of his pocket. Yes, Rozina and her mother were Dutch, but Friedrick's father had been a captain in the Nazi party, and while Friedrick was officially just too young, born in 1929, he knew he had taken part with his father. His father had been arrested after the war but shot himself before his trial. He wasn't sure Rozina was as innocent as she looked. He knew she hankered after being a countess, which was the promise Sebastian made to get her to marry him. She was several years older than him. He met her in Africa while he was on national service. Then Hugh met Margaret and they had Xavier. He knew they were both very, very angry. Then Sebastian had become an MP and he thought they had accepted the situation, but now? He was glad that Xavier would be coming back to Devon with them. He wished now he had insisted that Xavier board at Eton all the time, not just weekly. He hoped Xavier would be safe at Royston House. He would monitor the situation.

CHAPTER 6

The journey home was done in near silence. Peter was thinking about the situation with Sebastian, and Ivy was trying to distract Xavier – he was upset at leaving Savannah and Bedford – while Marcus seemed fretful. She hoped he wasn't coming down with something. Margaret was contemplating how to build some stables at their home, Veronica Cottage. The house had been built at the top of the field, on the main Barnstaple – South Molton road, next to the garage. The field sloped steeply down. Some had been made into terraced gardens, but there was some left at the bottom. She decided that the stable should be built behind Peter's garage; that would be easiest for electric and water. She was pleased she had thought of that. The last bit beyond that could be flattened and turned into an arena. That left a square of land for her horse, probably not enough. She would have to look to rent somewhere else, especially if she got a pony for Xavier as well.

They pulled up outside of their usual resting point hotel. Margaret was still not used to not being greeted by Bradley when they arrived. She cringed inwardly as she had always thought he just worked there; it was not until it was up for sale a few years ago that she realised he owned it. He had always come out to greet them, initially due to her parents' status but latterly because they had become friends. She had not even realised it was for sale because that journey, when it had gone on the market, was made in panic from her father's house in Devon to Royston House. She had been running from Peter. They had finally declared their love for each other for her to ruin it by doing something unexpected, and because it was so unexpected, Peter had shouted at her. She had rushed out of the room before he could explain and left hurriedly the next morning, leaving Ivy to follow with Xavier. It was Ivy who told her that the inn was for sale. Margaret was upset. She hoped the new owners would not change things too much and that she would like them. She was amazed to learn that it was her best friend and confidante, Elizabeth, who was going to buy it. Elizabeth had tried to persuade Mr Bradley to stay on, but he was not well and wanted to retire.

This time they were greeted by one of the new owners, Roberta. She led them through the reception area to the extended dining room. Some small nooks had been made for a more private, cosy feel. She led them to one by the large window.

"Will you join us, Bobbie?" asked Peter.

"No, I'm sorry, I can't." Bobbie smiled apologetically. "As you can see, we are very busy. I will try and get Ben to come and say hello when he has a minute."

The party settled down at the table. They looked out of the window at the extensive gardens. Previously they had always eaten in an upstairs room, but Elizabeth had revamped the hotel, and now they ate in the dining room.

The waiter came to take their order. Marilyn arrived with their drinks. She sat down with them.

"I can't stay long, but I wanted to make sure I said hello," she explained.

"How are you?" asked Peter pointedly.

"I can't believe how happy I am," she said. "Since your father and Susan's wedding, it has been a blur. Things have moved quickly. I can't thank everyone enough."

Margaret inwardly cringed at the mention of the wedding. Her father had remarried to Susan. She hated her and her daughter Angela. Mainly Angela, as she knew she had designs on Peter. She never got over their break-up even though it came from Angela herself.

"I wish I had left Larry before," continued Marilyn. "I know everyone was telling me to, but I just didn't have the strength. Ben gave me the strength and incentive. And now look, we are running our own hotel. Well, not quite our own, but you know what I mean."

They said they did and asked after her girls.

"They have settled down so quickly, and they adore Ben. He keeps making little treats for them. Do you know he used to make them treats while he worked at Taw Lodge, when they came in after school to wait for me to finish on my work days? He is so good with them. We are getting married as soon as my divorce comes through. They can't wait to be bridesmaids."

She beamed at them.

"It is all thanks to Beth. I am so glad she married Bill. I loved working at Taw Lodge, getting all the rooms ready, but it is so much better having one's own hotel. I know Beth and Bobbie own it, but as housekeeper they let me organise the rooms and staff. Larry used to say I was useless at everything." She was called away.

"Beth has everything organised well," said Margaret. "I couldn't run anything like this."

"She was lucky that Marian Bradley stayed on to help her. Though she was happy to leave to look after her father when Beth gave half the hotel to Bobbie. Then with Ben and Marilyn joining them as chef and housekeeper, it made it easier. Bobbie still has a lot to do though, looking after the reception, dining room, bar and gardens."

Just as they finished lunch, Benjamin came out to greet them. They chatted for about 10 minutes then resumed their journey to Devon.

*　*　*　*　*　*　*　*

Margaret was sitting elegantly on the sofa, watching Peter pace up and down.

"Come and sit down," she said, patting the cushion beside her. He sat down. Usually they ended up kissing while seated together, but Peter was too restless. Margaret went to hold him, but he jumped up and started to pace up and down again.

"You will wear the carpet out. Why don't you go outside and pace up and down," she said jokingly, but Peter took her at her word and stepped through the open French doors onto the terrace. He continued to pace up and down, reached one end of the terrace and looked down over the garden. He watched Ivy playing with Xavier and Marcus on the lawn below. The house was built on top of the hill. When he built it, he had made three terraces for the garden. The first was paved with tables and chairs and stretched the whole length of the house along the lounge and dining room, with French doors all the way along. There were steps at either end that led down to the next flat level, which was lawn, and steps in the middle that led to the final flat level, which was the smallest and had a series of pathways and flowerbeds.

Margaret followed him outside and put her arms around his waist. He absent-mindedly hugged her to him and kissed the top of her head. They had been so happy. Now it was all going to be ruined. Peter would not let that happen. He could feel that Margaret was tense even though she appeared relaxed. He had been so angry with her when she first told him. He wished he had stuck to his guns, but Margaret had been so persuasive, and he wanted to please her.

Sally brought out the coffee Margaret had ordered, and they sat drinking it in silence, watching the boys playing.

Margaret's eyes scanned the bottom bit of the field, which she planned to use for her horse. The stable had been started in the right-hand corner, behind Peter's garage. Soon they would start to fence the arena. She sat in the sun, enjoying it warming her face. Margaret stole a glance at Peter. She loved him so much. She just wanted him to be happy but... Margaret sighed, remembering the envelope that had come in the post six or seven weeks ago.

She was sitting down for breakfast, opening the post as normal, when the envelope appeared in the middle of the pile. It had been re-addressed in her mother-in-law's hand, from Royston House. She didn't know who it was from; it was handwritten and postmarked London. She turned it over. There was an address on the back, but she didn't recognise it. She picked up her silver paper knife and slit it open.

Margaret read the letter, her mouth open. She reread the letter. She had no idea what to do. She was astounded. Her first instinct was to go and see Peter, but she realised that he would probably just destroy it. Margaret finished opening the rest of her mail. She needed to speak to her father. She finished breakfast and rang the bell, and went upstairs to get ready. Usually she drove to her father's even though it was just a mile down the road, but today she needed the walk. She would get him to run her back.

Margaret said goodbye to Marcus; Xavier was at school. She went down the back path from the house to the garage. She saw Peter working on a car in one of the bays, with Jeremy. She tried to act normally and said she was just popping to see her father. Luckily Peter was grappling with a difficult problem and was distracted, kissed her and said he would see her at lunch. She nodded to Jeremy and left quickly.

It was downhill to her father's house, but she was still puffed out when she arrived at The Firs. She needed more exercise and looked forward to the arrival of her horse. She rang the bell and went straight in.

"Good morning, Emma," said Margaret to the maid, who arrived to take her coat. She took off her jacket and handed it to Emma. "Where is Father?"

"Sir and madam are in the garden," she replied. Margaret was annoyed; she did not want to see Susan. She went through the small drawing room and out to the garden. Her father and stepmother were seated on a small patio in a corner, which afforded a lovely view of Barnstaple. They watched her approach and rose to greet her as she arrived. She kissed her father and just nodded to Susan.

"How are Xavier and Marcus?" her father asked. "I hope there is nothing wrong." Margaret shook her head, sat down silently and waited. Her father sighed and looked apologetically at Susan, who tactfully rose and said she would see about some tea.

Margaret waited until she was out of sight and then took the letter out of her bag. She handed it to her father. He looked at her. Since he had married Susan the previous August, Margaret rarely came to the house. *It must be something important for her to come uninvited and to walk here*, he thought. He looked at the letter and then at Margaret.

"I don't know what to do," she said simply.

He began to read.

53

Dear Mrs Eastman,

This will come as a big shock that I have written to you. I am sorry if this causes any problems, but I did not know what reaction I would receive from Peter. This is a very difficult letter to write.

I don't know how to continue. To put it bluntly, I believe I am Peter's father.

We lost touch back in 1940. I have been trying to find him since, as soon as I was able. My son's name is Peter Sidney Eastman. He was born on 5 July 1934, and his mother's name was Veronica.

Please help. Please do not tear up this letter. Please respond even if he is not my son and you know of his parents.

Yours sincerely

Aaron S. Eastman

Charles slowly put down the letter and looked at Margaret. They sat in silence.

"I wish your mother was here. She would know exactly what to do. The poor man, searching for his son."

"I will write to him and tell him Peter is not his son," said Margaret, "but, as you say, the poor man. Searching for 25 years. I will be very tactful."

Susan returned, followed by Emma with the tea tray. She poured out the tea and handed it around. She looked quizzically at Charles. He peered round at Margaret, who seemed very annoyed.

"Oh, alright, tell her if you must," she said angrily.

Charles explained to Susan, showed her the letter and told her what Margaret proposed to do.

"But suppose it is Peter's father," she said. "What does Peter say?"

"I haven't told him yet."

Susan nodded.

"But you will have to tell him," she said. Margaret was more annoyed; she knew Susan was right. Susan continued. "Speak to Elizabeth first. She will help." Margaret was now angry. She had just come to that conclusion and was annoyed that Susan had as well. "What was Peter's father's name? Aaron is not that common."

"Aaron Samuel Eastman. Marcus is named after him. Marcus after you," she nodded to her father, as that was his second name, "and Samuel after Peter's father." It had taken a lot of persuasion on her part for Peter to agree.

"Well," said Susan, "you have to at least investigate a little more." Margaret stood up. She furiously snatched the letter out of Susan's hand.

"Yes, thank you, and goodbye," she said rudely.

She stomped back into the house. Charles looked apologetically at Susan. She nodded and signalled he should follow her. Charles and Margaret drove back to Veronica Cottage in silence. As they entered, they were greeted by Marcus and Ivy. Charles spent a lovely hour playing with Marcus. Margaret kissed her father as he left.

Luckily Peter was distracted when he came in from the garage for lunch. He was still wrestling with the car's issues. Margaret was already going to see Elizabeth the next day. It was Ivy's day off. When Ivy had her day off, Margaret always took Marcus and Xavier, when he wasn't at school, to Elizabeth's.

Margaret waited until Marcus and Chloe were playing happily, then showed the letter to Elizabeth.

"I don't know what to do," she said. "My first instinct was to destroy it. I don't want Peter hurt again. He is so against his father, understandably so, but…" She trailed off.

"I think he needs to know. He wants answers. He could never understand why his father abandoned him and his mother. Maybe he can get some answers," said Elizabeth.

Margaret nodded, but raised her eyebrows in surprise that Elizabeth knew what Peter wanted, he had not said anything to her, but Elizabeth and Peter had always been close.

"But suppose it isn't his father. And we put him through all of that for nothing."

They drank their tea, thinking of what to do.

"It does seem very likely that this man is Peter's father. He knows a lot of detail."

"I will write to him asking for more information. Why did it take him so long to contact Peter?" asked Margaret. Elizabeth was considering their options. She had a strong feeling about this.

"Yes," said Elizabeth, "but be careful. We need to handle this properly." She didn't want Margaret charging in and upsetting Peter, causing a rift between him and Margaret. Elizabeth had always felt very protective since he had arrived, so bewildered and confused. "Don't give him your address yet. We don't want him turning up unexpectedly. Write back to Mr Eastman, giving him... What about Lady Agatha? He already has her address. Do you think she would help?"

Margaret nodded.

"She is very fond of Peter."

"Give her a ring. Explain the situation. Write the letter to Mr Eastman, put it inside another envelope addressed to Lady Agatha and ask her to post it. Then he can reply to Lady Agatha, and she can send the letter on to you. We really need something more concrete. When Bobbie was trying to prove that she was Uncle Arthur's daughter, she had photographs. Ask him to send a photograph of him and Peter, but Peter would be very young. Though Peter should recognise his father."

"I will speak to Lady Agatha as soon as I can. I want to make sure Peter is out of the way. Thank you, Beth. You have helped me again. I don't know what I would do without you. I constantly thank the day that father knocked your mother down. That sounds horrible, but you know what I mean. I could not have managed without you. You have always been there for me. If your parents had not come to London, we would not have become friends." Margaret shuddered at the thought and gave Elizabeth a hug.

It was a few days before she could be sure that Peter would not interrupt her phone call. He had gone over to his South Molton garage, which he was worried about. He told Margaret that he was going to hire another mechanic to work with Jeremy so that he could spend more time at his South Molton garage. Since his last manager had left, his assistant, Colin Fordham, was running it, but Peter had a feeling it was too much for him.

Peter went over to South Molton on the Monday to spend the whole day with Colin, so Margaret took advantage of him being absent to speak to Lady Agatha. She was only too happy to help.

A week later Margaret received another letter, re-addressed by Lady Agatha from London. In it was a photograph of a man, a woman and a baby.

How long she spent looking at the old sepia photograph she didn't know. She could not stop looking. She could not tell if the baby in the middle really looked like its parents, but it did remind her of another.

Staring back at her was the spitting image of her son, Marcus. She knew people didn't always have to look like their parents when little but grew to resemble them when older and some looked like them when born, as did her other son, Xavier. He was exactly like Hugh but as he had grown older had begun to look less like him. She had got tired of Hugh's relations saying how much he looked like Hugh in a surprised voice.

She was startled out of her trance by Peter's voice. She hastily stuffed the photograph back into the envelope and went out to the hall. She forgot Peter was coming back early from the garage because he planned to go over to the South Molton garage to interview for a part-time receptionist/typist/secretary. He had spent time with Colin, and while he was a good mechanic, he could not keep up with the paperwork and he forgot what parts he used and how much time he spent on each vehicle. He had also not claimed enough overtime or taken all his lunch breaks, Peter angrily discovered, so he gave him an extra payment to cover his time. Peter decided he needed help for the garage next door and had already employed someone.

Peter had come in the side door and was in his office. Margaret met him as he came out.

"Good luck," she said. Peter grimaced. He was tired of trying to find staff; he just wanted to work on cars. Margaret walked him to the door. He gave Margaret a kiss and ran his finger round her face.

"See you tonight," he said and went out the front door. Margaret turned back, glanced at the dining room and was horrified to see a bit of paper on the grey carpet. The white back showed up startlingly. It was clearly another photo. She rushed over and picked it up, relieved that Peter had not spotted it. She looked at it. It was a picture of the same three people; the baby was older, and the man and woman had swapped places, but they were the same.

CHAPTER 7

It was Charles's 70th birthday the following week, so Margaret arranged an evening party at The Firs. Just a small one. She planned to tell Peter about everything then, when she had everyone to support her.

They had just finished the meal when Susan directed everyone into the lounge. Normally Margaret would have resented this. The Firs had been her home, with her parents, and she disliked the fact that Susan and Angela had moved in, but she was distracted by what was to come.

Margaret guided Peter to the large sofa and sat next to him at one end. Angela quickly sat the other side of Peter. Edith and Elizabeth moved a couple of small fireside armchairs closer, with the help of David and Charles.

"This looks like a conspiracy," said Peter, laughing, as they sat in a circle, Charles, Susan and David on the other sofa behind them. William, Elizabeth's husband, had been unable to come.

"It is," said Margaret dryly. She could hardly speak.

Peter turned to look at her. She could see a frightened look in his eyes. She couldn't meet them and instead sat looking at her hands in her lap. She sensed Peter stiffen beside her.

"Peter," said Edith. "Look at me." Peter slowly looked at her. "Maggie has something to show you. We are all behind her with this, and you."

Margaret picked up her handbag and took out the first photograph. She gave it to Peter. He reluctantly took it. He glanced at it, then jumped up.

"You've been in my tin," he exclaimed. "How could you?" He looked around accusingly at everyone.

Margaret sat back on the sofa. Elizabeth sat next to her in the spot vacated by Peter. They clasped hands.

"Peter," said Edith again. "Look at me. No one has been in your tin. No one has been in your tin," she repeated. "Do you understand?" Peter looked at Margaret and Elizabeth, their eyes wide with apprehension. They all knew how sensitive Peter was about his tin. It was his sole possession from the bomb blast that killed his mother and destroyed their home. He never let anyone look in it.

"Neither of you have been in my tin?" Neither girl could speak, but both shook their heads. "Then how did you get this?" he asked, pacing up and down.

"Maggie received it last week in the post," continued Edith. "But it began a couple of weeks before that. Come and sit down and listen." She patted the armchair next to her, left empty by Elizabeth. Peter reluctantly stopped pacing and did as he was told. "When Maggie received the first letter, she did not know what to do. She was going to tear it up but showed it to Charles instead. Then she spoke to Beth. They decided that they should reply and ask for more proof. The photographs then came, and David and I were brought in."

"I knew something was up these past weeks, but I had been preoccupied with the garages," said Peter. "Was everyone in on this?"

"I wasn't," said Angela. Margaret had been pleased to hear that. She was sure Susan had told her. Peter ignored her and continued.

"So where did this photograph come from? I haven't seen it before. I just assumed it was from my tin."

"Your father," said Margaret in a small, squeaky voice.

The tension in the room was almost unbearable. She tightly shut her eyes. She sensed Peter get up and start pacing again. Finally he stopped and came over to her.

"You had better tell me all about it."

Elizabeth moved back to her original chair, and Peter sat down beside Margaret. Margaret opened her eyes, took a deep breath and started to explain. Peter did not interrupt until she had finished. She waited with bated breath for him to speak.

"Well," he said finally. "That's that. Now what about another cup of coffee." He looked at Susan, who duly obliged. Everyone was staring at him. "What?" he said defiantly, staring back at them all.

"Don't you want to meet your father?" asked a stunned Elizabeth.

"No," said Peter flatly. "Why should I? He abandoned Mother and me. Just walked out and never came back."

"Don't you want to know why?"

"No," said Peter again. "I know why. He just stopped loving us and moved on." Margaret's heart nearly broke to hear the anguish in his voice. She took his hand and a deep breath.

"I think you should meet him. I can't bear to see you suffering like this. Find out what happened, then if you decide not to take it further, it will be your decision. You can decide this time."

Peter looked at her, studying her face. He took her hand and kissed it.

"You are so wise. But it brings back so many painful memories."

"I know. But I... we are all here for you this time. You won't have to face him alone."

"Let me think about it."

They travelled home in silence. When they were in bed, Peter turned to her.

"This evening, after dinner when we went into the lounge, and you all surrounded me, I thought... I thought you were going to leave me. I thought you were going to say you wanted a divorce. I know I have been neglecting you lately, but I hope to spend much more time with you now the garages are dealt with. I didn't know what to say. I didn't want another 'hiccup'."

Margaret pulled him to her.

"Oh, Peter. I love you so much. I definitely do not want a divorce, but another 'hiccup', who knows?" She smiled at him knowingly. He laughed and started wildly kissing her.

The next morning, as they were finishing breakfast, the phone rang. Peter answered it. Margaret could hear him reassuring the person that everything was okay. He came back into the room smiling.

"That was Beth. She has been worried about us all night."

They laughed together. Last night was the best night they had had together for some time.

"So," said Peter, "where do we go from here?"

"I thought that we could meet your father."

"No. I don't want to see him, not after what he did to Mother and me."

"But, Peter, don't you want to know why?"

Peter shook his head.

"It hurts too much." Margaret went to him, put her arms around his waist and hugged him. They were disturbed by Xavier running in the room.

At lunch, Margaret resumed the conversation about Peter's father.

"Now you've had time to think, have you changed your mind?"

"No," said Peter, then he had a sudden thought. "You haven't already arranged anything, have you?"

"No," said Margaret, shaking her head.

"Good. I don't want him turning up here."

"He won't. He doesn't know where you live." Peter looked puzzled. Margaret explained, again, about Lady Agatha acting as a go-between.

"Is there anyone who doesn't know?" he said indignantly and left the room. Margaret sighed. This was going to take longer than she thought.

She enlisted Elizabeth and Edith's help. At his birthday party, he finally cracked. The pressure of everyone there and always talking to him about his father became too much. Margaret finally got Peter to agree to see his father.

Strike while the iron is hot, she thought and invited Peter's father to stay the next weekend. She put their address on the letter this time and their telephone number and sent it direct without the mediation of Lady Agatha. Then she waited with as much trepidation as Peter. Every time she mentioned the details of the visit, he glared at her. Peter's father was due to arrive Saturday afternoon and planned to leave Monday morning. Margaret had given the details of The Coaching Inn to break their journey.

Peter's father told Margaret he had married again, and his wife was coming too.

They had had a phone call the previous evening from Peter's father. Margaret took it. He said they had left that afternoon and were staying the night at The Coaching Inn and would be with them for lunch. Margaret hastily rang Mrs Bancroft in case she needed to go shopping for the meal, but she was reassured that she had enough to feed everyone. Then Margaret rang her father and asked him to come over. She thought it better if there was someone else there.

Peter resumed his pacing. Why had he let himself be talked into this? He wanted nothing to do with his father. His father had just abandoned them; that was all there was to it.

The doorbell sounded, and Sally showed the guests through to the terrace.

Margaret greeted her father with a kiss but ignored Susan.

"Thank you for coming," she said. "I just felt it would be better with you here." Charles kissed her back and hugged her reassuringly. He tilted his head apologetically to Susan, and she just sighed. She always knew Margaret resented her marrying her father, but she had loved Charles since she met him. She hoped that eventually Margaret would accept her.

They sat in silence and waited.

The doorbell rang again. This time Margaret and Peter went into the hall, followed by Charles and Susan. Sally opened the door and a couple entered. Margaret signalled to Sally, who curtsied and left.

Margaret took a step forward, holding out her hand.

"Hello, I'm Margaret," she introduced herself. The man stepped forward and shook it.

"I'm Aaron Eastman," he said, "and this is my wife, Esme." Margaret shook her hand and turned to the party in the hall.

"My father, Charles Sutherland, and his... wife, Susan." They shook hands. She turned to Peter, who was standing away from them. "And Peter." Aaron held out his hand, but Peter refused to take it. Eventually Aaron let it fall to his side.

"Let us go into the lounge," said Margaret in a false jolly voice. She led the way across the hall. "I will see if lunch is ready." She quickly left the lounge and sped into the kitchen. *I need a drink*, she thought.

Peter was watching his father while pretending to stare out the window. He was standing at the French doors. The others were making small talk, asking about the journey. His father was as he remembered him, older, his black hair now with some grey hairs at the temple, his blue eyes not so sparkling.

Margaret entered and announced lunch was ready. They all trooped into the dining room. Sally served the home-made steak and kidney pie, then left. They started eating. Margaret could bear it no more.

"I think we need to start clearing the air. First off, Peter, is this your father?"

Peter nodded to her.

"Good, at least we have the right person here." She tried to make the atmosphere lighter. Susan and Esme gave a small laugh.

"Now, for an explanation. I know it will take some time, so we will go slowly. We have all weekend." She glanced at her father for help.

"No accusations, just cold hard facts to start with," Susan spoke. Margaret glared at her. "We need to start on the day Aaron disappeared." Margaret glared at her again.

"Everything was normal until you left?" Margaret nodded to Aaron. She could not bring herself to mention his name yet. He nodded. She looked at Peter. He nodded too.

"So," she addressed Aaron, "you left the house to enlist?" He nodded. He suddenly had a lump in his throat. He put down his fork.

"Yes," he said croakily and took a sip of water. "I had returned from work and was determined to enlist that evening. It was January 1940. Roni, er, Veronica, your mother," he turned to Peter, "didn't want me to go out. She didn't want me to enlist, not then with so much happening. She wanted me to wait until I was called up. But I was determined, so I left." He took another gulp of water, and Esme squeezed his arm. "I was not well that day. I had not been well for a few days. I was going to enlist and then take a few days off work.

"Anyway, I set off, after having the row with your mother. I arrived at the enlisting office, very hot and tired. I felt exhausted. I just wanted to get it done and go home to rest. I remember signing on because the person dealing with me had a mass of ginger hair and a bushy beard. Then I remember walking along the street. Suddenly there was a mass of people pushing me. I couldn't breathe. I tried to get away from them and walked down a quieter street. I fell off the edge of the kerb. I tried to get back on the pavement but fell over again. A couple came along, and I asked them to help, but they thought I was drunk. I managed to stagger back to the main street and then collapsed again. I hit my head. This time somebody did stop. They called an ambulance. I wasn't making much sense. I remember feeling frightened that I would die on the street like Mother." His voice started trembling as he recalled the memory. "I didn't want to die like that. Like Mother." His hand shook, spilling some of the water. "I wasn't thinking clearly; I was just remembering Mother. They asked me my name, but I didn't answer. They tried to find my wallet, but I had lost it. They became insistent." He remembered faces and people all around him. He had felt so hot, so helpless. He remembered his mother. "They were pressing me, and I was still thinking of Mother, so before I passed out, I said Frances Sittall."

He sat back, exhausted. Everyone was silent. They waited for Aaron to recover. No one spoke until they had all finished the pie. Margaret rang the bell.

"Who is Frances Sittall?" she asked.

"My mother," said Aaron as Sally came into the room. She quickly cleared the table. Margaret knew that she and Mrs Bancroft would be gossiping in the kitchen. Sally returned with a trifle for dessert.

"I don't remember any Frances Sittall," protested Peter, "though the name Sittall is somehow familiar."

"No," said Aaron, "you wouldn't. She died before you were born in a horrible accident that also maimed and nearly killed your Aunt Ruth."

"Aunt Ruth? No. I don't remember her either," Peter said defiantly, staring at his father.

"Let Aaron explain a bit more," said Susan. Margaret stared at her fiercely. Peter stared insolently at his father.

"I will tell you about our family. I was born in 1911 to Frances and Sidney Eastman. I already had a sister, Ruth; she was born in 1908. My father, Sid, served in the war. He was awarded a medal for bravery. You were named after him, Peter."

"At least one member of my family acted honorably then," said Peter rudely.

"Peter," exclaimed Susan. Margaret wanted to admonish Susan, but no words would come. Peter looked down at his trifle and continued to eat.

"No, he needs to say what he feels," said Aaron.

"What happened to your father?" said Charles. "I was in the war but very young. I was in the navy." Charles chatted to give Aaron time.

"I don't remember much of my father. He went to war when I was three. But I do remember a holiday. He came home because he had been wounded. That was when he got his medal. He was in the middle of a field, in a barn being used as a makeshift ward until the wounded could be moved, in France, close to the line. The Germans had sent out a scouting party and found them. They set fire to the barn. Father kept going into the barn to rescue the wounded until it collapsed on him. He saved several lives. That was in 1917. When he came home, we all went down to Poole. Two of his comrades, brothers, lived there, but unfortunately, they died of their injuries. Whether Dad went there to find their families, I don't know. I just know it was the last time I spent with him. When he went back to war, he was killed. He was a hero."

CHAPTER 8

Margaret rang the bell for Sally. She said they would take coffee in the lounge. They went next door and sat down.

Aaron resumed telling them about his and Peter's family.

"Dad had been good friends with his parents' neighbours. They moved next door to Grandma and Grandpa just before the turn of the century. They invited my grandparents over for tea, and my father went with them. While they were there, the neighbours' son, came home; he was studying law and spent time in the middle of London. He had brought some work with him, and he and Dad became friends straight away. He is the reason why both Dad and I studied law. His name was Vernon Sittall. He was older than Dad. It was when they were visiting a client that they met Mother. They both fell in love with her, but she chose Dad. They all remained friends after Mum and Dad married. Vernon was wonderful when Dad died. Mum married him in 1922. It was on a trip to London to celebrate their fifth anniversary, and also me deciding to study law after finishing school and Ruth's engagement, that the accident happened." He took a drink of coffee and a deep breath. "We had just come out of the underground station at Leicester Square. We were running late. We had met Vernon at his office in Kensington, but he was taking longer with his client than expected. So we rushed out of the packed underground. Vernon and I were in front, anxious to get to the theatre before the play started; Ruth's fiancé was going to meet us there. Then we were going for supper. Suddenly we heard a shout and a commotion." He paused again, and Esme patted his leg. "We stopped and turned round. We realised that Mother and Ruth weren't with us. We tried to find them. We pushed our way through the crowd." He paused, wiping his mouth with his hanky. "They were lying there on the ground. Mother had a pool of blood around her head. Ruth was lying half under the bus." He stopped, wiping his face. Esme put her arm around him.

"You're nearly done. Keep going. You need to tell them." Aaron nodded. He hated these memories.

"Mother and Ruth had tried to follow us across the road from the station. We should have taken better care of them. Mother slipped off the kerb and fell hitting her head on the road. She died instantly. A bus was coming and swerved trying to avoid her but hit Ruth, who was trying to get to her. Ruth had a broken hip and leg. We were not sure if she would walk again. She could initially with crutches, but after a few years she had to use a chair. I have a picture of her, and Mum and Dad." Esme delved into her handbag and passed a couple of pictures around.

"I've met your aunt," Charles said to Peter as he studied the photograph. "She ran over my foot. It was at an award ceremony. Constance had to go. I wasn't invited but went anyway." He was good at getting into places he wasn't invited; that was how he met Constance. "It would have been just after the war, the second war, 1947 or 1948, before Constance started to get ill. Your aunt reversed into me but told me it was my fault," he finished indignantly. Everyone laughed.

"That sounds like Ruth," said Aaron, laughing. "She got a medal for looking after the disabled navy officers. She opened up her home to care for them, even though she was in a chair."

Peter was staring at the photographs, staring at his aunt.

"I don't remember her," he said sadly.

Margaret stood up.

"I think that is a good place to stop. I think we all need to take in what has been revealed so far. We will continue tonight. I have invited Elizabeth, William, Edith and David tonight as well."

Peter left immediately, mumbling about the garage. Charles and Susan said goodbye. Margaret walked them to the door and kissed her father.

Aaron brought in the cases and went upstairs. Margaret returned to the lounge and found Esme there.

Esme smiled at her.

"You have a lovely house."

"Thank you. Peter built it for me."

"Wow. How long have you been married?"

"Three years."

Esme took a deep breath. She was now coming to the point. She noticed Margaret's animosity towards Susan and the effect it was having on Peter, and thus Aaron.

"And how long has your father been married to Susan?"

"Nearly a year," was the sulky reply. Esme carried on.

"How long had you known Peter before you married?"

"About twenty... one years."

"How long has your father known Susan?"

"About the same."

"When did your first husband die?"

"About five years ago."

"When did you mother pass away?"

"About five years ago." Esme looked at Margaret until she was forced to look back at her.

"So both you and your father lost your spouses about the same time and married people you had known about the same length of time." Margaret nodded. She hadn't realised that before.

"How long has Susan been a widow?"

"About 20-odd years."

"So your father had known Susan a long time. Since she became a widow, the same time that you had known Peter. They had been friends, just as you and Peter had been friends."

"Peter and I had never been friends. I mean, I pretended I didn't like him," she added honestly.

"And it was the same for your father?"

"I don't know. I think he always liked Susan."

"Did your mother like Susan?"

"Yes, I think so."

Here was the 64-million-dollar question. Esme tried to keep relaxed. She couldn't take her time; she only had a few hours.

"Was your father having an affair with Susan while your mother was alive?" Margaret looked horrified.

"No, of course not."

"How do you know?"

"He told me." Margaret thought back to the chat she had had with her father, when he told her that he and Susan were getting engaged, shortly after her wedding to Peter. He had reassured her that he and Susan had liked each other and been friends, and she had supported him through her mother's ill health, but he had always been faithful to her mother. She believed him.

"But would you believe Susan?"

"No." Margaret thought back to her confrontation with Susan, after her conversation with her father. She demanded to know if her father and Susan had had an affair. Susan, of course, denied it, but she knew.

"So you believe your father that he was loyal to your mother, but you don't believe Susan, and think she was having an affair with your father," Esme said and added gently, "They can't both be right." Margaret stared at her. Put like that she realised how silly it sounded. She was confused. Esme continued. "Do you think your father was lying?"

Margaret shook her head. She knew her father was telling the truth. Then Susan must be telling the truth as well. She felt as if a weight had fallen from her shoulders. How could she have been so stupid?

"I think you wanted to believe the worst of Susan because you are so loyal to your mother. Your father and Susan's relationship was similar to yours and Peter's. Very, very good friends, maybe a bit in love but loyal to your spouses."

Margaret nodded, tears in her eyes now as she thought what she had put her father through.

Esme felt she was getting somewhere.

"I have been so horrible to him. He needed my support, and I wasn't there. I just made things worse for him."

"I'm sure he understands, and Susan." Margaret tensed again at the sound of Susan's name. Esme continued, a little bit longer then she needed to get to Aaron. "Apart from the relationship she had with your father, why else don't you like her?"

"She and Angela always seem to be antagonising me. I know it is deliberate."

"Who is Angela?"

"Susan's daughter, from her first marriage."

"Why would Angela deliberately antagonise you?"

"Because she is in love with Peter. She always has been since he arrived."

"How old is Angela?"

"Thirty-three."

"So Susan wasn't married too long to her first husband then. Angela was about 10 when he died. That is very young. They hadn't been married long?"

Margaret thought. She couldn't remember.

"I think Susan and her first husband were married for about 15 years."

"So Angela was born sometime after they married."

"No, yes. I'm sorry." She rubbed her hand against her temple. "At Father and Susan's wedding, I overheard someone saying that at least this was not a shot-gun wedding like Susan's first one. I remember because I had no idea what a shot-gun wedding was. I asked Peter, and he explained."

"So, Susan was expecting a baby when she married first time. So, Angela must be older than 33, or does Susan have another child?"

"No," said Margaret slowly. "She only has Angela. I know Angela is about four years older than me." She thought back to the time when she was 14. Peter had been over to see Charles and Constance; he was 17. She was hiding on the landing, waiting for him to go. There was a knock on the door as he was about to leave. It was Angela.

"You are just the person I want," she said, looking up at him. At 17 he was over six feet. "I want to give you this," she continued provocatively. Margaret felt herself stiffen and took a deep breath. Peter took the envelope. "It is an invitation to my 18th party. I hope you can come. We could have a lot of fun." It was all Margaret could do to stop herself running down the stairs and slapping her face. She watched as Peter glanced up at the landing, very slowly lifted Angela's chin and gave her a long kiss. Margaret clenched her fists. At last they broke apart.

"See you at the party," Peter said and firmly, but gently, manoeuvred Angela out of the open door. He shut it behind her.

"You can come out now," he said. Margaret waited for someone to appear, when she realised he was talking to her. She moved from her hiding place.

"How could you?" she said angrily, stomping down the stairs.

"Are you jealous?" said Peter, laughing. "Do you want me to kiss you?" He took a step towards her. She was staring at him. Just in time she rushed upstairs to her room. She could hear him laughing. She flung herself on her bed. How she hated him.

"No, Susan only has Angela," Margaret said firmly.

"And you hate Angela. It is not Susan, but Angela." Margaret suddenly realised it was Angela she hated, and she nodded. Esme continued. "So what happened to Susan's first baby?"

Margaret stared at her. *What had happened to Susan's first baby?* Margaret continued to stare at Esme and said,

"What happened to Susan's baby?" Esme shrugged.

"What happened to Susan's baby?" Margaret repeated, more to herself this time.

Esme coughed. "Could I go to my room now?"

"Oh, yes, of course," Margaret said. "Follow me and I will show you."

They went out of the lounge and across the hall to the impressive sweeping staircase. At the top, in the middle of the landing, were her and Aaron's suitcases.

"Why were they left here?" asked Esme. "Where is Aaron?"

They heard the sound of voices from the floor above. They turned and went up the smaller staircase. At the top they looked round the smaller secondary landing. They saw Aaron on his hands and knees with Xavier on his back.

"I think that is enough now, Xavier," admonished Margaret. Ivy came in from the bedroom where she had put Marcus to rest.

"Sorry, madam," she said, taking Xavier's hand.

"No, it's my fault," said Aaron, slowly getting up. He looked hot and tired.

"I want to play with Marcus's grandad some more," said Xavier. Margaret raised her eyebrows to Aaron at Xavier's form of address.

"Sorry, I didn't know what else to say when he asked who I was." Margaret nodded.

"I will show you to your room." She took them back downstairs to the first landing and led them to the bedroom over the dining room, with an adjoining Jack and Jill bathroom. She left them to rest; she was going to do the same. She went into her room, but the question returned. *What happened to Susan's baby?* She had to get an answer. Suddenly she knew; she would speak to Elizabeth.

Margaret went downstairs to Peter's office. She rang Elizabeth. Elizabeth wanted to know how it went. Margaret said she would explain everything that evening, and did she know about Susan's baby.

"Susan's baby? You mean Angela?"

"No," said Margaret impatiently. "Susan's first baby."

"Susan's first baby?"

"Yes."

"What about it?"

"Exactly."

"What are you talking about, Maggie?"

Margaret sighed.

"When Susan got married to her first husband, she was expecting a baby. What happened to it?"

"Oh," said Elizabeth. "That baby."

"Yes, that baby." Margaret was getting quite cross now. She sensed Elizabeth was playing with her because she wouldn't give her any information about Peter's father. "Please," she begged.

Elizabeth smiled to herself.

"I will tell you what I know. Susan and Arnold – that was her first husband – had to get married because they were expecting. Susan's father insisted on it to avoid a scandal, though I think it was too late by then. Anyway, on their wedding night Arnold got drunk and assaulted Susan. He always had a temper. He attacked her very badly. She lost the baby. She nearly died herself." There was silence. Eventually Margaret spoke.

"Poor Susan. Poor, poor Susan. Why didn't she divorce him?"

"Apparently, and this bit is more hearsay, she wanted to get her revenge. So she pretended that Angela wasn't his. She is, of course, but Arnold always had his doubts." Margaret was thinking.

"Maggie? Are you there?"

"Yes, thank you, Beth. Do you know anymore?"

"Not much, only that a couple of years after Arnold died, just about the end of the war, there was some gossip about her and Sir Nicholas Mortimer. They remained friends for several years, but nothing came of it. Angela started dating his nephew when he came to live with his uncle." Margaret heard the tone of Elizabeth's voice change from teasing to steely at the mention of his nephew, but she ignored it.

"Thank you, Beth. I will tell you everything this evening, I promise. Come a bit early if you can." Margaret slowly put the phone down. She was so sorry for Susan; she had had no idea.

Poor, poor Susan. Margaret's hatred had completely disappeared, and she was full of compassion.

CHAPTER 9

Margaret was awakened by Peter coming into the room. She hadn't meant to fall asleep, just rest. She glanced at the silver alarm clock by her bed. Half past five, just enough time to get ready.

She looked anxiously at Peter. He looked very tense.

"Would you like me to run you a bath?" she said.

Peter nodded and slumped onto the bed. Margaret crawled over and sat beside him. She gave him a hug. Usually he would respond by pushing her back on the bed and covering her with kisses until she demanded he stop. But he just sat there listless.

"Everything will turn out okay," she said. "You have taken a big step today. I am sure we will get all the answers tonight."

"But will they be the right ones? All these years I have spent hating him. Not knowing." Margaret gave him another reassuring hug.

"You have all of us on your side. Just listen to him, hear his story. If necessary, we will check the facts. Then this time it will be your decision to see him again. But you have discovered your Aunt Ruth. Do you remember her?" Peter shook his head. "Maybe you could ring her tomorrow. Perhaps the sound of her voice will ring some bells." This time Peter nodded. Margaret smiled. She hoped she was doing the right thing. She pushed herself off the bed.

"I'm going to run your bath," she said. "You smell of oil and the garage." She went into their bathroom and heard Peter get off the bed. "I hope you haven't made the bed dirty," she shouted, laughing so he would know she wasn't serious.

"No, but I might make you dirty," he said, making her jump as he came up behind her. He had stripped off ready for his bath. His arms encircled Margaret. He pushed her slip straps down and started to kiss her shoulders. Margaret tried to push him away.

"We haven't got time," she said. "I need to get ready."

"You could always join me in the bath," he said cheekily.

Margaret was relieved; he was getting back to himself. She was so tempted but firmly refused. She heard Peter laughing as she went out the bathroom. She went over to her wardrobe and got out the dress she was going to wear that evening. She decided on an off-the-shoulder golden brocade cocktail dress, styled her bronze hair up into a loose beehive and chose a simple diamond necklace and earrings. She was just doing the finishing touches in front of her dressing table when Peter came out the bathroom with just a towel round his waist.

"You look beautiful, as always," he said, going over to her. He stood behind her and put his arms over her shoulders. She screamed and stood up.

"Don't do that – you are all wet. Look, you have made my dress wet." She pointed to a small patch on the bodice.

"Maybe I should kiss it better." He took a step towards her. She took one backwards and nearly fell over her dressing table stool. Peter grabbed her to stop her falling over. This time she didn't push him away but ran her fingers over his chest.

It was Peter's turn to resist. He sighed, then overcame his urge to make love to Margaret. He settled for a long lingering kiss. As they broke apart, Margaret reassured him again.

"We are with you. This time you have all of us to support you."

Peter nodded. He already felt in control. He watched Margaret leave. He had had a good think this afternoon. Initially he had wanted absolutely nothing to do with his father and had only agreed because Margaret had been so forceful, along with Elizabeth and Edith. He felt that Constance would have added her voice as well, if she was alive. He had been determined to have no further contact with his father, no matter what he said, but he had a feeling it wouldn't be that easy. He dressed slowly and finally went downstairs. He had just entered the lounge when the doorbell rang.

Margaret sped past him. She beat Sally to the front door. She opened it and let everyone in. She grabbed Elizabeth's arm.

"Excuse us a minute. I need a word with Beth. Please go into the lounge." She pulled Elizabeth into the office.

"Did you find out anymore?"

"No," said Elizabeth. "Mum didn't know much more than I told you this afternoon. What is this all about?"

"Nothing. Just something Esme said this afternoon. Shall we join the others?" Margaret opened the door and led the way to the lounge. Elizabeth followed, determined to find out everything soon.

They joined the party in the lounge. Peter was serving the sherry. He gave a glass to Elizabeth and Edith. They could wait no longer and demanded to know what had passed. Margaret quickly summarised the lunchtime conversation.

As she was finishing, the door opened slowly, and Aaron and Esme entered. Esme was glad that she had purchased a new dress when she saw what the other ladies were wearing. She was not usually one for dresses and was going to wear her tweed suit but decided to splash out on a short sleeveless black dress. When she put it on upstairs, she had felt uncomfortable. She had added a jet and pearl necklace that Aaron had given her for her last birthday. Halfway down the stairs she had wanted to go and change; now, in the room with everyone else, she was glad she had worn it.

Aaron and Esme were introduced to Elizabeth and William, and Edith and David. Margaret indicated to Peter to offer Aaron and Esme sherry. He pulled a face but did as he was asked. They made small talk again while they waited for Charles and Susan. Peter smiled to himself, as it was almost the same conversation he had heard before lunch, asking about their journey down and so on.

The doorbell rang again, and this time Margaret did not rush off to answer but waited in the lounge. Charles and Susan were shown in by Sally. Margaret kissed her father as usual but this time greeted Susan as well; she gave her a quick hug. Everyone in the room was stunned. Edith looked at Elizabeth and both raised their eyebrows. Elizabeth would definitely be having words with Margaret at the first opportunity.

Margaret quickly offered Charles and Susan sherry to cover her embarrassment.

Aaron coughed and was about to speak when there was a knock on the door and Ivy and Xavier came in.

"He can't wait any longer to say hello to everyone," said Ivy.

Margaret and Peter had already said goodnight to Marcus before they came down but agreed to let Xavier down to say goodnight and see everyone. He had wanted to join the party. Xavier went round giving everyone a kiss or a hug, then he and Ivy left the room. Aaron was about to speak again when there was another knock on the door. Sally entered.

"Mrs Bancroft says the soup is ready." She curtsied and left the room. Everyone followed her into the dining room. A big tureen of soup sat on the side table. Everyone took their places and Sally served the soup. As soon as everyone had a bowl, she curtsied and left. Margaret smiled. Her training was paying off; Sally had not spilled a single drop of soup.

"Please can I say something," said Aaron nervously, then he looked at Esme, who nodded. "I need to tell you something before we go on. I wanted to tell you at lunch, but it didn't happen. I want to tell you now because I don't want you to think I am hiding anything, and we may not get that far in the story." He took a deep breath and continued. "Esme and I have a daughter. You have a sister, Peter."

Everyone waited for Peter to speak, but he sat in silence. Edith decided to break the silence. She was sitting next to Peter and could feel him tense.

"What is her name?"

"Phoebe. She is 16."

Still no reaction from Peter. He just continued to eat his soup. This time Susan broke the silence.

"Maybe you should continue your story, Aaron."

"Yes," agreed Margaret eagerly. She wanted to go to Peter but left it to Edith and Elizabeth, who were sitting either side of Peter to support him, at the other end of the table. Everyone looked at Margaret. Usually she disagreed with everything Susan said. "Please continue."

"Where was I? Oh, yes," he remembered. He hated remembering. The image of his mother lying in the pool of blood and the sound of Ruth moaning in pain haunted him for a long time. "I was lying on the ground barely conscious, and people were asking my name. All I could think about was Mother, and I mumbled her name, and how I didn't want to die like that. Next thing I know I am being put in an ambulance and someone is saying, 'Don't worry, Mr Sittall, you are in safe hands.'" Aaron took a sip of wine.

"The next thing I remember is waking up in hospital with no memory of anything." There was a gasp of astonishment from everyone except Peter, who gave a snort of disbelief. "Everyone there called me Francis Sittall. I would answer to the name, but it didn't feel right. I had to learn to walk, read, everything again. I had been in a coma for six months, and I spent another few months building up my strength before being moved to a different hospital. I insisted that all my records went with me. I didn't want them getting lost; they were the only things I had that were mine. At the next hospital there was somebody there who was interested in amnesia cases. We agreed it had been caused by my illness – I had a very vigilant case of meningitis; I can't remember the full medical name – and that there must have been a traumatic incident but, of course, I couldn't remember at that point. I stayed there until April 1941, when I was moved out of London to a psychiatric hospital near Swindon. I was under the supervision of Sir Boyd Jennings. Then I met Esme."

"Sorry to interrupt," apologised Margaret. "I will get Sally to clear and bring in the main course, then we can hear about your meeting with Esme." She looked at Aaron, and he nodded. Margaret rang the bell. Ten minutes later they were sitting down to the main course, waiting to hear about Aaron and Esme's meeting.

"I was in a room with four other men. They had lost their memories as well, due to the war, though. One man had been there as long as I had, but others came and went. Anyway, that afternoon I was sitting reading a book when I heard the matron come back for something she had forgotten. It was her afternoon off, and I had already said goodbye." He paused for a moment, then continued. "I got up to greet her again, when she was followed in by Esme. I was bowled over; my heart was going. I immediately went to introduce myself." Again he paused and had another sip of wine. He took a deep breath. "I introduced myself as Aaron Eastman. This caused a stir. Initially everyone went silent. Esme held out her hand and said who she was, but then the matron intervened. She insisted I was Francis Sittall, but I was equally insistent that I was Aaron Eastman." He stopped speaking and mopped his head with his napkin.

"I can take up some of the story now," said Esme. "I heard about Aaron's case; it was the worst case of amnesia we had seen. But I hadn't seen him, as he was Sir Boyd's patient. But that day, Judith, Judith Stokes, the matron for Aaron's ward, and I had arranged to go to a dance being held for the soldiers stationed nearby. Judith had forgotten her handbag so returned for it. Usually she left it in the staff room but had taken it to the nurses' station on the ward. So as we walked in, I saw this handsome man stand up and come over to us. As he introduced himself, I couldn't breathe. I could hardly say my name. Then Judith was arguing about his name. I had to calm them both down. Aaron then nearly collapsed, but we got him back on the bed. He fell asleep immediately. We left, but the dance was ruined for me." She turned and smiled at Aaron. "All I could think about was you." Aaron gripped her hand. He took up the story again.

"I awoke next morning. I think they gave me something to knock me out. My head hurt. I had a special appointment with Sir Boyd. He didn't usually work Saturday's but came in specially. I told him what happened. He didn't argue, just asked if I remembered anything else. But I didn't. My head was still hurting, so they gave me some strong pain killers, and I was a bit woozy for the next few days. At my next appointment with Sir Boyd, Esme was there. He had asked her to join us." He was interrupted.

"You aren't a nurse, are you?" said Edith accusingly, interrupting. Everyone looked at Esme. She shook her head. "I thought not," said Edith with satisfaction. "You are not a matron either, are you?"

Esme shook her head, smiling.

"No, I am a psychiatrist. I worked alongside Sir Boyd. How did you know?"

"Mum senses all sorts of things like that. I thought you were a nurse on the next ward," Elizabeth said.

Margaret was digesting this news. She glanced at Esme, who caught her look. Esme smiled and shrugged her shoulders. Margaret returned the smile. She stood up to ring for Sally.

When they had settled down for dessert, Aaron continued.

"With Esme there as reassurance, I tried to piece everything together. I started to recall events leading up to Mother and Ruth's accident. Esme traced Ruth in Poole. I couldn't remember exactly where she lived, but she was easy to find. I spoke to Ruth on the telephone. She was in tears – we both were. We spoke many times over the months to Christmas." Aaron paused and looked at Peter. "Ruth had been telephoning your mother after my disappearance, but she could not do much in her situation, you do understand." Peter shrugged. "Also, she was looking after Vernon. He visited you and your mother shortly after my disappearance. Do you remember him?" Aaron looked at Peter.

"I don't know. So many people turned up."

"He was tall, about 6ft, heavily built with a big blond handlebar moustache. He also had a limp due to an accident when he was a boy, which is why he failed the army medical." Peter was looking puzzled.

"I don't know. I think I have a very vague recollection of him."

"He drove a green MG Roadster, very flashy."

Peter smiled for the first time that evening.

"I remember the car. When he left, I went outside to look at it. He let me sit in it. I think that was when I fell in love with cars."

Esme took a photograph out of her bag and passed it along to Peter.

"Yes, that's him. He promised to help. He promised to return. But he didn't."

"No," said Aaron. "On the way back to Poole – he lived with Ruth – he suffered a major stroke and crashed the car. He was taken to Southampton Hospital, and then transferred to Poole. Because of the stroke he was unable to speak or move much. He then suffered a heart attack. Ruth nursed him as best she could; she also had the injured sailors, so she was very busy. He died in March 1941. Ruth tried to ring your mother, but the phone was cut off, and she had no further contact with her or you."

Margaret summoned Sally and told her to bring the coffee through to the lounge.

When they were all settled, Aaron continued.

"With Ruth's help I was beginning to piece everything together. We went slowly because they didn't tell me much. They wanted me to remember, but I couldn't. They decided that a visit to Ruth might help. As she couldn't come to me, Esme and I set off to Poole. We took the train. Sir Boyd was happy to entrust me to Esme's care. When we arrived at Ruth's house, it did jolt a few memories. Then meeting Ruth again was amazing. While I was there, I did experience some more memories. This is when I remembered you and your mother." Aaron paused for a drink. "I remember you running around the garden and your mother chasing after you. I was excited at the discovery, then Ruth told me that she had lost contact with you. I was determined to try and find you. When we arrived back at the hospital, I remembered more about the day I left. When I saw Sir Boyd the next day, I told him that I remembered enrolling and needed to join my regiment immediately. He said I wasn't well enough, but he would contact them. A few days later I had a visit from the military police; they were going to arrest me for desertion."

There was a knock on the door, and Sally came in.

"Ma'am, if you please, we have finished in the kitchen."

Margaret muttered her excuses and followed Sally into the kitchen.

"Thank you, Mrs Bancroft. That was a lovely meal. And thank you, Sally – you did well. Hello, Mr Bancroft." She smiled at a man sitting at the kitchen table. "Thank you for taking Sally home."

"Are you sure you don't need me tomorrow?"

"Yes, Mrs Bancroft. We are going to Father's for lunch and then have a quiet tea here with the boys."

"I have cooked a chicken for you – it is in the fridge. You can have it cold with a salad. I have also made an apple pie. You can have that hot or cold and there is a jug of cream as well."

Margaret locked the back door after they left and went back to the lounge. While they waited for her to return, Charles was talking to Aaron about cricket, excited that he lived close to Lord's cricket ground.

Aaron resumed.

"Thanks to Sir Boyd and Esme, they didn't take me away. The next few months were taken up with my trial. I had contacted my old law firm, Cooper, Scott & Sittall. Luckily, I won my case, as I was able to prove that I had been in hospital under a false name and sustained memory loss. Both Sir Boyd and Esme testified for me. I was free to search for you." He looked at Peter. "But then I received instructions to report to my base the day after next, so I had to hurry. I had left the hospital and moved in with Derek Scott, my business partner, and his wife, Vera. Their children were away. Their son Robert was fighting in France, and their daughter Julie was a Land Army girl in Wales, so they were happy for me to stay. Esme arranged to come as well. We took a trip to our old home. I wasn't expecting much as Ruth had said she couldn't reach you there. Her letter had been returned, marked unknown. I spoke to the lady that was living there, but she didn't know anything. I went to the flat below, where Mrs French lived. She remembered us. She thought I had been killed, so at first she thought I was a ghost. She remembered you and your mother departing very suddenly. She did not know where you had gone." Aaron sighed. "There is one more thing I must ask you, Peter. What happened to the baby your mother was carrying? I didn't like to ask Mrs French, as she was getting confused."

Peter looked at his father.

"I don't know. I don't remember a baby."

CHAPTER 10

"But your mother was expecting. That was one of the reasons we wanted to move house."

"I remember the house. We didn't move there. I can't remember any baby."

"I think with all the stress of your father leaving, she may have miscarried, Peter," said Edith quietly. "Think back; was your mother ill?"

"Yes," said Peter. "She was. About a month after Father left, she got Mrs French to take me to school as she wasn't well. Mrs French stayed with me that night as Mother was in hospital. She was home when I got back the next day but was still ill. She got better after a few days. I didn't realise that she had miscarried. Poor Mother. To go through that alone. It was all your fault." He shouted that last bit at his father.

"I'm sorry," was all his father could say.

"Peter!" admonished Margaret.

"No, he's quite right. It is my fault. I should never have gone out that night. I should have listened to Roni. But it is a double-edged sword because I now have Esme and Phoebe."

No one knew what to say.

Margaret broke the silence.

"And I would not have Peter or Marcus. Because Peter would have stayed in London. I would never have met him."

Peter looked at Margaret. He hadn't thought of that.

David and Edith stirred. Edith spoke.

"We have a million questions but are quiet exhausted. I think we will leave now." They stood up.

"Before you go, can I take everyone's photograph? I promised Ruth I would. I understand that you will not be at Charles and Susan's tomorrow?" said Aaron, he looked at Edith and David.

"No," replied Edith. "I'm afraid we have to go to David's Aunt Maud's 100th birthday. His cousin insisted and I don't feel we can miss it."

"I brought my camera down earlier." Aaron retrieved it from the side table. "Can I have the ladies sitting on the sofa and the men standing behind?"

Edith sat on the right of the sofa, next to Elizabeth. Margaret sat next. Susan hesitated about sitting on the left end next to Margaret. Usually if she went near Margaret, Margaret would move away. But this time, Margaret patted the cushion, so Susan sat down. It was a bit of a squash, but they sat comfortably.

"I don't know why I have to have my picture taken," said Peter sulkily. At that moment, there was a cry and a thump. Aaron, who had been walking backwards to try and get everyone in, fell over a footstool. Everyone laughed except Peter. Aaron stood up and checked his camera was still working.

"Perhaps the gentlemen could sit on chairs. You are all so tall it is difficult to get your heads in."

"Get them from the dining room," ordered Margaret.

The men dutifully filed out. Peter was still moaning.

"I don't want him to take my picture."

William quickly grabbed a chair and went back to the lounge.

"This is not for you, Peter, but for your aunt," said David, who departed with a chair. Charles picked up his chair.

"Your Aunt Ruth is an innocent in all of this. If she wants a photo, then she should have one. And your sister, Phoebe; it is not her fault either." He left.

Peter stood with his hands on his chair. He reluctantly picked it up and returned to the lounge.

"No," said Aaron. "Please can I have the men sitting behind their wives? You are all mixed up." William was behind Susan, David was behind Margaret, Charles Elizabeth and Peter Edith. It was Aaron's turn to laugh as the men played musical chairs. Finally they were sorted, and Aaron took his pictures.

"Thank you," he said. "We are visiting Ruth next weekend, so I can take them and show her. I would like to get some of you and the boys tomorrow." He looked at Margaret. She nodded.

* * * * * * * *

Sunday morning breakfast was usually a noisy affair held in the kitchen. But this Sunday breakfast had been laid in the dining room by Sally and Mrs Bancroft before they left the previous evening. Peter was cooking the breakfast in the kitchen. Ivy was in the dining room trying to persuade Marcus to eat some cereal when Aaron and Esme came in.

"Good morning, sir, madam," said Ivy as they entered.

"Good morning, Ivy. And how are the boys this morning?"

"Can we play horses again?" asked Xavier.

"No," said his mother as she entered the room. "I don't think that's a good idea. Marcus's grandad," she raised her eyebrows, "is here to see Papa Peter, not play with you, young man." She tickled him as she passed on her way to get a cup of tea. Xavier giggled.

"Mum has promised a real pony," he declared.

Aaron and Esme looked at Margaret.

"Yes, I have," she confirmed as she sat down. "I am getting some stables and the field ready. I hope to have a horse as well. I miss Savannah – she is stabled at Royston House. I don't want to move her."

"Phoebe is horse mad. Of course, living in London makes it difficult for her, but when we visit Ruth, we visit the stables just outside Poole and she rides there," said Esme.

Peter came in with the breakfast and put it on the sideboard to keep it warm.

"Please help yourselves."

He got himself a cup of tea and sat next to Margaret.

"Peter, after you have rung your aunt this morning, maybe you could ring Phoebe? Would that be alright?" She looked at Aaron and Esme.

Esme nodded. "She would love that."

Peter was about to say something. He wasn't sure he wanted to speak to his father's relatives, but he thought about what Charles said and bit his tongue. He was right; it was not their fault. Anyway, he now had a sister. He had had Elizabeth and Margaret, but neither of them really felt like a sister. Now he had one all of his own.

Breakfast got more and more noisy as Aaron and Xavier decided to have a singing contest, and Marcus wanted to join in. Margaret admitted defeat and declared she was going to get dressed. She had come down in her burgundy nightdress with matching bell-sleeved robe. Esme was astonished to see such detail on nightwear; there were lace panels on the shoulder and red embroidery on the front and cuffs. She felt dowdy in her cream twin set and plaid skirt.

Peter cleared the table with Esme's help. Aaron went up to the nursery with Ivy, Xavier and Marcus.

When Margaret came down, Peter was in the lounge reading the Sunday newspapers and Esme was looking out over the garden.

"I will give you a tour," said Margaret, standing beside her.

Esme was pleased to see Margaret was casually dressed, just wearing a pale-green blouse and slacks, but she could see that they were still expensive.

Peter stood up and put down the paper.

"I will ring Aunt Ruth now." He felt strange saying that. He had a real aunt now, not borrowed ones.

"I will give you the number," said Esme, hunting in her bag for her phone book.

"Where is Aaron?" asked Margaret.

"Still with the boys, I think," replied Esme, still rummaging in her bag.

"I'd better go and rescue him." Margaret left the room and went to the top floor. She found Aaron and Xavier trying to do a jigsaw.

"I hope he isn't being a nuisance," said Margaret.

"No, he is a lovely lad. He does you credit."

Margaret smiled.

"Come downstairs for some coffee – you too, Xavier. Where is Marcus?"

"He is asleep," replied Ivy as she came out of the bedroom.

"You may leave now, if you wish," said Margaret. Ivy usually had Sunday afternoon off, getting a lift from Mr Bancroft when he picked up Mrs Bancroft after she finished preparing lunch. Ivy always got dropped off at The Firs, as she was friends with the maid there, Emma. But today she arranged to visit Ross and his wife Lucy and would have to walk as her car was being repaired and Mrs Bancroft wasn't working, plus Emma was busy at The Firs. Ross was the handyman-cum-gardener who lived at Landkey with his wife, Lucy nee Bowden, Elizabeth's friend from her village. Ross and Lucy had invited her to lunch. She said goodbye to everyone and left.

Margaret made some coffee, and they sat on the veranda enjoying the view, watching Xavier play on the lawn. Peter returned from the office when he finished talking to Ruth. He was pleased he had rung her, though she was in tears most of the time. He suggested they should arrange a visit soon.

"I would like to speak to Phoebe now, I think." He was hesitant. Peter hoped they would get on. He didn't know how she would feel about him.

"That's a marvellous idea. We hoped you would want to speak to her, but we told her that it may take a bit of time for you to get used to the idea that you had a sister," said Esme. This time she didn't need to search her bag for her phone book. She knew her number by heart.

"Who is looking after Phoebe while you are here?" asked Margaret, suddenly realising that she could be in London on her own. Margaret hoped not. She remembered how wild she had been at 16.

"My parents are staying with her," replied Esme. Margaret breathed a sigh of relief.

Peter returned to the study. He slowly dialled the number and listened to the ringing tone.

"Hello," said a soft voice thick with emotion, making the Sloane Square accent more prominent.

* * * * * * *

They all piled out of Peter's black Zephyr when it stopped outside The Firs. Emma opened the door immediately and showed them into the lounge.

Everyone greeted each other enthusiastically. They were just settling themselves down on the patio outside when they had to get up to greet the new arrivals.

"Mum is so cross she can't come," said Elizabeth. "And that she had to go to Aunt Maud's party, but she is 100." Elizabeth shrugged her shoulders. "Also, I'm sorry that Bill can't come – we are having problems with the chef. It has not been the same since Ben left."

Everyone settled down on the patio again.

"Mum, can me and Xavier go and play in the wood garden?" asked Duncan. He and Xavier were inseparable. They went to a public school a few miles outside Barnstaple and had all their lessons together.

"Yes," replied Elizabeth, quickly glancing at Margaret, who gave a nod.

"Can we take Jet and Max with us?"

This time Elizabeth glanced at Charles, who nodded.

"Yes, but take care," she shouted after them as they ran off followed by Charles's dogs. Max, a chocolate Labrador given to Charles by Susan when they became engaged, ran ahead of them, but Jet, Charles's black Labrador, followed slowly behind and then gave up and returned to Charles. Charles stroked his head.

"Never mind, old chap. He will be old like us one day."

Emma came out with a tray of drinks: sherry, water and Edith's elderflower cordial. Esme asked what it was.

Elizabeth explained that it was made by Edith, but it was an acquired taste. Esme said she would try some. Emma gave her a glass. Esme cautiously tasted it.

"It's got a strange flavour, but it is not unpleasant." She had another sip. "It is definitely growing on me."

Elizabeth and Margaret exchanged glances, remembering another time Elizabeth had tried to introduce someone to Edith's elderflower cordial. Margaret's sister-in-law, Rozina; she had made comments about both the cordial and Peter. They could laugh now but at the time were very cross.

Angela made a dramatic entrance; she had been waiting for everyone to arrive. She flounced out of the French doors onto the patio, her yellow shirtwaist dress showing off her small waist and emphasizing her black hair. She had not done up the top button and was showing some cleavage. She dramatically pulled a chair next to Peter and sat in it.

Charles quickly introduced her to Esme and Aaron. Angela accepted a glass of sherry from Emma and turned to Peter.

"My car is in need of your attention. It is making a strange noise."

"Would you like me to look at it?" asked Peter.

"Yes, if you could take a quick look before lunch." They stood up and Angela took Peter's arm and led him into the house.

Esme and Aaron exchanged looks this time.

"Any further revelations will have to wait until lunch as we have lost Peter," said Susan.

"How are your stables coming along?" Susan asked Margaret. Usually she did not initiate a conversation with Margaret, as she either ignored her or cut her short, but after Margaret's greetings last night and today, Susan thought she would risk it, especially if she asked about the stables, which she knew Margaret loved.

"They are finished, and the fences are in place. I had thought that I would just have a horse, but Xavier is very keen on getting a pony. I am not sure we have enough space. The field is a bit small for two animals."

"You can use my field," said Susan generously.

"Your field?"

"Yes, the one opposite the entrance to Peter's garage."

"You own that field?"

"Yes, and a few more."

"But..." Margaret was at a loss, staring at Susan.

"Isn't that just typical of you, Maggie! Why do you know so little about people? Susan owns two whole farms."

"Part farms," Susan muttered under her breath.

Margaret looked astonished. She turned to Elizabeth.

"Beth, you know what I'm like. I hate to pry and gossip."

"I know, Maggie." Elizabeth grabbed her hand reassuringly. "We know what you've been through and understand you. And we still love you despite it." Margaret laughed as Elizabeth hoped she would.

Esme was dying to ask what they were referring to but refrained. That would keep for another day.

"I own these fields behind the wood garden." Susan waved her hand in the direction of the garden. It was at the end of the garden, at the top of the hill. It was not really a wood but some small trees and three big ones in grass. It also had a gate through to the next house. "And across Manor Road and Venn Road to join with Ronald's farm." She turned to Esme and Aaron. "Ronald is my stepson, Angela's half-brother. He looks after both farms for us. He inherited North Taw Farm from his... father." She hesitated at the thought of her first husband and turned back to Margaret. "I will speak to Ron. I'm sure there won't be a problem."

Margaret looked at her, speechless.

"I don't know what to say."

"Is it big enough?"

"Oh yes, more than big enough."

"Well, just say yes."

"Yes, thank you." Margaret stood up, and much to everyone's astonishment, she went over to Susan and kissed her cheek. "Thank you." She slowly walked back to her chair, thinking. "I would like to make a new gate, opposite the garage entrance. The current gate is at the bottom on Manor Road."

"Yes, that's fine. Do what you have to."

Suddenly an upstairs window was flung open, and voices could be heard, followed by the soft vocals of Bobby Darin singing *Dream Lover*.

"Sorry, that's Angela playing her music," apologised Susan. Esme glanced at Margaret, and she returned the glance with a shrug.

The gong sounded for lunch. Elizabeth and Margaret went to get their offspring, Chloe and Marcus, who were playing on a blanket on the lawn.

Everyone was trooping back into the house when Max rushed passed them followed by Duncan and Xavier. Last to arrive was Peter, with Angela, finally doing up her button. Esme was aghast at the implication. She had grown fond of Margaret in the two days she had been here and hated the fact that Peter was having an affair with Angela, and that she was being so brazen about it.

CHAPTER 11

When everyone was seated, Emma brought in the vegetables. There was a pile of plates in front of Charles, and she put the joint of beef in front of him. She took the plates around as Charles carved the meat. She left when everyone had a plate. After everyone had finished helping themselves to the vegetables, Aaron resumed his story.

"Where was I? Oh, yes, we were speaking to Mrs French. She did not know where you had gone. Roni had visited her that day you left, giving notice on the flat. She was having breakfast and heard the letter box flap. She was surprised because the post had already been delivered. She went to the front door and saw the envelope. It had the key to the flat in it. Mrs French opened the door and saw you and your mother waiting by the side of the road. She was about to call out when a van pulled up and you got in. That was the last she saw of you." Peter nodded as he tried to put a spoonful of lunch into Marcus's mouth while avoiding his flailing arms.

"I remember the van."

"We asked Mrs French which company had moved you, but she said you only had two suitcases. She said that it was Maurice Reed's van. Maurice lived at the end of the road. He always... liked Roni, but she hated him. She would go out of her way to avoid him, another reason to move. I was surprised she asked for his help, but I suppose she had no choice."

"I didn't like him either and I know Mother didn't. He flung the suitcases in the back, and I sat between him and Mother in the front." He remembered Maurice trying to get his mother to sit in the middle, but she insisted that he did. Now he was realising why.

Aaron continued his story.

"We visited Maurice. He had not been called up, or if he had, he had found a way of avoiding it. He was still obnoxious. He admitted driving you both to the East End, but he didn't have an address. Initially he pretended that he did and was keeping you and your mother company, but I knew Roni. We persisted and he owned up that he had no idea where you were. He told us where he had taken you. He said he dropped you off the north side of Central Park."

"I remember getting out of the van by a park. I don't know the name of it. We waited there until he drove off and waited about 10 minutes before crossing the road. We walked for about five minutes. Mother was dragging the suitcases, and I tried to help as best I could."

"I had to join my regiment, so I left Esme and Vera Scott to try and search for you. That would have been June or July 1942." He looked at Esme for confirmation.

"Yes, I moved in with Vera and Derek and worked at the local hospital. We didn't know what to do. We went over to Central Park to get an idea. The bombing was terrible. We drew up a plan of action. We would just knock on doors asking if anyone knew you or your mother."

"But by that time, Mother was dead, and I was in hospital."

"Yes, but we didn't know that. We started at the northwest point of the park and circled out. It took some time as I was working long shifts and Vera had her voluntary work. But after a couple of horrible encounters, we felt we were not getting anywhere, so we decided on a different tack. We put a card in the local shop windows asking for information. We didn't say much, just if anyone knew of you to contact Cooper, Scott & Sittall Solicitors and a telephone number. Oh, and that there would be a reward.

"A couple of weeks later, Derek had a phone call from a Mrs Sibley. She said that her mother had read the card and had information. Derek made an appointment a few days later. He was very sceptical, thinking that they just wanted the reward. But after speaking to Mrs Sibley and her mother, Mrs Finn, he was less so."

"Mrs Finn. Mrs Finn. I remember now. She was so kind to me when we moved in. I hated the school and didn't go." Margaret remembered how he had spoken about being bullied because of his clothes and accent. "She looked after me when Mother was at work. I used to help with their market stall. I used to help her and her son. Wait, she did have a daughter; she lived a few streets over, and she helped from time to time. What was she called?" Everyone was silent while he was thinking. "Mary," he spoke at last. "Mary Sibley."

"Yes, that was her name. Derek took their details and said we would be in touch. We wrote to Aaron, but it took some time for the letter to arrive. We heard nothing until Christmas. Aaron wrote that he would try and get some leave as soon as he could. Well, he did come home a couple of months later but only because he had been injured. He was awarded a Military Medal for his bravery. He was driving a lorry of supplies in a convoy when it was hit by German bombs. He rescued as many of his comrades as possible and continued driving despite the continued attack and brought them to safety. He saved 20 men, but he had been shot in the leg and had burns to his arms and chest from when he had run into another lorry to rescue his captain."

Peter looked at him, startled. He didn't want to know this. He wanted to continue to hate his father. Esme continued.

"As soon as Aaron was able, we arranged a meeting with Mrs Finn. We took some photographs, and she confirmed it was you and your mother. But she couldn't tell us much more. The last time she saw you, as she was running to the air raid shelter, you were standing outside your house clutching your tin box waiting for your mother. When the all-clear sounded and she came out, the houses were gone. An ambulance pulled up where your house had been. She ran as fast as she could and just caught a glimpse of you disappearing into the ambulance. She remembered a posh woman asking her if she was your mother; she said no but that your mother would be coming down the street. She pointed. She was in shock, not realising that it was too late for your mother. The posh lady and another man went over to where she pointed and found her under a pile of rubble, just her hand sticking out.

She had died instantly. Sorry about the descriptions." Esme apologised to Peter and Margaret. Esme paused, still feeling the emotion of the moment over 20 years ago.

"We had no idea where you had gone, Peter. We tried to track you down, but it was confusion everywhere."

His father continued. "I was redeployed. I had to leave Esme and Vera to carry on trying to find you and your mother."

"Eventually, we did trace your mother. And when Aaron finally came home, when the war finished, we got a proper headstone made."

"I would like to visit her grave," said Peter quietly.

Aaron nodded.

"We thought you would. We would like you to visit us and we could go together, as a family."

Xavier and Duncan began to fidget in their chairs.

"Can we get down now?" asked Duncan.

"Don't you want any pudding?" asked Susan. "It's jelly and ice cream." The boys looked at each other and both nodded their heads enthusiastically. Susan rang for Emma.

Angela, who had been sitting quietly, unusual for her, had been fascinated by the story and decided to make herself known.

"Peter, you must introduce me to your sister. I am dying to get to know her."

Esme wasn't sure she wanted her daughter to get to know Angela. Everyone ignored Angela and carried on their own conversations, except Peter, who as much as he tried not to be, was sitting next to her. She grabbed his arm to get his attention.

"How delightful to have a sister, well, half-sister. I have a wonderful half-brother. It is much better having half-siblings than stepsiblings." She glanced at Margaret.

Esme expected Margaret to say something, but she was dealing with Marcus. Esme, who was just across the table from her, was going to defend Margaret, but Peter spoke first.

"I think your stepsister is the most amazing and beautiful person in the world." Margaret looked up and smiled at him. "But I do think it is a good idea to get to know Phoebe." He then said something he never thought that he would say. He looked at

Esme and Aaron. "Why don't you come back in a couple of weeks and bring Phoebe with you?"

"That's a superb idea," interposed Angela, before Esme and Aaron could say anything. She kept her arms around Peter's arm.

The lunch party trooped out of the dining room and back onto the patio. Esme hung back to try and speak to Margaret. She followed her through the door; they were almost the last to leave. Peter and Angela followed. She heard Angela speak to Peter in a loud whisper.

"Do you want to come back up to my room?"

Esme could stand it no longer. She realised why Margaret hated Angela, and she was disappointed in Peter as well. She was beginning to wish that she and Aaron hadn't traced him.

"Peter, I'm sure your father will want to finish his story, and you must still have lots of questions. Let's sit in the sun and enjoy our coffee."

She was pleased to see Peter shake off Angela's arms and follow them outside. Once they were all settled, Aaron continued.

"I had no more news of you until a couple of years ago. I should have traced you then, but I wasn't sure. Esme's sister, Noreen, was at her dentist's in Reigate and flipping through the society magazines that they had. They were a few months out of date – she was looking at the wedding pictures as her daughter was getting married at the end of the year. She suddenly spotted the name Eastman under one of the photographs. She stared at it but was then called into the dentist's room. She mentioned this to Esme when they met for Esme's birthday in August. Unfortunately she couldn't remember the name of the magazine or anything else about the wedding. Luckily when she went back for her six-month check, she found the magazine; it was at the bottom of the pile and a bit worse for wear. She was full of guilt as she tore the page out and stuffed it in her bag. She showed it to us at Christmas. I thought it was you, but I really wasn't sure. I was afraid to get my hopes up. When we visited Ruth in February, we showed her. She was all for tracing you but, I'm ashamed to say, I didn't have the courage. She badgered me over the summer, and finally I decided I would try and trace you. I looked up Margaret in

Who's Who." He glanced at Margaret. "I couldn't find you. I was probably looking under the wrong name. There wasn't much to go on from the magazine. The caption read…" He turned to Esme, who took the creased and worn page out of her bag. The photograph filled half a page; it was a picture of Peter and Margaret leaving Bishop's Tawton Church. The picture of Peter was not so clear as he had his head turned sideways, but Margaret was looking straight at the camera. "Here, read it for yourself." He handed it to Peter. Peter could see why his father hadn't been sure, with his head turned.

Peter read, *Wedding of Lady Margaret, widow of Sir Hugh Browne, to Peter Eastman, in Devon.* He agreed there was not much to go on and handed the page to Margaret. She scanned it anxiously and was relieved that it said so little.

"I had looked up Lady Margaret Browne," said Aaron, "but found nothing." Margaret didn't like to say that her entry was under the name of Lady Margaret Sutherland. She hadn't bothered to change it. She was only there because of her grandfather, Lord Cranley. Currently, her second cousin held the title. "While Noreen was staying with her daughter in East Grinstead in April, she was watching the local news programme and caught the bit about Sebastian Browne. About his son's christening. They showed some photographs and mentioned you and Margaret again. She rang us immediately. I got to work and found out about Sebastian. Being an MP, it was easy. I found out his brother Hugh had died." He looked apologetically at Margaret, and she smiled her acceptance. "Then I traced the address of Royston House. I didn't know if you were still there, but I hoped the letter would get to you. Which it did."

Aaron sat back, his story told.

"The rest you know. I was so pleased to get the letter from you, Margaret. I wrote to you because I didn't know how Peter would react."

No one broke the silence for several minutes. Most people were watching Peter. He didn't notice. He was deep in thought, as he had been all weekend. Peter felt drained, now that his father's story was over. He had expected to dislike his father on sight and to repudiate all of his lies, but that hadn't happened. Peter now remembered how his father used to play with him and take him to the parks and museums. He was confused. He needed to think.

"I think I would like to go home now. Sorry," he addressed Susan. "I have to go to the garage."

"Don't apologise. We all have a lot to think about," said Susan, smiling at him. "We are all here for you if you need to talk."

Peter smiled his thanks and stood up. Everyone else stood up too. Angela grabbed Peter's arm again.

"I could help you at the garage. I can bring my car in now."

Esme sighed. She was now getting annoyed.

"What Peter needs is to be on his own." She knew she sounded angry, but she couldn't help it.

"How do you know what Peter needs?" demanded Angela. She pointed her finger at Esme. "You've only known him a few minutes. What do you know about the way he feels?"

Elizabeth wanted to join in. She could see how Peter was feeling and so wanted to comfort him but felt helpless.

"Esme is a psychiatrist. She probably knows more in her little finger than you do in your whole body."

The expression of horror on Angela's face brought a smile to most people's faces. Elizabeth was still angry and was about to say more when she was interrupted by Peter. He walked over to Elizabeth as she was talking, he took her hands and looked into her eyes.

"Beth, don't worry. I just need a bit of time." He put his arms around her. Esme glanced at Angela, whose expression had gone from horror to sheer jealousy. Peter smoothed back Elizabeth's hair from her face. "I will talk to you as soon as I can."

"Sorry, Peter," she said in a quiet voice and kissed his cheek, suddenly aware of everyone else. "Where are the boys?"

"Still in the wood garden with Max," said Charles. "I will go and get them." He strode away, and as he passed Elizabeth, she could see that he was struggling as well. *This is going to affect all of us*, she suddenly realised.

* * * * * * *

When they arrived back at Veronica Cottage, everyone went their own ways. Peter apologised and disappeared to the garage. No one minded. Esme went to her room; she needed to freshen up. All day she had felt uncomfortable in her old twin set and plaid skirt, especially compared to Angela. She threw her bag on the bed. She wanted to study Angela. No one had brought out so much hate in her. She had never seen someone like her. All the patients she had treated, and she had never disliked any of them so intently. She had not liked them all, but they had excuses; they were ill. But Angela, well!

Margaret said she would put the kettle on and went off to the kitchen with Marcus. Aaron looked at Xavier.

"I know you wanted to play with Duncan, but will I do instead?"

Xavier had been moaning all the way home that he hadn't wanted to leave. He wanted to stay and play with Duncan, and Max, he added afterwards as no one seemed to be listening. He wasn't happy; he felt squashed in the back of the car with Margaret, Esme and Marcus, but in reality, with Marcus on Margaret's lap, he had plenty of room.

"Do you know how to play knights?" he asked.

"No," said Aaron, "but you could teach me." Xavier nodded.

"I need to get swords and horses," he said, dashing off to the nursery.

Aaron wandered into the lounge and over to the windows. He could just see the garage roof over the high hedge separating it from the house. He hoped he and Peter could be friends. He had almost cried when he had received the last letter from Margaret with her address on, Veronica Cottage. That swept away the last vestiges of doubt that Aaron had that he had found his son.

Margaret entered with Marcus.

"I'm sorry, but do you mind looking after Marcus while I bring in the tea?" Aaron said he didn't mind at all. Margaret opened the French doors to the veranda. Aaron took Marcus and sat outside, waiting for Xavier.

Marcus was trying to get down the steps at the end of the terrace, as he had spotted a ball on the lawn and wanted to play with it. He had had a short nap while at Charles and Susan's and was now full of energy. Aaron got up to help him. This brought back so many memories of helping Peter up and down the steps to their flat in London. He started to play with Marcus and the football. He didn't notice Peter watching surreptitiously from behind the gate that divided the garage and house.

He was remembering how his father used to play with him like that. Aaron and Marcus's game was interrupted by Xavier running down the steps waving two swords and trying to bring two hobby horses with him. It had taken him a while to sort out how to carry them, but the stairs were easier than the uneven stone steps. He neared the bottom when suddenly he went head over heels. He let out a shout. Aaron was immediately by his side, full of concern. Peter was about to enter the garden to help but refrained. He watched as Aaron carefully made sure that Xavier wasn't hurt and praised Xavier's bravery at not crying.

"If I am going to ride a proper horse, I will probably fall off at some point. So I have to be brave." He felt like crying inside; his knee hurt him. Aaron had cleaned it up, but it was going to have a bruise.

"Shall we play swords and knights? You will have to tell me what to do."

"Marcus needs to go away. He will just get in the way."

"No," said Aaron gently. "He can play here if he wants to, but we will move him out of the middle of the lawn." He carefully picked up Marcus and the ball and took them up the other end. "We will just have to learn how to avoid him. In real battles you have to learn how to avoid hurting people that are not part of it." Xavier nodded. He gave a horse and a sword to Aaron.

Peter wondered about that. How many battles had his father been in? How often had he had to avoid wounding people? He assumed that his father was not referring to German soldiers but perhaps wounded colleagues or the local communities.

He spotted Margaret coming out with the tea tray. He smiled to himself. She still looked uncomfortable at doing simple tasks like making tea. He didn't mind; it was all part of being with Margaret. He watched her looking at Aaron and the boys, then her gaze went beyond them to the field. He saw her smiling broadly as she thought about the horses she could now have, then her gaze swept over to the garage. She spotted him hiding. She smiled shyly at him but didn't say anything. Peter felt his heart leaping. She was still his Margaret. To everyone else she was self-confident and strong willed, but once they got in their bedroom, she was so innocent and naïve it took his breath away. He suddenly couldn't wait until tonight. They had not made love the past couple of nights because of the tension caused by his father's visit, but tonight would be different, he vowed.

CHAPTER 12

Margaret called to Aaron that his tea was ready. He acknowledged with a wave of his sword. He was immediately stabbed, gently but firmly, in his stomach.

"I win," shouted Xavier, dancing around.

"Yes, you do. And as I am dead, I am going to have a cup of tea." He went up the steps to the veranda and put his sword and horse by the French doors.

Xavier was now teasing Marcus with his sword.

"Stop that, Xavier. Put the sword away. Play with Marcus nicely," admonished his mother. Xavier duly put his horse and sword down and began to kick the ball around with Marcus. He always just kicked it out of reach of Marcus, taunting him. Margaret sighed. She poured out a cup of tea for herself. She looked towards Peter. He was now inside the gate, playing with the boys.

"Where is Esme?" asked Margaret.

"I'm here," she said as she stepped outside onto the veranda. "Oh, Xavier is out here. I thought I heard him in the nursery." She accepted a cup of tea from Margaret. Margaret also poured out Peter's but knew it would probably go cold before he drank it.

She was right. It was 15 minutes before they finished their game of football. It didn't matter that the tea was cold; Peter drank it anyway.

"It is nearly time for tea," said Margaret. "I need to make the salad and everything." She tried to sound confident but cringed inwardly. Preparing meals was not her strong point.

"I will help," said Esme. Margaret smiled at her gratefully. *It will be a good chance to have a quiet chat*, thought Esme.

"Put your toys back in the nursery, Xavier," ordered his mother. "And make sure you wash your hands. Do you need someone to help you?"

"No, I will ask Ivy to help."

"She is back?" Margaret was relieved though confused. Usually Ivy didn't return until it was time to get the boys to bed.

"Yes. She can help me, if she has stopped crying."

They all looked at each other. Margaret stood up.

"I will go and see what the matter is."

She climbed the stairs to the nursery. She could hear someone quietly sobbing. She knocked gently and cautiously opened the door to Ivy's room.

"Please leave me alone," came the muffled voice from the bed. Margaret ignored it and carried on into the room. She slowly sat on the side of the bed.

"Ivy, please tell me what happened." Margaret hated to see her like this. "I am not going until you have," she said firmly.

Ivy sighed and sat up.

"Let me wash my face first." Margaret nodded and watched her go out the room and into the bathroom. Margaret stood up and wandered around. It was the first time she had been in Ivy's room since they had moved in. She had been in when Peter first showed her around the house he had built. But everywhere was empty then. Ivy had chosen the blue décor and pine furniture she wanted, and Margaret purchased it, but she had not seen it since. She stopped by the dressing table, in front of the window that overlooked the front drive. It was messy with make-up. Ivy must have been in a hurry, she thought. She picked up a photograph of a couple in their wedding outfits. Ivy's parents, she assumed.

Ivy returned, her face washed, but Margaret could see she had been crying again. Margaret sat on the bed and patted the mattress next to her. She was not much older than Ivy but felt like her mother at that moment. Mostly Ivy wore her uniform and Margaret only caught glimpses of her out of it as she left or returned on her days out, and she always had her long chestnut hair tied back. Now it was hanging loose over her shoulders.

"Take a deep breath and tell me what happened."

Ivy sat down. She had a handkerchief in her hands which was wet with tears.

"As you know, I arranged to have lunch with Ross and Lucy." Margaret nodded, but she didn't really know. She vaguely remembered Ivy saying something about it. "Usually Emma and I lunch together at The Firs but, because Emma was busy today, Lucy asked me to lunch with her and Ross. Anyway, today I walked to Ross's house in Landkey. I was a bit tired when I got there. They gave me some wine. Actually, I had a lot of wine. Lunch was delayed, and there was some problem with the cooker. It was finally cooked just as Ross's brother came in." She started to cry again. Margaret gently encouraged her to go on.

"What is his brother like?"

Ivy sighed.

"He is very handsome. I..." She trailed off again, crying.

"What is his name?"

"Mark. Mark Lennox." She finally stopped crying. "When we finished lunch, I helped Lucy with the dishes. It was clear that Lucy was tired, with the baby being due any moment. Due to the wine I had drunk, I was a bit unsteady on my feet. Mark offered to drive me back. He said that he had to drop something off at their mother's first – she lives in a tiny cottage on the outskirts of Swimbridge – and then would bring me home. I accepted. We had to park in a gateway to a field as the cottage was on the road and we would block the road. When Mark came back, he didn't drive off straight away. We sat looking at the field. It felt comfortable. He leant over to kiss me." She started to cry again. "I let him." Margaret tried to reassure her.

"If you like him, and he likes you," she started, then realised she wasn't sure what to say.

"Yes, no. That wasn't the problem. He... No, it was me. I don't know what came over me. Maybe it was the wine? But I... and now he hates me."

Margaret was confused. She wished Elizabeth was here.

"What did you do?"

Ivy was in a panic. She suddenly realised it was her employer she was talking to, and she was supposed to set an example; she was in charge of young children. She just shook her head and said nothing.

Ivy was thinking about that afternoon. How could she tell Margaret what she had done? She was sitting in the sun, in the car, waiting for Mark to return. She was dozing slightly, due to the wine. When he did return, he leant across and put his arm around her. She felt comfortable and happy. He slowly kissed her, so she kissed him back. He ran his free hand up and down her leg. She moved her legs apart. He ran his hand inside her thighs. She moved her legs wider and felt him respond. Her body was taking over. She felt relaxed and in a dream-like state. She couldn't believe how she felt. She wanted more. She asked him for more and moved her hand over to his legs. She could feel him responding and started to open his trousers so she could feel more of him. She said that perhaps they should move in the back and be more comfortable. He said he had a better idea. He drove a short distance to another gate. He opened the door for Ivy to get out, grabbed the blanket from the back seat and led her through the gate. It was all over quickly. Ivy wasn't sure what to expect, but she was a bit disappointed. Tears started to form in her eyes. Mark looked at his watch. Suddenly, his mood changed. He pulled himself away from her and ordered her off the blanket and back in the car. He drove fast through the villages. Ivy had trouble trying to sort her clothing out. She was in tears. As soon as the car stopped on the drive, she opened the door and rushed away. She heard Mark shout her name, but she just kept running. She got to her room as quickly as she could. She flung herself on the bed. When her crying eased, she heard a car in the drive. She looked out the window, afraid that Mark had returned, but it was Margaret and the family. She tried to quieten her crying as she heard Xavier come upstairs. He was making a lot of noise getting his toys, so she hoped he hadn't heard her.

"I won't be seeing him again," Ivy finally said.

"Did he... hurt you?" asked Margaret. "Like your previous employer." Margaret remembered her interview with Ivy, when she and Hugh were looking for a nanny for Xavier. She had asked her mother-in-law, Lady Agatha, for help. One of Lady Agatha's friends knew that her daughter's nanny was looking for a new position. She passed Margaret's details on. Initially, Margaret interviewed her on her own, as Hugh was returning from Brunswick House in London. Ivy had turned up smartly dressed in her brown uniform but very nervous. Margaret had tried to put her at ease. Ivy was employed as a junior nanny. When her employers had their fourth child, the senior nanny had declared that she needed help, so they employed Ivy straight from college. During the fifth pregnancy, her employer became very ill, and her husband needed to be at home more than usual. His attentions turned to Ivy. He kept visiting the nursery when the senior nanny was out with the older children. He became more and more attentive. Ivy didn't know what to do. He repulsed her; he was overweight and smelled of stale tobacco. Ivy gave her notice, and she now felt confident enough to lock the door. Initially, Ivy had just told Margaret that she wanted to run her own nursery, not be an assistant anymore, but when they heard Hugh arrive, she became agitated. Margaret coaxed the truth out of her. She immediately gave her the job. When Hugh came in, Ivy was relieved he was different from her previous employer. She liked him immediately and started as soon as she could.

Margaret was trying to coax the truth out of her now.

"Do I need to call the police?" Ivy was horrified.

"No. Please don't," begged Ivy. Margaret was relieved; it obviously hadn't gone that far. Ivy continued. "Please don't worry. I will bounce back. I just need time."

"If you are sure," said Margaret doubtfully. Ivy smiled and nodded.

"Yes," she said firmly. Margaret stood up helplessly. She didn't want to leave but didn't know what else to do. She felt there was more to it than Ivy was saying.

"If you need us, we are here," she said finally before leaving Ivy alone.

Ivy was relieved. Now she could forget all about it. But she had really liked him. She had never felt like this about anyone before. She had had limited opportunities to meet men. When she arrived at Royston House, there was a small staff. Most were a good few years older than she was, but she enjoyed Simon's company. He was employed as a groom, and she used to sneak out to the stables to see him. They had some cosy chats in the tack room, but after Hugh died and they moved to Devon, he married someone else and now had a baby.

Ivy sighed. She was completely off men. She started crying again at the thought of not seeing Mark. Ivy was so embarrassed. She suddenly thought, how would she be able to face Ross, Lucy and Emma? She could imagine them all laughing at her. Ivy looked at the clock. She had about an hour before she had to resume her duties. She tried to pull herself together.

Margaret walked slowly down the stairs. She felt a failure. She had tried to help. The best she could reassure herself with was that she had not made it any worse. Peter was waiting for her in the hallway. Margaret shrugged her shoulders.

"I don't know. I tried. Something happened between her and Mark, Ross's brother. I don't think anything too serious but..." She trailed off.

"Do you want me to talk to her?" asked Peter, putting his arms around Margaret. Margaret shook her head.

"Not at the moment. Let's just wait and see what happens. Oh my goodness," exclaimed Margaret. "I need to get tea ready."

"Don't worry," Peter reassured her. "Esme has it all under control." Margaret relaxed a little.

When they entered the kitchen, they saw everything ready. They had decided to eat on the veranda. The food was carried through, and everyone settled down to eat.

Ivy came out just as they finished. She was dressed in her uniform and her hair was in its usual bun. She scooped up Marcus to give him his bath and get him ready for bed.

Xavier demanded that both Peter and Aaron played with him. Esme was finally alone with Margaret. She was trying to work out how to bring up the subject of Angela. Margaret started to clear the dishes, and Esme helped. They took them to the kitchen.

"I think Peter is beginning to accept his father," Esme started to say. "When we set off for this weekend, the best we hoped for was at least that he didn't send us straight home." Esme had told Aaron not to get his hopes up too high and that it might take many meetings before Peter acknowledged him, because from what they had learned, Peter had had a rough time after Aaron left, and he might blame Aaron.

"No, at least he is talking to Aaron. I wasn't sure what to expect either, knowing how Peter felt about Aaron. But I think he realised it is not his father's fault," Margaret replied.

Esme nodded.

"Families aren't easy." Esme was watching Margaret closely. "I suppose I am, well, Peter's stepmother. Not a wicked one, I hope." She laughed, and so did Margaret, as she had hoped.

"No, I don't think you are wicked."

"What about your stepmother? Is she so wicked?"

"I thought she was. You made me realise that I didn't know her at all. I hadn't realised what she had been through. I just thought she was after Dad's money. Also, I felt such loyalty to Mother, but now I know better."

"What about Angela?" Esme asked quietly.

"Angela is a whole different kettle of fish. She enjoys making fun of me at every opportunity."

"And what about Peter?"

"Peter doesn't like her either. She had always been after him. They did go out together for a time. But even though Angela finished it, she has always tried to get him back."

"And he has never..." Esme didn't know how to ask, "gone back to her?"

"No, she tries hard. Like today at lunch."

"When she enticed him away to see her car and play music in her bedroom."

"Yes, but Peter never succumbs."

Esme stopped washing up and looked at her doubtfully.

"Can you be sure? She is very beautiful."

"Oh yes. I know Peter." Margaret stopped drying and looked at Esme. "You didn't fall for that act, did you? She has perfected it over the years. Well, if you don't know Angela – she always does that, grabs Peter, and insinuates stuff. He is too much a gentleman to physically push her away, but he never does anything."

"But this lunchtime," persisted Esme, "we heard them in her bedroom."

"What we heard was the radio, and then Angela being provocative. Just ignore her."

"But Peter didn't return until we went in to lunch. He came in with her; she was doing up her button."

Margaret sighed. She and Peter knew what Angela was like. She decided to tell Esme about the conversation she had had with Peter. It was just after they had become engaged. She wanted reassurance about Angela, why he let her act like a lover. Peter had sighed and explained that he felt sorry for her. He said that he and Angela had been dating, but she had started to see Julian Mortimer also, and at a New Year's party in 1954, Angela had broken up with him. It was to be announced that Julian had got engaged. Peter said that Angela started to walk up to Julian, a big smile on her face, ready to say yes, when just before she got there, Julian turned to another girl at his side and introduced her as his fiancée. Everyone cheered and pushed past Angela. Peter saw her face, just for a split second, how hurt she was. Then he saw Julian watching Angela with a smirk on his face. Peter reached out to her and led her away. Margaret sighed and continued to speak to Esme.

"He said he just felt so sorry for her. Today, after Peter had inspected the car, which was making a strange noise, he told Angela to bring the car in tomorrow. After he left her, he played with Xavier and Duncan."

"Is that what he told you?" Esme wanted to believe him.

"Yes and no. Peter told me that Angela would be bringing the car tomorrow, but also Xavier told me. He said that Peter had come to see how they were getting on in the new tree house that Dad had had built for them. They laughed as he tried to get his 6ft 3in body through the small hatch. Apparently, it was easier getting out – he just fell out." Margaret smiled at the thought.

Esme was so relieved she laughed loudly.

"What are you ladies laughing at?" asked Peter as he came into the kitchen. He wanted to make sure that Margaret was not flustered. Margaret was not cut out for domestic tasks and could make the simplest chore complicated. But today, with Esme's help, she seemed to have coped. The china was sitting on the side, but it was stacked neatly. She obviously couldn't remember where it went. He watched her open several cupboards before he opened one for her, indicating that it went in that one. She shrugged and obediently put the china away. Finally they were finished, and Margaret was thankful when she could leave the kitchen. It was not her favourite place unless she was eating with her family.

CHAPTER 13

Everyone was anxiously waiting their arrival. They were trying to relax by reading the newspapers. Previously, when they were due to arrive, Peter had been pacing up and down. Now he was seated but still tense. Finally they heard the sound of a car on the drive. They went out to greet the new arrivals.

Margaret and Esme immediately embraced each other. Aaron held out his hand to Peter. Peter hesitated for a moment then shook it. He was still unsure of his feelings for his father. He had spent 25 years hating him for abandoning him and his mother. Now he realised that things were not as he imagined.

Someone else slowly got out of the car, uncertainty showing all over her face. Esme put her arm around her and led her forward.

"Peter, this is your sister, Phoebe."

Peter looked at Phoebe. She was short, only 5ft 3in, slightly shorter than her mother but with the same blonde hair and a slimmer figure. She had the same blue eyes as him. He was uncertain what to do; he hadn't many dealings with 16-year-old girls. Margaret stepped in to help.

"Welcome, Phoebe." She gave her a hug. "I am Margaret. I believe you like horses." Phoebe nodded. She was a bit overwhelmed by Margaret. She had been told all about her, but now, to see her... She was stunned by her elegance and poise. She felt unkempt beside her. Margaret took her hand and led her into the house. "Tomorrow, would you like to see the horses?"

"Oh, yes, please," said Phoebe eagerly, forgetting all her awkwardness. "How many do you have?" They went off into the house chatting.

Esme looked at Peter, smiling now. She had sensed how nervous Phoebe had been.

"Margaret is a wonderful person."

"Yes, she is," said Peter emphatically. "I am so lucky to have her." Peter bent down to pick up a couple of suitcases. Esme had seen the sincerity in his eyes; she now knew that any doubts she had had about him and Angela were completely unfounded. She followed Peter and Aaron into the house.

Margaret was leading an overawed Phoebe into the house. She led her upstairs, explaining the doors as they passed them to try and relax her. At the top of the stairs, they turned right to go along the open railed landing.

"This is the back guest room," Margaret explained as they passed the first door on their left. "These stairs go up to the nursery. This is the first main guest room, your parents' room." Margaret opened a door as they turned right around the corner. "And this is your room." She opened a door about halfway along the landing. "Opposite here is a small box room and that door in the corner leads to our room, mine and Peter's."

Margaret led the way into the second guest room and went over to the window. Phoebe followed. She looked out over the garden.

"You have two horses," she exclaimed. "Can I ride them?"

"Not this time. Chaos, the black and white pony, only arrived two days ago and the grey mare only arrived this morning. I would like them to settle in a bit first. But next time you come, we will arrange something." Phoebe smiled happily. Margaret walked across to another door and opened it onto a small corridor. "The door at the end leads into your parents' room and the side door leads into the bathroom." They jumped as the door to the landing burst open, and Aaron came in carrying her suitcase.

"Come down when you are ready," said Margaret, following Aaron out. "We are having a light meal on the veranda." She smiled and shut the door.

"Thank you for looking after her," said Aaron. "She was worried about meeting you."

Margaret tipped her head in acknowledgement.

* * * * * *

113

Margaret was just checking over the buffet when she heard a sound from under the table. She bent down to look, and two pairs of eyes stared back at her.

"Come out," she ordered. Xavier and Duncan scrambled out. "What are you doing under there? You could have pulled the cloth off." She sighed. "Go and play outside." The boys ran off, almost colliding with Elizabeth, who was coming in with Marcus in her arms, followed by Chloe. Margaret was glad that Elizabeth had arrived early. She had been struggling to entertain Phoebe. They had spent the morning at the stable, but this afternoon she felt that Phoebe was bored. They had been discussing Aaron's departure and what happened after.

When the war ended, Aaron resumed his legal career. He was now a partner in the firm, and they had changed the name. It was currently Scott, Eastman and Hall. Peter recalled seeing the name on his and Margaret's trips to London. He never dreamt it was his father's business. He only noticed because of the name Eastman. He would never have taken any notice otherwise.

Aaron and Esme had got married in 1947 – they got engaged as soon as the war ended. It was a bigger wedding than Aaron's first one to Peter's mother. Then only Vernon Sittall and Derek and Vera Scott were there. Vernon walked Roni down the aisle and Derek acted as best man. Aaron gave Peter a picture. There weren't many.

"Did none of Mother's relatives go?" asked Peter.

Aaron paused slightly.

"Your mother was always very secretive about her family. I asked her if there was anyone she wanted to invite. She first mentioned that maybe her brother but then shook her head and said, very definitely, no. I was so young, only 22, and I didn't want to upset her. She was beginning to have doubts; she kept muttering that men didn't always mean what they say. I was desperate, so we married quickly, but I should have questioned her more closely. I was so busy studying as well." He sighed and looked at the picture. "It was a lovely day. After the ceremony, Vernon treated us all to a wedding breakfast at the Dorchester, then we walked round the park and went home." Esme took his hand. He smiled at her, but there were tears in his eyes.

"Your marriage to Esme was different," said Margaret gently, seeing Phoebe getting uncomfortable.

"Yes," said Aaron, brightening up a bit. "It was bigger, not by much. There were still shortages and rationing. There were about a dozen guests?" He looked at Esme. Esme nodded and continued.

"Yes, my parents and grandmother. My sister Noreen and her family, and my other sister, Glynis." She paused, catching her breath. "Also my friend Judith, who was a matron on Aaron's ward, and her fiancé." She reached in her bag for some photographs and handed them round.

"We were grateful to Derek and Vera, who provided the wedding breakfast. Mother had made the cake." Margaret looked at the photograph and saw a single-layer cake decorated in flowers. "We partly honeymooned with Ruth, then we had a few days on our own exploring the Dorset coast as far as Lyme Regis. She wasn't able to come to the wedding, so we went to her." Margaret took the photograph offered by Esme. There was a group of four people.

"Who is the man?"

"That is Ruth's husband. She met him during the war. He was one of the patients sent to her. He had lost an eye and an arm. Ruth says they fell in love at first sight, but Eric tells a different story. I'm sure you will hear all about it when you visit."

"Yes, we will be visiting on our way home from seeing you. Can we still come in four weeks?" Margaret looked at Esme, who nodded. "We shall only stay two or three days. I don't want Xavier and Marcus tiring you. Then we will visit Xavier's grandparents, and after that go onto visit Ruth and Eric. But I am confused – I thought you said that Ruth was engaged at the time of her accident. What happened?"

Aaron spoke.

"After the accident, as soon as he found out that Ruth would not be able to walk properly and would end up in a wheelchair, he broke off the engagement and said some hurtful things. But that is not all. We heard a month later that he had got engaged to an American girl. Though he got his just deserts, he was a stockbroker and had advised all his clients to invest in America, then the Wall Street Crash happened, and everyone lost their money." Aaron could not keep the satisfaction out of his voice. He was glad after the hurt caused to Ruth.

Ivy appeared.

"I thought I would get Xavier and Marcus. I thought they would need a rest before the party tonight," she said half apologetically.

"Good idea," agreed Margaret. She gave Marcus to Ivy and called to Xavier. He protested, but they knew he would have a short sleep once he got upstairs.

Margaret suggested that they all have a rest as the evening would be tiring. Everyone had so many questions.

Phoebe was first downstairs. She stood in the lounge looking over the gardens. Peter entered and was about to leave and shut the door, but he took a deep breath and called Phoebe's name. As he had been told, she was innocent in all of this.

She turned to him, nervousness showing all over her face. Peter went to the bureau and took out a small package. He handed it to Phoebe. She opened it and held the contents in her fingers.

"It's beautiful," she said.

"Here, let me put it on you," said Peter. He carefully took the silver chain and stood behind Phoebe. He gently put the chain round her neck and closed the clasp. Phoebe fingered the silver horse with its diamond detail.

"It looks lovely," said Peter. Phoebe went up to him to give him a thank you kiss. "Let's sit down; it will be easier. Do you like it? We wanted to get you something for your birthday. I know it's late, but there are exceptional circumstances. We missed out on so many birthdays."

"It is beautiful. I am so glad I came. Not just for the gift," she said, horrified how it might have sounded. "But to meet you all."

Peter realised what an ordeal it had been for her, and that she might not have wanted to meet him.

"I am so glad you did come," he reassured her. "And whatever happens you will always be my sister. Nothing can change that. I have never had a sister before. Beth and Maggie tried when I first arrived – well, Beth did. Maggie was Maggie. But it didn't feel quite right. But with you it is different." He was rewarded with a big smile.

They didn't hear the door open and close again quietly. They sat chatting, Phoebe telling him about Aunt Ruth. They were interrupted by the doorbell. They went into the hall. Margaret had opened the door and chaos had ensued. Elizabeth had arrived with her family. Duncan had immediately asked for Xavier, who had come flying down the stairs. The boys had knocked over Chloe in their exuberance, and she was now crying. William and Peter shook hands, and Peter introduced them to Phoebe.

Elizabeth studied Phoebe, standing awkwardly in her square-necked white chiffon dress with bishop sleeves and empire waist trimmed with ribbon. She looked beautiful, but she had the same stance and look that Peter had when they first met. Elizabeth was overcome.

"Sorry," she said, "you look so much like Peter when he first arrived. Can I give you a hug?" Phoebe nodded. "Welcome to the family. It isn't usually this chaotic." She caught Margaret's raised eyebrow. "Maybe it is." Everyone laughed. Esme was pleased to hear Phoebe laughing and relaxing. Elizabeth and William greeted her and Aaron.

They were outside, enjoying the evening sun, and Edith and David had arrived and greeted everyone. The doorbell went and the last arrivals came out onto the veranda. Phoebe was introduced and disappeared into her shell again. She was just beginning to relax, realising that everyone liked her and was pleased to see her. From what her parents had told her, she thought that everyone would be snobbish and not want to have anything to do with her. They had tried to reassure her, but she still had her doubts. That morning spent with Margaret and the horses had shown her that. Though Margaret gave the appearance of being grand, she was very down to earth. She had enjoyed her company and learning about the horses.

The afternoon had been tense when the 'grown-ups' had been discussing the past. She hadn't liked the way her father had got upset. She thought he was going to cry, but he didn't. She was uncomfortable. She was pleased when Ivy interrupted, and Margaret said they should go to their rooms. She thankfully escaped and rushed to her room. She stood at the window for ages, watching the horses. At last she lay on her bed. She knew she wouldn't sleep and was surprised when her mother woke her to get dressed.

Her new white dress was hanging up. She hadn't wanted to have a new one. She wanted to wear her old pink one, but her mother insisted, which was surprising as usually she managed to get her own way. She had been debating whether to leave the dress behind and just bring her old one – she felt comfortable in that one – but her mother had checked and made sure the new one was packed. As she dressed, she knew her mother had been right. She was first downstairs and apprehensive when Peter had found her in the lounge, but after their talk she was so much more confident.

She had felt momentarily uneasy when Elizabeth and her parents had arrived, but they had made her feel welcome. She had different feelings about the last guests' arrival.

She soon discovered that she could hide in a corner as she was not the centre of attention.

She could feel her jaw begin to drop open. It was only because she was drinking her lemonade that it did not actually happen. He was the most beautiful man she had ever seen. He must have walked straight off the catwalk.

Everyone had stood up to greet the new arrivals. It took some time for everyone to settle down again. She compared her brother to him. While Peter was taller and very good-looking, he could not hold a candle to Vince.

Aaron, Esme and Phoebe were introduced. Esme was curious. The engagment seemed to happen very quickly. Nothing was said when they visited before or this visit, but she had to admit they were preoccupied.

"How did you meet?"

"We met at school." He smiled at Angela. "She was the most beautiful girl in the school and village." Angela smiled back, preening herself. "I was devastated when she left to go to her posh school, and so was every other boy." Angela had a very satisfied look on her face.

"Not every boy," muttered Peter under his breath. Phoebe nearly choked on her drink. Vince gave him a glare.

"You have done very well for yourself," Vince said, waving his arms in the direction of the house and garage. "For a poor boy from the East End." Angela nodded.

"Please get your facts right," interrupted Elizabeth. "Peter only lived in the East End for a short time, and his mother was killed there. He was born in Knightsbridge." She was annoyed. Now she remembered why she didn't like Vince. He and Angela were a good match. "By the way, how is your sister, Vince?" There was a sharp intake of breath from some people. Angela was about to reply when Margaret interrupted.

"Shall we get some food before Xavier and Duncan demolish everything?"

Margaret pulled Elizabeth back as everyone went into the house.

"Don't let them upset you, Beth."

Elizabeth sighed.

"I know, but I just couldn't help it. I remember how Vince, his cousin, Alan Taylor, and David Bowden used to gang up on everyone. Luckily, they were a few years older than us and left before us so that our final years at Bishop's Tawton were torment free."

They joined the rest of the party in the house.

Elizabeth's parents, Edith and David, were talking to Vince and Angela, mostly Edith.

"How are your parents? It was a good turnout at Mrs Taylor's, your gran's, funeral."

"Yes, Mum and Dad didn't expect so many people. Gran was very popular. Mum was so pleased that you could take Gran's dogs. They really didn't know what to do and didn't want to put them down."

"We were happy to help. Smudge and Peanut have settled in well. It is nice to have a dog around again. Your parents must be glad that you could get leave and support them."

"Yes, but I have to go back Monday. I hope to be back at Christmas."

"It is a lovely ring, Angela."

"Thank you." She took the opportunity to flash the diamond around the room.

Esme was talking to Susan.

"It is a beautiful ring."

"Yes, she loves anything flashy. Unfortunately she didn't have very much when she was young. My first husband was not overly generous. She has always been envious of those that have nice things. It is my fault. I did something I shouldn't and to make up for it, I have always indulged her. I let her have her own way too much."

Esme patted her arm.

"I think there were mitigating circumstances."

Susan shook her head.

"No, I was pretty horrid back then."

"Understandable, with your first husband..." She didn't know how to finish. Usually her training stood her in good stead, but Susan was not a patient.

Susan smiled at her.

"Thank you. We should form a stepmothers' guild – you are stepmother to Peter and me to Margaret." They embraced to seal the bond.

"Now, tell me about Vince. Last time I came he wasn't mentioned, now he and Angela are engaged."

"It was all a bit quick. We had known him since he was a baby. Living in Bishop's Tawton, everyone knew everyone. My first husband had a farm on the edge of the village; we lived there until his death. David and Edith still live there. Elizabeth and William also live there – their hotel is at the other end of the village from the farm." Esme nodded. She knew that villages could be a close-knit community. "When they were 11, they all went to different schools. Vince started to train as a policeman, following his father's footsteps. His father, Malcolm, is an inspector. After he did his national service, he decided to join the army.

"He saw Angela again at his parents' silver wedding anniversary party, but she was going out with Peter. Apparently, she ignored him all evening. Then they met a few months ago. Vince was on leave and Angela was out with friends when they bumped into each other. This time Vince wasn't taking no for an answer. Apparently, he bought the ring and decided to propose next time he visited, which was now, due the passing of his grandmother, so when he arrived, he and Angela were engaged."

They looked around the room. Elizabeth, Edith and Margaret were sitting on the sofa and armchairs with Phoebe, obviously telling her all about Peter as a child. Vince and Angela were in a corner, arm in arm, looking out the window. Peter was with Charles, Aaron, David and William. They were having a very intense discussion. Judging from the arm movements, cricket was involved.

Esme had one more question.

"I understand that Elizabeth and Angela don't get along. But what was that comment Elizabeth made about Vince's sister?"

"Vince's sister is Doris. About 10 or 12 years ago, Angela and Peter were seeing each other. Angela broke off the relationship, as she was also seeing Julian Mortimer. His uncle and I had... spent some time together, but he didn't match up to Charles, so nothing came of it. He owns several businesses and was training Julian to take over. Angela felt he was going to propose, which he did but not to Angela. He led her on but then proposed to someone else." Susan took a sip of wine. "He wasn't very nice about it and humiliated her in front of lots of people. Peter helped her through."

"But what has that got to do with Vince's sister?"

"Julian broke off his engagement a couple of years later and started dating Doris when she opened her hairdressing business. They got engaged just before Margaret and Peter got married."

"So, Angela will have to put up with bumping into Julian. Do he and Doris have any children?"

"No, Julian broke off the engagement just before Christmas 1964. The wedding was set for the New Year – he almost left her at the altar." Esme's hand flew to her mouth.

"Oh no, poor Doris, and poor Angela."

"Anyway, that is the past. Hopefully, Vince and Angela will be very happy. He dotes on her, which is what she needs."

Susan sighed and raised her glass to Esme.

"To us." Esme responded with a smile.

"To the stepmothers' club."

CHAPTER 14

The following day they were having lunch at the Taw Lodge Hotel. Ivy was looking after the Eastman children and the King children at Elizabeth and William's house. Usually she had Sunday afternoon off but didn't mind swapping for another afternoon. She was glad to be away from Veronica Cottage. The past two weeks had been a nightmare for her. Since she arrived back after that embarrassing encounter with Mark, she had been living on her nerves. She was afraid he would turn up and confront her and tell everyone what had happened. She was very apprehensive when she went to visit Emma on her day off. Emma knew something was wrong, but Ivy wouldn't say anything to her. She was afraid she would bump into Ross, but he was nowhere to be seen. The next morning, she had gone down to the kitchen, as usual, to get Xavier and Marcus's breakfast. On her way back, as she crossed the hall to the stairs, the post arrived. She put down the tray and picked it up. She was about to put it on the hall table when a postcard caught her eye. She looked at the picture and then began to place it on top of the pile when something told her to turn it over. It was addressed to her. Her blood ran cold. She stuffed it in her apron pocket and resumed her journey to the nursery. It wasn't until later that morning that she was able to read it. Xavier was downstairs with Margaret, and Marcus was having his sleep. She went to her room and read the postcard from Mark. He was in Blackpool with his mother. He always drove her up to stay with her sister for a week, but this year his uncle had passed away, so he was staying an extra week for the funeral. Ross was unable to go due to the imminent arrival of his and Lucy's baby. He stayed at his cousin's house, as his aunt only had a small terraced house. He said he couldn't wait to see her when he got back. Ivy was tempted to rip it up, but she didn't. She put it in a drawer and shut it firmly.

Ivy was busy looking after the children, and was ready to put her plan into action.

The adults were lunching at Taw Lodge Hotel. William was with them but not lunching.

"Since Beth stole my chef and housekeeper away to her hotel, I have had lots of issues. Beth has been very good stepping in to help with the housekeeping, but it is only temporary; she has so much else to do. The chef is the big issue. He is very able to do breakfasts and lunches, like today, where it is roasts, but he doesn't do so well on catering for weddings and things."

At that he was called to the kitchen again.

"What did he mean you stole his chef and housekeeper?" asked Esme.

Elizabeth explained about her cousin, Roberta, and Roberta's half-brother, Benjamin, and William's sister, Marilyn.

"It is a lovely place to break the journey," said Esme. "We will try and speak to your family on our way home. It has been very busy the times we have visited. The food is really excellent, so I can understand why. The new chef here has a lot to live up to."

"Marilyn and Ben hope to marry as soon as her divorce comes through."

"Is there no one else to help? What about William's parents?"

"They have semi-retired to the hotel in Torquay."

"You have another hotel?"

"Yes, Bill does. This one is his parents'. Bill owns the one in Torquay. He bought it a few years ago to prove a point." Elizabeth thought back to that dreadful time. After Margaret's disastrous adventure and William rescuing her, then disappearing and reappearing. On the night of Margaret's dreadful venture into adulthood, he had had an argument with his parents and decided to prove a point. "When we married, his parents decided to retire to Torquay, so they sort of swapped hotels."

Esme nodded.

"And you have no brothers or sisters? Just a cousin who took your staff from here." Esme smiled. Elizabeth laughed.

"It sounds dreadful when you put it like that, but in essence, yes. So now I am working at the hotel. I always did like to help out, but I have less time since the children came along."

They were interrupted by Charles and Susan, who were leaving. Angela and Vince decided not to come, much to everyone's relief. They wanted time on their own as Vince had to return to his unit the next day.

Edith and David were next to leave. Everyone else went to Elizabeth's house. No one was in a rush to leave. She made some tea. Eventually the party broke up and the Eastmans returned to Veronica Cottage.

Ivy was relieved that it was quiet. She half expected a car to be there. She rushed upstairs with Marcus and pottered around slowly, getting him ready for bed. Eventually she took him down to say goodnight to everyone. While he was being passed around and kissed goodnight, she asked Margaret if she could have a word.

Margaret looked surprised but agreed. She led the way to the kitchen. Margaret looked at her quizzically. Ivy stood, her fingers tracing the pattern on the worktop. Finally she spoke.

"I would like to take some leave."

"Yes, of course, when were you thinking?"

Ivy paused and looked down at the tiled floor.

"Tomorrow," she said in a quiet voice.

"Tomorrow!" exclaimed Margaret.

"Yes, I'm sorry it is such short notice, but I can't stay here. I have spoken to Sally. She is willing to stay." Margaret was at a loss. She just nodded.

Ivy rushed out of the kitchen, hurriedly took Marcus from Peter and went upstairs. Margaret followed slowly.

Peter looked at Margaret enquiringly when she entered the lounge. He was doing a jigsaw with Xavier and Aaron.

"Ivy wants to go on holiday."

"That's alright, isn't it?" Margaret nodded. "When does she want to go?"

"Tomorrow."

"Tomorrow." He was as surprised as Margaret. "That is very short notice. I don't know if Sally is available."

"Yes, she is. Apparently, Ivy had already spoken to her."

Everyone else had paused what they were doing. They sensed something was amiss.

"Well, did Ivy say why she wanted to go at such short notice?"

"No, but I think it has something to do with her visit to Ross's house and his brother. She was upset when she got back and has been acting strangely since."

"Shall I talk to her?"

"I don't know. Maybe she will be better when she returns from her holiday."

* * * * * * * *

The next morning there were lots of goodbyes. Phoebe was leaving in a much happier frame of mind than when she arrived. She was looking forward to seeing everyone in a few weeks. She kissed her nephews, Xavier, who immediately wiped his face, which made everyone laugh, and Marcus in Sally's arms. Aaron and Esme were next. Esme gave everyone a kiss. This time Xavier didn't wipe it away, due to a look from his mother. Lastly, Aaron kissed everyone except Peter, who held out his hand. Aaron shook it warmly with both his hands.

Everyone waved as the car pulled out of the drive.

Then it was Ivy's turn. She came out with a heavy suitcase and put it in her car. It was her car that caused all the trouble. It had been in Peter's garage two weeks ago, waiting for a part, which is why she had to walk to Ross's house and get a lift back from his brother.

Ivy kissed Marcus and gently ran her finger down his face. Sally took him inside.

"Thank you, Margaret, and Peter, for everything," she said, addressing them by their names. Margaret and Peter looked at each other.

"You are coming back, aren't you?" Margaret asked, panic in her voice.

Ivy was crouching down in front of Xavier. She stroked his hair out of his eyes.

"Goodbye, Xavier." She kissed him and stood up.

Xavier sensed something was wrong and started to cry.

"You are coming back?" he asked anxiously, echoing his mother.

Ivy looked round at them. She could see the worried expressions on Margaret and Peter's faces. She wasn't sure she would be back, but she couldn't stay. Her heart was breaking as she looked down at Xavier. He grabbed her waist. He was sobbing more intensely.

"Don't go," he begged. Margaret started to pull him away. She had tears in her eyes. Ivy looked at her; she didn't want to go. She was undecided if she would be back.

Ivy crouched down again and spoke to Xavier, who was clinging to Margaret.

"I will be back. Look, take this." She unclasped a locket she had round her neck and gave it to Xavier. "It has a picture of my... brother in. It is very precious to me. I always wear it under my uniform." She opened it up. There was a picture of a young boy. "That is Daniel. He died." There was a catch in her voice. "You can give it back to me when I return." *They can always post it back to me*, she thought.

Xavier stopped crying. He looked at the silver locket in his hand, realising how important it was to her. He nodded.

Ivy got in her car. She paused as she drove out. Then, determinedly, she pulled away.

* * * * * * *

It was a happy party in Peter's Zephyr that pulled up outside the house in St John's Wood, a semi-detached house with three floors. Phoebe had been sitting on the wall outside waiting for them. Xavier was first out, followed by Margaret. Peter got out and relieved Ivy of a sleeping Marcus. Aaron came out to greet them. He led them down the side of the house, and as they stepped through the gated pathway, they were ambushed by Bull, an Alsatian dog. He apologised that Esme couldn't greet them, but she had a client. She didn't usually work on a Saturday, but this was an emergency. They followed him round the back of the house and into the large airy garden room. They could see the kitchen off to the right and a door leading to the hall. Aaron said he would show them where they would be sleeping. By the time they freshened up, Esme should be finished with the client. He opened the door to the hall and stairs. There was another door leading to the front door. This had some bolts on. Aaron explained that the front room of the house was Esme's surgery. They had partitioned the large hall and made a small waiting room. The bolts were security for Phoebe when she was on her own. She would put them across to stop any patients from coming through. They trailed behind Aaron to the first floor. There were three bedrooms and a bathroom. The big front room was Aaron and Esme's. Xavier was to have the small front one. Peter and Margaret had the back bedroom next to the bathroom. Ivy and Marcus would share the spare room on the top floor. Phoebe had her room on the top floor, at the front. There was a small bathroom next to the spare room.

When the visitors came down to the garden room, the dividing door was open, and Esme was waiting for them. She apologised for having a patient. She invited them through to the garden room and explained more about her practice. Aaron had tea and coffee ready. After she and Aaron were married, she worked at the hospital but wanted to be at home when they started a family. They bought the house because it was adaptable. They partitioned the hall and extended into the garden. After Phoebe was born, Esme only worked one day a week at home, and Vera looked after Phoebe. As Phoebe got older it was easier for Vera to come to them, and the bolts were added to the door for safety. They decided to get a dog for security at night; it would sleep in the surgery. Esme had a few drugs there. When Bull arrived, he was so clumsy he knocked everything over like a bull in a china shop and the name stuck.

Xavier was exploring the garden with Phoebe. Ivy was helping Marcus to keep up. Bull was running from one to another. He knocked Ivy and Marcus over, but they got up again, laughing.

Esme was shocked at the change in Ivy. She couldn't wait to find out what had happened.

Esme had prepared a meal for them. She apologised, but there would be two extra guests; she couldn't keep them away. At 6 o'clock the doorbell rang. Peter and Margaret stood up to greet them. Peter suddenly recognised them.

"Mr and Mrs Scott!"

They shook hands. Mrs Scott was dabbing her eyes.

"You do remember us," she said. They took the wine offered by Aaron.

"Yes, I do now. You came round a few days after Dad disappeared," Peter addressed Mr Scott, "with another man. And I had seen you before, a few times, when you came to collect Dad in your car. It is coming back to me now. I couldn't recall you before, Mr Scott. I remember your big blue and black car."

They sat at the table as they were talking, and Esme got the dinner.

"Please call us Derek and Vera. Yes, my Hillman Minx. The other man was our partner. Unfortunately he has passed away. I tried to help Roni, but she was a very independent person. I did ring every few weeks, not as often as I would like, which I do regret, but I was so busy with the ARP." He looked apologetically at Peter, asking for forgiveness.

Peter stared at him, thinking. He was brought back to earth by Vera.

"I used to pop in to see your mother every week, but after a few months, she started to make excuses. I told myself that she had Mrs French to help as well. It is such a shame about Mrs French, but your father has looked after her well. I am very sorry to say that I did not go back round to see your mother after September. I am so sorry, Peter. I should have done more to help."

Peter looked at their anxious faces.

"You should have done more, but it is not your fault. I understand about the war and now, looking back, I realise how independent Mother was."

Aaron went round refilling the wine glasses. He was shaking and nearly spilled it. Esme was anxious. She knew this was hard for him, for everyone. Margaret declined the wine – as previously, she was drinking water. Phoebe picked up her glass and waved it at her father. He had not refilled her glass.

"No, Phoebe, one glass is enough," he said firmly. Phoebe was about to argue when Margaret interrupted; she was next to her.

"Don't be too anxious to have alcohol. It can be devastating if you are young." Margaret spoke quietly, but Esme heard the desperate sadness in her voice. Phoebe lowered her glass. She, too, could hear the melancholy note in Margaret's voice.

"Let's have dessert," said Esme, trying to break the downturn in atmosphere. "I have tried to make lemon meringue pie, but it is not very good. There is also a trifle but with a hole in as Xavier and Marcus have already had some." Everyone laughed as she intended, and the tension was broken.

Peter was thoughtful.

"What happened to Mrs French? Margaret and I were in London a few years ago, and we went to look at the old flat. We bumped into her, but she seemed confused. I had wanted to introduce myself, but she brushed us off."

"I'm sorry to say she has dementia. It started about 10 years ago. We had to put her in a home about five years ago as she could not be trusted on her own. It was a very difficult decision but the only one we could take." Peter nodded.

The rest of the evening passed pleasantly, with light-hearted stories and anecdotes. It was broken twice by Ivy bringing the boys down when it was their bedtime.

"I can't believe you are a father, Peter," said Vera. She found herself left with Peter as Margaret had gone with Ivy and Xavier, and Phoebe had disappeared to her room. Aaron and Derek were talking about a case and Esme was in the kitchen. "When Aaron said that he may have found you, I was astounded. I was sure you had been killed with your mother. But you were alive, married and with a family. I was relieved." She took his hand. "I can't tell you how upset I was when you vanished. First your father, and then you and your mother. Initially I had hoped that you and she had gone to join him, but I soon realised that was a stupid idea. Then, when your father turned up all that time later, well, you could have knocked us down with a feather. And it turns out he lost his memory and was living under the name of his mother. You just can't believe it. Esme and I tried hard to find you while your father went to war. We did find your mother, Peter, I am so sorry she was killed. We tried to find you, but there was no trace. We really did. Please believe me."

CHAPTER 15

Peter was shaken. He had heard the story now several times, but this was the most poignant. He held Vera's hand. Until now he had still blamed his father, but hearing it from Vera, it gave him a different perspective. Vera's account was detached at the same time the deep association was there. He suddenly realised all the other people affected, not just him. He was glad he was going to Ruth's next weekend. He had been doubtful about going, not sure that he believed his father, thinking that there may have been a conspiracy, but now the doubts had been swept aside and he was truly understanding and coming to terms with everything.

"Thank you for telling me. I do believe you." He broke the mood. "I think Esme may need some help." He stood up. Vera stood as well.

"Yes, I think you are right." She was relieved. She had been worried that he would blame her for not looking after him and Veronica more. She had tried, but Veronica was very stubborn and insistent that she was taking care of everything. It had been easy to walk away and concentrate on her children, Derek, the war and everything else.

* * * * * * * *

The next day, they all walked around Regent's Park. Margaret and Peter reminisced about time spent there in their childhood and more recently when they were discovering their love for each other. They laughed at the boys' antics and playing with Bull. Aaron declared that he didn't know why they had him. He was useless as a guard dog, and he would probably lick the burglars to death. Phoebe was sullen as they left the house; she had wanted her friends to come. She wanted to introduce them to her brother, who was so handsome all her friends had fallen in love with him immediately seeing his picture, and sister-in-law, who was so sophisticated, and they wanted to emulate her style. But Phoebe had been firmly told no. It was a family affair, this time, for everyone to try and get to know each other. Phoebe had protested that Derek and Vera had been there the previous night, and that was not any different. But she had come round thanks to Margaret's help, and by the time they returned to the house, she was joining in with the boys and Bull.

Monday saw the party split up. Ivy had the day off. Margaret, Peter and the boys were going to visit some places on their own, and to their surprise, Phoebe asked to go with them.

Their first stop was the flat, just off Berkeley Square and then to Berkeley Square Park, where they had their first true kiss. On the way to Brunswick House, they passed some other places that they reminisced about. Margaret and Peter had not visited Brunswick House since they had got married. They knocked on the door. It was opened by Withers. He was so happy to see them he forgot his usual calm manner for several minutes. He exclaimed how Xavier had grown. He was introduced to Marcus and Phoebe.

He went to get the tea and coffee that he had prepared in advance and served them in the lounge. The boys and Phoebe went to play in the garden. Margaret and Peter asked if they could go to the kitchen to see Mrs Coghlan. Withers' face clouded over. He explained that her husband was not well and as Sebastian was not visiting due to the Parliament summer break, she had taken time to nurse him. They asked where she lived, and if they might visit. Withers went to ring her.

Margaret and Peter were left alone. Their thoughts returned to the last time they were there. They had spent their days together, exploring London. It was when Margaret started to discover that Peter was not who she thought he was and a new realisation that she loved him. They had not been alone as Margaret's brother-in-law had been there as well. He was married to Hugh's sister and was in the middle of an art exhibition. They laughed at how his fellow artist had tried to pretend that they were having an affair. It was also a time when Peter started to learn about his past. They had visited a couple of times previous, but Peter had wanted nothing to do with the London he had lived in, then with Margaret's help had started to remember. They stood at the window in each other's arms, watching the children playing.

Withers interrupted them with a cough. He was so pleased to see how happy they were together. Initially, Withers had thought that he would dislike Peter, but from the moment Peter had arrived, he had proved himself. Withers had been won over completely after Hugh's death. He had been very impressed with the way Peter handled everything, how discreet he was. Withers knew that if it had been left to Sebastian, all sorts of secrets may have come out as Sebastian hated his brother.

"Mrs Coghlan doesn't want you to visit as Mr Coghlan is so ill, but she will be here in about 10 minutes if you can wait." He had been pleased to see them look upset when he said they couldn't visit as it showed they cared, but also when they smiled again at the news of Mrs Coghlan's visit. Fifteen minutes later there were tears in the kitchen as she was welcomed by everyone. They had more tea in the kitchen. Withers tried, half-heartedly, to get them back upstairs, but they refused, as Mrs Coghlan would not go upstairs. Both Withers and Mrs Coghlan insisted they stayed for lunch. They had a picnic in the garden.

* * * * * * *

Phoebe had declared that she wanted to visit Margaret's charity with her mother and Margaret. Margaret had planned to visit her charity house that afternoon. Esme had asked if she could come, and now Phoebe was coming too.

Margaret had become interested in the charity after she bumped into her former maid Claudia after leaving her doctor's surgery where she had an antenatal check-up when carrying Xavier. Margaret had been shocked to see her maid, as she thought she was in France with her fiancé. She discovered that Claudia's now ex-fiancé was actually married and had abandoned

Claudia, who was expecting his child. Margaret went with Claudia to where she was staying, a house for unmarried mothers, and discovered that it was about to close as the landlord wanted to sell. Margaret stepped in and bought the property so that the charity could continue.

Esme had initially been surprised that Margaret was interested in that sort of charity but had been quick to offer her services. She was looking for a new interest to use her skills and this seemed just right.

They arrived and were warmly greeted by Claudia, who was now the manager and ran the house. There were 12 girls there, ranging from 15 to 20. Esme was shocked to see the young girls with their large bellies or carrying around their babies. She knew she had made the right decision and could offer so much. She was introduced to each of them. It was mainly the same story: they had been seduced then abandoned by the man and their families. Esme had not wanted Phoebe to come, but seeing her interact with girls, mostly around her own age, and how they responded to her, she knew it had been the right decision. Phoebe had led a sheltered life; it was good she was exposed to the 'real' world, and this environment provided that, safely.

On the way home, Phoebe declared that she wanted to become a paediatrician and help those girls and their babies. Esme was delighted that Phoebe had finally decided on a career.

Esme parked in the drive, and they went round the back of the house to the garden. They stopped to take in the scene. Peter was sitting on a garden chair surrounded by a group of girls. Xavier was playing with Bull, and Marcus was asleep on a blanket. Peter spotted them, and they laughed at the relieved expression on his face. He quickly waved and stood up. The girls turned as one to see who had arrived.

"Poor Peter." Esme laughed. "It looks as if he has had a hard time with Phoebe's ABC friends." Then she turned to Phoebe, who was looking aghast. "I told you not to invite them."

Margaret interrupted. "ABC friends?" she whispered enquiringly.

"Adele, Mirabelle, or Belle, and Camilla."

The girls stood up slowly; they had been seated on the grass. The two parties greeted each other.

"Mummy," shouted Xavier, running up to Margaret, followed by Bull, who nearly knocked Esme over.

Peter walked quickly over to Margaret and whispered in her ear. "Thank God you've come back. Help me." Margaret smiled. Phoebe was indignant. "Adele, Mirabelle, Camilla! What are you doing here?" she demanded. The girls looked at each other, then Adele spoke.

"We just had to visit your brother." She looked coyly at the other two. Camilla continued, brazenly.

"We wanted to make sure he was as handsome as you said."

"And he is," said Mirabelle, going red when she realised everyone was listening. Marcus woke up and, seeing his mother, toddled over to her. Margaret bent down to pick him up, which gave her the opportunity to hide a big smile that was forming. Phoebe sighed, also embarrassed. Mirabelle spoke again.

"We just wanted to check. You made out that he was some sort of Adonis," Mirabelle insisted. Now it was Phoebe's turn to go red. "We needed to know. And now we do. And you were quite correct." They started to laugh, and the four girls ran off to Phoebe's room, giggling.

"Phew," said Peter. "What?" he demanded as he saw that Margaret and Esme were laughing as well. "Xavier, come and help me with all these women." But Xavier was playing with Bull again.

Margaret and Esme went into the kitchen to prepare the evening meal. Aaron arrived home. He had been annoyed he had to work, but it was a big corporate case he couldn't ignore. He joined Peter and Xavier in the garden.

Esme called Phoebe for dinner. She came downstairs with her friends. They started to giggle again and act sheepishly and flirty.

"It was nice to meet you, Peter. I hope we can meet again soon."

"And you, Mrs Eastman. You are as elegant as Phoebe said."

"And as handsome. Well, they are," insisted Camilla when she saw her friends' faces. They all giggled.

Phoebe hurried them out the door before they could say too much more to embarrass her.

They had just finished the meal when the doorbell rang.

"I'll go," said Phoebe. It was a good excuse to leave.

When she returned, they looked at her expectantly. Phoebe had a strange look on her face. She opened the door wide and stood back. She let the visitor enter the room.

"Ah, there you are, Ivy," said Margaret. "You've changed your clothes. I like the red; it is not a colour you usually wear. I was just about to put Marcus to bed." Margaret stood up, holding Marcus to give him to Ivy, when she noticed everyone was staring at her.

"That is not Ivy," said Peter. He was always amazed at Margaret's lack of knowledge regarding people she knew. He knew that she did not like prying into peoples' lives and did not like people prying into her life. He sighed and turned to the new guest.

"This is Holly, Ivy's twin sister. Am I right?"

Margaret looked at Peter, stunned, then back to Holly.

"I am sorry. I didn't realise that Ivy had a twin sister. Where is Ivy?"

"Here," came a voice from the hall. Slowly Ivy emerged. "Sorry, I have had a bit of an accident." She came in on crutches. "I tripped over and twisted my ankle."

"She was desperate to get back to you, but I insisted she went to hospital, which is why she is late."

"That doesn't matter," said Peter. "What did the hospital say? Have you broken it?" Ivy shook her head.

"It is badly twisted. They say I just need rest. I told them that was impossible. Let me take Marcus. I will resume my duties now." She held out her arms, difficult with the crutches.

"No," said Margaret. "If you need rest, you should have it. Somehow, I will look after Marcus." She looked at Peter, panic on her face. Peter smiled at her.

"Don't worry. We will all help." Margaret looked relieved.

"I have told Ivy to come and stay with me. I can look after her and make sure she rests. It will not be easy for her while you are travelling and visiting."

"I think that is a very good idea," said Peter, and Margaret nodded her agreement.

"I can't," protested Ivy. "How will you manage?"

"I will help," Phoebe announced. "I can come with you to Royston House and then onto Aunt Ruth's."

"I don't know," said Esme. "I'm not sure I like the idea of you gallivanting all over the place. And how will you get home?"

"I can catch the train. I won't be gallivanting; I will be with Peter and Margaret."

"What do you think, Aaron?"

"I think it will give Phoebe and Peter a chance to get to know each other properly. We can meet her at the station. Ruth and Eric can put her on the train in Poole."

Esme was not convinced but did not object anymore. Phoebe gave her a hug.

"I need to pack as we are leaving tomorrow. I will put Marcus to bed then pack." She took Marcus from Margaret and danced out the door. Explaining to him what was happening, he was chuckling as she danced with him.

"I need to pack as well," said Ivy, and she slowly turned to head upstairs.

"I will do it," said Holly. "You can't climb the stairs like that. Luckily, we live in a bungalow, so Ivy won't have to climb stairs. I will get Phoebe's help." She looked at Esme, who nodded. Holly left the room.

Ivy sat on a chair. Thankful to sit down, her ankles were aching though she didn't want to admit it.

"Why didn't you tell me you had a twin sister?" asked Margaret, half accusingly.

"I did," replied Ivy. "At the interview. Hugh asked about my family, so I told you." Margaret was surprised. She thought back and realised she hadn't listened to much of the interview between Hugh and Ivy. She was going more on her feelings; after all, Ivy would be looking after her baby.

"How did you know, Peter?" she asked him accusingly.

"When we got engaged and I became responsible for Xavier, Ivy and I had a chat, as I would now be her employer. I wanted to make sure she would be happy to continue to look after Xavier and our children as they came along." Margaret gave him a big smile. He always looked after her.

Ivy was distracted by Xavier trying to use her crutches.

"Careful! Don't fall over and break anything."

"Let's go in the garden until Ivy and Holly are ready to leave," said Aaron. "It won't matter if you fall over there."

Margaret watched her son and father-in-law. Then she turned to Ivy.

"Why did your parents name you Ivy and Holly?"

"We were born on 28 December, and Mother heard someone singing that song." She shrugged and grimaced. "So we were landed with the names Holly and Ivy. We had a hard time at school."

Margaret saw Peter shaking his head in disbelief. She continued. "I did know when your birthday was," she said in defiance to Peter. "I just didn't know you had a sister." She was about to ask more when Holly returned.

* * * * * * *

Phoebe couldn't wait to see the horses. They had left London just after lunch and arrived late afternoon. She had been impatient to see them but had had to wait until everyone was settled in. At last Margaret was ready. She led the way out of the back of the house to the stables. Savannah and Bedford were in the field. Phoebe clasped her hands together when she saw them.

"Can we go for a ride now?"

"No, it is too late; we need to get ready for dinner shortly. We can have a ride tomorrow." Margaret was as excited as Phoebe to go riding. She was looking forward to riding Savannah again.

There was a formal dinner for their arrival. Xavier was allowed to join them, and a maid sat with Marcus while they ate. Xavier was a bit overwhelmed with all the paraphernalia and glad to get to his room afterwards. His and Marcus's sleeping arrangements had quickly been rearranged. They were not sleeping in the nursery now. Margaret and Peter did not feel it right that

Phoebe should be sleeping up there with the boys. So, Xavier had Hugh's old room, Marcus had the one next to Margaret and Peter's room and Phoebe had one of the rooms opposite, known to Margaret and Peter as the 'secret door' room due to an incident they had had to deal with a few years ago after Hugh's death, involving his valet.

The next morning Margaret and Phoebe went to the stables as soon as breakfast was finished. Simon, who looked after the horses, was already there. He had the horses tied up in the yard and was grooming Bedford. Margaret and Phoebe helped him finish and saddled up. They set off down Royston Lane. *It feels good to ride Savannah again*, thought Margaret. At the end of the lane they turned left. Margaret planned to ride to Gray's Wood via Walton's Bridle path; it would take about an hour to an hour and a half. Simon had assured her that he had exercised the horses and they were fit to tackle the ride. From the feel of Savannah underneath her, he was true to his word.

They arrived back at the yard tired but happy; it had been a lovely, uneventful ride. Xavier was waiting for them with Simon. Margaret left Xavier and Phoebe helping Simon with Savannah and Bedford. She went in the back door, nodded to the maid then to the cook in the kitchen as she went through to the hall. She was about to climb the stairs to go and change when she was stopped by Lady Agatha.

"Sonia has just rung. She confirmed that they will all be over this afternoon for tea." Margaret smiled acknowledgement and secretly to herself at Lady Agatha's expression. She could tell that Lady Agatha found all of Sonia's children coming en masse a trial.

Luckily, it was a nice afternoon, and the children could play outside. Phoebe was overwhelmed with the number and kept getting their names wrong. Margaret and Peter were surprised to see Fleur Fitzgerald turn up with them. They had met her previously in London when Wolfe, Sonia's husband, was exhibiting his work. Fleur was a fellow artist at the same exhibition. They glanced at each other, raising their eyebrows.

They were not sure if he and Fleur were having an affair, but Sonia seemed happy to have Fleur around. Wolfe was in Scotland as he had a commission to paint a lord's family similarly to the way he had previously painted his family. Margaret could bear it no longer; she was bursting with curiosity. When Lady Agatha left to go to her grandchildren, she took the opportunity to speak to them. Peter shook his head. He could see that she was going to speak and dreaded the ensuing argument.

"It is nice to meet you again, Fleur," she started. "I see you are helping Sonia with her girls."

"Yes," replied Fleur, "she is so lucky to have so many. We hope to have one soon." She put her hand on her belly.

"Maybe you will have a son. I only seem to have daughters." Sonia smiled at her. Margaret and Peter were shocked. Sonia laughed at their discomfort.

"Surely you knew that Fleur married Wolfe's brother. Fleur has been a godsend while Wolfe is away." Sonia smiled at everyone.

CHAPTER 16

Friday morning Peter's Zephyr was filled, again, with luggage and people for the last leg of the journey. It was only a three-and-a-half-hour journey to Poole, but they stopped just outside Ringwood to freshen up.

Peter took a deep breath when they got back in the car. Margaret sympathised with him.

"The worst is over now. Your aunt is so looking forward to seeing you."

"What if she blames me for Mum's death... and Dad?"

"Why would she?" Margaret looked at Peter, puzzled. What was going on in his head? "Your aunt will not blame you. You were only a child. Please, Peter, do not blame yourself." She was trying not to sound desperate. Peter turned to look at her.

"I know, but I still feel I could have done more. Now I know Dad was ill, I feel as if I let them down."

Margaret leant over and hugged him.

"There is no way you are to blame, and you did everything that a young boy could do in the war. Xavier is about that age; would you expect him to know everything? Please relax and enjoy being reunited with your aunt." She could feel some of the tension go out of Peter.

"You are right. I will try." He started up the car and Margaret moved back to her seat. She looked at the three faces behind her and smiled. They were all looking tense, sensing something more than understanding. They returned her smile and tried to spot the ponies as they drove through the New Forest.

Peter followed Phoebe's directions when they got to Poole, eventually pulling up outside his aunt's house.

"Does it look familiar?" asked Margaret. Peter shook his head, but there was a slight feeling.

He slowly got out the car. The children waited for him, for once, instead of rushing out. Margaret took Marcus from Phoebe and nodded to her to go up to the door. Phoebe skipped up the path, knocked on the door with familiarity and opened it. She called out to her aunt.

Peter and Margaret followed, more slowly. They waited outside. Phoebe poked her head around the corner of the house.

"They are outside, in the garden."

Peter and Margaret followed her around the side of the house. There was a large lawn and several fruit trees. To one side was a patio area with a table and chairs. Phoebe led them over. Peter stood still and looked at his aunt. She had tears running down her face. She dabbed her eyes with a handkerchief.

"I thought I would never see you again."

Peter crouched down beside her wheelchair.

"I'm sorry," he said.

"No, it's not your fault," she said, stroking his head. "How you've grown. That's a stupid thing to say. You are so handsome. I can see Aaron and Roni in you."

"Here, lad, sit in this chair." Peter stood up and took the offered chair next to his aunt. His aunt took his hands in hers.

"I'm sorry. It is so nice to see you." She started to cry again, then after dabbing her eyes said, "You must be parched. Eric, can you make some fresh tea and bring some biscuits?"

"I'll help, Uncle Eric," said Phoebe, and they went off to the kitchen.

"Now," said Ruth, "introduce me to your family."

They were sitting comfortably having their tea. No one liked to say too much.

"I think Marcus's nappy needs changing," said Margaret. "We need to unload the car."

"Of course," said Eric, standing up. "I will help and show you to your rooms. We do not have anyone staying here at the moment. As soon as we knew you were coming, we cancelled all the bookings," he explained as they walked to the car. They sorted the luggage and returned to the garden as quickly as they could.

Ruth had taken the tea things into the house and started to organise the meal. She shooed everyone out into the garden while she and Eric cooked. They joined everyone in the garden as the preparations allowed.

"It is a lovely surprise to have you here, Phoebe," said Ruth.

"Yes, I couldn't miss the opportunity to come and stay."

"And do some riding – that's more of a reason you came."

Everyone laughed at Phoebe's face. Ruth patted her hand. "I'm only joking."

At last the meal was ready and everyone went into the dining room.

"I think we should start to address the issues we have been skirting around," said Ruth. Peter nodded.

"When your father disappeared, I rang your mother everyday that I was able. We both kept ringing the hospitals and police stations, but there was no trace. Vernon, our stepfather," she looked at Peter, who nodded, "went up to London to visit your mother. He reassured her about money, but he had his accident on the way home. It was a difficult time." Eric went round the table and gave her a hug with his one arm. Ruth wiped her tears and carried on. "I had no idea what your mother planned or that she did not have any money. Vernon said he was going to sort it, so I thought he had. I didn't realise that he needed more time. Due to his heart attack and stroke, he could not tell me what to do. Then you and your mother disappeared. She always was independent. I don't mean that as a criticism; it was just her way. I kept hoping she would make contact. And your father. I lost all of you." She paused and took a sip of wine. She looked at Peter. "I really did try to find you. But with Vernon, the war and everything..."

Peter found it hard to speak.

"I do understand." He hadn't really, until now. He had thought that Ruth should have done more, but now, seeing her and listening to her, he finally realised how difficult it had been. "I know you did everything you could." He got up and gave her a kiss. "Really, I do."

"Thank you," she whispered.

Margaret changed the subject.

"So, how did you and Eric meet?" She knew the story but wanted to cheer her up. Ruth smiled at Eric.

"It was love at first sight. I know some people don't believe in those things, but it was."

"But when we met, I was covered in bandages," replied Eric indignantly. "You didn't know what I looked like, but I could see you and fell in love immediately." They smiled at each other.

"When Mother and I had our accident," Ruth took a deep breath, "Vernon bought this house for us. We didn't want to live in our old house. Too many memories. So we started afresh. Your father continued his studies in London, staying in the flat. Vernon and I came here and started a bed and breakfast business. We made a couple of bedrooms downstairs, revamped the kitchen and dining room. This is usually for guests," she waved her arm around the room, "but for today, it is accommodating us. We moved the tables together. Eric may only have one arm, but it is very strong." She blushed slightly before continuing. "We have five bedrooms, four on the first floor and one in the attic. Over the years we have installed bathrooms, so each room had their own. During the war, we offered the house to the navy for their injured sailors to recuperate and recover. We doubled them up and usually had about 10. We turned the lounge, across the passage, into a bedroom as well. We had two nurses staying; they had the attic. We had four or five different ones over the years. Then one day Eric came, and he never left."

"I couldn't. My family are in Norfolk, and I thought if I left, I would never see you again."

"He was a great help when Vernon died. I had no one. But then Eric stepped in."

"I had to. It was too much for Ruth. She saved my life. She gave me something to do, other than feeling sorry for myself."

"When he arrived, he was carrying on so much. Nothing was right, he wouldn't do his exercises, and all he did was moan."

"Then I saw how Ruth was coping and everything changed."

"He did his exercises and gradually got stronger, then he started to help the other patients. He knew what they had gone through and could sympathise with them."

Peter interrupted their reminiscing.

"Marcus needs to go to bed." He stood up. Phoebe also stood up.

"I'll do it – that's what I'm here for." She put her hand out to Peter.

"No, I don't mind." She picked up Marcus and left. Xavier took the opportunity to follow her. He was bored.

Ruth continued.

"When I received the phone call from the hospital saying that they had Aaron, I was so excited. It was such a relief. I thought that we would all get together, but it wasn't to happen. I had thought that Aaron knew where you were, and when I realised he didn't, it was like losing you all over again. Esme was wonderful. I was so glad when they married." She looked at Peter. "I really liked your mother and still miss her. When they found out that she had been killed, it was a very sad day for me, but she was found. That just left you missing." She turned to Margaret. "I met your parents."

Margaret nodded.

"Dad told me. There was a garden party to honour anyone who had received awards regarding the navy. Mother made sure she was on duty and got Dad in. She knew he would enjoy it."

"Yes, it was held the year after the war ended. I believe I bumped into your father with my wheelchair. We all ended up having a lovely chat. Of course, I was introduced as Mrs Burns – Eric and I had married in 1942. We have been married 23 years, which is such a long time when you say it out loud. If I had been known as Miss Eastman, your parents might have said that they had adopted a Peter Eastman, then I would have said that my nephew, Peter Eastman, had gone missing. We might have found you sooner." She began to cry. "What is it with names? I was introduced as Mrs Burns, not Miss Eastman, and your father, Peter, in his confused state, said his name was our mother's name, Frances Sittall. If only he had said Aaron Eastman, we would have found him almost immediately." She broke down completely. Eric took her away to recover. Peter was in shock. Though he knew it had affected everyone, he never really realised how much and the last vestiges of resentment at not being found disappeared.

He really believed now that everyone had done everything possible to find him.

* * * * * * *

They loaded the car for the last time after lunch on the Sunday. They left Phoebe with Eric and Ruth; she planned to travel back to London on the Monday as there were more trains. Margaret was shocked at the ease Phoebe was talking about travelling on her own. She had had a terrible experience travelling from London to Barnstaple and she had been older than Phoebe.

They drove directly home. Mrs Bancroft had been in and left a meal for them, and Sally was there to look after the boys. Ivy was due to return the next day. Initially she was going to return to Barnstaple by train, but it was arranged that Holly would drive her to The Coaching Inn and Mark would meet them and bring her back to Barnstaple.

Ivy was excited at her sister meeting Mark at last. They all piled into Holly's car – she had to bring her boys with her. Holly was looking forward to meeting Mark. She had been dying to meet him since Ivy had turned up at her house a few weeks ago. Ivy was staying with their parents, who lived a couple of streets away in Hammersmith. She came over the morning after her arrival very emotional. Holly was able to calm her down and put everything in perspective. All that was important, she told Ivy, was that she loved him. Ivy said she did but didn't know if Mark loved her, and that he probably had a very low opinion of her and would never want to see her again. Holly declared they needed to find out. Ivy did not have Mark's telephone number. Holly made her ring Emma. Then made her ring Mark when he returned from Blackpool. It took a lot of persuasion before Ivy agreed. Mark was very relieved to hear from her – he had feared the worst. He explained that as soon as he had taken his mother home, he had gone to see her. He was shocked to find that she had left. Peter sympathised with him, but they could not tell him where she was as they didn't know, nor did they know when she was returning. Mark had a couple of sleepless nights before Ivy had rung. He apologised for rushing off, but he had to be at work, in the pharmacy at the hospital, as he was going on holiday, so he could not be late. He was mortified to think that Ivy thought he had abandoned her. Ivy was happy to return to Barnstaple the following week and arranged to meet Mark. Everyone was relieved to see Ivy again and have her back to her old self, with a spring in her step. Mark was formally introduced to everyone at Veronica Cottage. Peter had met him informally at the wedding of Ross and Lucy a few years ago, but it was the time that he and Margaret were separated, so he did not enjoy the wedding. Margaret was at Royston House with Ivy.

Ivy was pleased that he was meeting her family. Ivy and Holly watched Mark and the boys play croquet on the hotel lawn. They smiled as he deftly caught a tennis ball that came over from the neighbouring court and threw it back. The boys cheered.

"He is a good one," said Holly. Ivy smiled and nodded.

"I can't believe it. I was so worried when he rushed off after we had... I thought he despised me. I was so relieved that he was just going to be late for work. It was his last shift at the hospital before taking holiday with his mother, so he needed to get everything in order before he left. He is the assistant pharmacist," she stated proudly.

Holly nodded. She was so pleased her sister was happy again. When Ivy turned up so upset, she was very concerned. Then when Ivy told her that her period was late, she tried to reassure her that she would help but, luckily, it started the next day, much to their relief.

* * * * * * * *

The two women were laughing as they went into the kitchen. They could not believe it. Margaret rushed down Elizabeth's garden path, eager to see her, Marcus in her arms. The door was opened before she got there. Elizabeth was equally excited to see her.

While they were hugging, both said at the same time,

"I'm pregnant."

"I'm having a baby."

"So am I."

"I am too."

Margaret put Marcus down to play on the mat and sat in the lounge with Elizabeth.

"I'm due in April next year."

"That's when I'm due as well. It is going to be fun being expectant together. That is something we haven't done before."

"Yes," agreed Margaret, "none of our previous pregnancies have coincided."

Finally they moved off the topic of their forthcoming babies and to other topics.

"It feels such a long time since we had our weekly chats. We have so much to catch up on," said Elizabeth. Margaret nodded her agreement. "So where do we start?"

Margaret brought her up to date and told Elizabeth about their visit to Peter's family. Elizabeth was relieved that Peter finally accepted his relations. She knew how difficult it had been for him. She remembered his arrival from London, and the journey to recovery. How he had come to rely on her in the early days as he settled in. She had watched his confidence grow as he matured. They had a very close relationship.

CHAPTER 17

"Now, that leaves you." Elizabeth stared at Margaret. Margaret raised her eyebrows. "Yes, you and Susan. Don't pretend to be surprised. Since it became public knowledge that she and your father were courting, then engaged, and finally married, you have hated her. Now, that is understandable, as you are loyal to your mother, but what about your father? And the big question: why did your attitude to Susan change almost instantly?" Elizabeth was defiant, waiting for Margaret to answer.

"Esme," was the one-word answer. Elizabeth looked puzzled. "Esme," repeated Margaret. "She asked me about Susan. I didn't know she was a psychiatrist and was just trying to help Peter and Aaron, but my bad feeling towards Susan was affecting Peter." Elizabeth's mouth dropped open. It was unusual for Margaret to have such an insight. Margaret laughed at Elizabeth's expression. "Esme explained while we were staying with them."

"But how did she get you to change your attitude?" asked Elizabeth.

Margaret shook her head. She did not want to say.

"This is me. You tell me anything. I know everything." Margaret smiled and sighed. She knew it was true.

"Well, first off, when Father told me that they were courting, he said that he had never been unfaithful to Mother, and I believed him. He said he had always liked Susan since he met her shortly after Peter arrived. He liked her company, but they knew the relationship couldn't go anywhere. But when I spoke to Susan, and she tried to reassure me of the same thing, I did not believe her." Margaret held up her hand. "I know what you are going say. Esme said the same. It sounds stupid, but that is what I believed – that Susan was having an affair with Father, but he wasn't having one with Susan." Elizabeth started to laugh, and Margaret joined in.

"Oh, Maggie! That is so like you to believe two opposite things. So Esme straightened that out." Elizabeth looked at Margaret again. "But there is more?" Margaret nodded. "Go on."

"I also thought that she was after his money."

"But Susan owns two farms, and she will inherit Elvine House from her parents." Margaret shrugged.

"I know," she said sadly, "but that is what I thought. It wasn't until she offered me the field for Chaos and Melody that I realised."

This time Elizabeth sighed.

"Oh, Maggie," she said again. "What are we going to do with you?"

"Also, I did not realise what a terrible marriage she had with her first husband." Margaret shuddered at the thought. "Esme was asking about Angela. Something I heard at Dad and Susan's wedding suddenly didn't make sense."

"I remember you ringing me, asking about Susan's first baby." Margaret nodded.

"I did not realise that she was pregnant when she married Arnold and that he hit her and caused a miscarriage. That was a shock. I feel so sorry for her. I am glad she found Father. But Angela, I still don't like her." Margaret sat back, relieved she had told Elizabeth. "I am glad she is getting married and moving away."

"Yes, and to Vince! Malcolm and Ruby are a bit put out. They don't like her, but they are making the best of it. Angela is planning a lavish Christmas wedding. No doubt we will be invited, waddling like a pair of ducks."

"How will you manage at the hotel now you are pregnant?"

"We have finally employed a housekeeper." Margaret raised her eyebrows enquiringly. "Rose Grayson. She has worked for us over the years as a chambermaid and barmaid. She surprised us by asking if she could have the job, but it is working out well."

"Rose Grayson. That name rings a bell. Is she any relation to Norman and Kathleen Grayson, that are at Elvine House?"

"Yes, she is their daughter-in-law, married to their son, Oscar. They have a daughter, Irene. Rose was working occasionally and helping Kathleen, but now they need the money as Oscar cannot work anymore. His war injuries are now too much, so he is taking early retirement, but he only has a small pension, so Rose has had to find a job. How is your staff?"

"At the moment everyone is happy. Jeremy has finally asked Sally to go out with him. She is dancing around the house, doing everything asked of her, which is making Mrs Bancroft happy. Ivy is singing as she goes now that she and Mark have sorted their problem out. I was so relieved when she came back. When Xavier gave her back her locket, he asked about Daniel.

"He was three when he died – he always had health issues. Ivy was six. She tried to look after him, but there was nothing she could do. That is why she became a nanny."

"What was the problem with her and Mark? If anyone can help, you can, after what you and Peter went through." Margaret opened her mouth to reply, but the telephone rang, and Elizabeth went to answer it.

Margaret thought about her and Peter's problem, known as the 'hiccup'. Peter had raised the issue on the third night of their honeymoon. They came back from the skiing slopes tired but happy, as they could finally manage to ski down the nursery slopes without falling over. Neither had skied before, so it was something they could both do together, starting on an equal footing. As Margaret was tired, she did not notice that Peter kept topping up her wine glass. Usually she did not drink much, if at all.

When they went up to the suite, Peter stopped her getting undressed.

"Tonight we are going to re-enact our 'hiccup'."

Margaret looked at him, suddenly very frightened.

"Come and sit on the sofa." He led her over and sat her down. He knelt in front of her. "We need to do this. I don't want to go through the rest of our lives having this hanging over us." Margaret nodded. She understood but was dreading it. "What I want to know is why you did it. When I said I wanted to make love to you, I meant when we were married. And if I did mean there and then, I still would not have expected you to do that."

Margaret stared at him, helpless. She felt so humiliated. "Is it to do with Hugh? Come on, no secrets. I liked Hugh, but I also knew what he was like." Margaret just continued to stare at him. No secrets, he said, but how could she tell him her big secret when it was not just hers? Peter continued. "Was that how you and he made love? He got you to do that. I know you didn't make love for a few months, and never after you got pregnant, and I know you were very innocent when you married, just that one incident." He paused. He could see her looking at him intently. "When we make love, we do not do it the way Hugh wanted it, do we?" Margaret shook her head. "Now that I understand, I think it was wonderful that you were willing to give yourself to me, just like that. At the time I did not understand. Did you enjoy doing that to Hugh? Come on, no secrets." He saw her hesitate. Margaret shook her head, tears forming in her eyes. "Oh, Maggie, I love so much, that you were prepared to do that for me. But I want you to do that now. I promise I will make it more enjoyable." Margaret suddenly felt the familiar shiver go up and down her spine. She let him remove her shoes and dress. He took off all his clothes except his trousers. He sat beside her and started to kiss her until she relaxed. "I want to make love to you," he said and guided her hand to his trousers. She slowly undid them, and this time she felt the anticipation grow inside her instead of the dread of what was to happen like during her first marriage. This time he did not stop her until finally he could bear it no more and pushed her back onto the sofa, removing the rest of her clothes as fast as he could, and made love to her.

Afterwards, Margaret felt elated, as if a great weight had been lifted. She knew Peter had been right. She turned to him and smiled.

"I now know the difference. This time was better, because you were gentle and helped me." She shuddered. "Hugh did not help me at all. He just thought of himself."

"Don't blame him. That was his way. He did love you; he just didn't know what you needed."

"And I suppose you do," she said, feigning indignance while smiling at Peter.

"Yes, I am an expert at knowing what you want, even before you know it." She recalled how they made love again when they got into bed. She was glad that Peter had exorcised their ghost 'hiccup'.

Margaret's thoughts were interrupted by Elizabeth returning from the hall.

* * * * * * *

They were complimenting each other on their new arrivals. They had resumed their weekly meetings a month after the birth of their babies.

"Faye is beginning to lose her dark hair. I think it is turning red like yours."

"That's what Peter says, but I don't think so. I want her to take after him, not me. Anyway, who does Fabian take after? I can't decide."

Elizabeth looked down at her son.

"I don't know. He has Bill's bluey purple eyes but my features. He is growing so quickly, but then he was large at 8lbs, while Faye only weighed six and a half." Margaret laughed at the envy in her voice.

They both looked at their babies, Fabian the older by 10 days and already nearly twice the size of Faye.

* * * * * * *

There was quite a crowd in the village church for the christening of the babies. Margaret and Elizabeth had initially only invited their immediate families, but word soon spread, and the list grew as they had requests to come. Afterwards, there was a buffet lunch at the Taw Lodge Hotel.

"What made you choose their names?" asked Phoebe.

"We just went with what we liked," replied Elizabeth. "Bill liked Fabian, and I wanted William. Duncan is named James after Bill, so it seemed appropriate to have William." Phoebe nodded, and she turned to Margaret.

"We wanted something different, so picked Faye. The second name was more difficult. We just couldn't agree. We had many conversations, but finally we both agreed to name her after our mothers, using their second names, hence Faye Isobel Harriet. A bit of a mouthful, but there you are!"

"Can I hold her?" Margaret nodded and gave her to Phoebe. Elizabeth was called away. Margaret sat in her chair, sipping her coffee, remembering the conversations they had had about names. Faye they both liked and agreed on quickly, but Margaret wanted to call her after someone in Peter's family as well. Both mothers had already had a road and house named after them, so she asked about Peter's mother's family. Of course, Peter had no idea. She asked if there was any information in his tin box. He refused to even think about opening it. He was determined, and Margaret had had to give up. It was hidden at the back of the wardrobe. Peter had been clutching it when his house was bombed, and his mother was killed. He let Constance open it to get his birth certificate out, but it had remained shut ever since. Margaret thought about opening it but could not bring herself to do so without Peter's permission. She finally rang Aaron to get the information.

Phoebe spoke again. "I'm glad Angela isn't here."

"I'm glad she isn't her as well."

"Who isn't here?" asked Elizabeth when she returned.

"Angela!" Elizabeth nodded in agreement.

"But it would be fun. I hear she is expecting. We could keep running our hands over our flat stomachs." Elizabeth and Margaret remembered how, at Angela and Vince's wedding, Angela would keep making snide remarks about how fat they were. "Well, you could, Maggie. I don't know how you manage to regain your figure so quickly. I still have all the weight from all three pregnancies." Margaret laughed at her expression.

"But Bill loves you. He wouldn't have it any other way."

Elizabeth looked over to him and smiled. She could see William was having an animated conversation with Peter and Ronald about the World Cup England had won the previous month. He was vigorously kicking an imaginary ball. She gasped as he spun round and nearly fell over Christine and Jessica, who were walking past. William just managed to keep his balance and put his arms around Jessica, who he had bumped into.

"Sorry about that. Are you alright, not hurt?" he asked.

Jessica looked at his striking eyes and felt his arms. She trembled inwardly and just shook her head, unable to speak.

Christine looked cross.

"Come on, Jess. Put him down," she hissed angrily, then to William, "Sorry, you know what impressionable teenagers are like."

She grabbed Jessica and they ran off giggling.

William turned back to Peter and Ronald.

"You've made a conquest there, mate," said Ronald. William pulled a face and looked for Elizabeth. He spotted her watching and gave a shrug. She smiled back at him.

* * * * * * * *

Angela looked round at everyone. She was enjoying all the attention. She should have had a baby before. She was only slightly annoyed that the christening was overshadowed a bit with Vince's sister's announcement, the previous week, that she and Jeremy had become engaged.

"How is Sally taking the news of the engagement?" Elizabeth asked Margaret while they were sitting together at the christening.

"Terribly. It was bad enough when he broke up with Sally to go out with Doris. But now, we have had a few bits of broken crockery. It is worse now that Ivy and Mark have announced their engagement."

"Ivy and Mark are engaged! When did that happen?" exclaimed Elizabeth.

"Last night. She told us this morning." Elizabeth studied her friend.

"You are happy for them, aren't you?"

"Oh, yes, very, but what am I going do when she leaves?" Elizabeth laughed.

"Oh, Maggie, that's just like you. Thinking of yourself." Margaret pretended to take offense.

"When are they thinking of getting married? Next week?"

"No, Ivy said not for a couple of years, until Faye is older. I suppose I could manage then."

"Oh, Maggie!" exclaimed Elizabeth again, her smile making Margaret realise she was teasing.

"How are Peter's garages coming on? He has amassed quite an empire now." Margaret laughed.

"He is happy. He loves playing with his cars. The Exeter garage is now up and running. Jeremy is happy being the manager of the garage here. He has done a good job this past year." Margaret and Elizabeth looked at each, suddenly realising that it was about a year ago he broke up with Sally, a maid, and started going out with Doris, who had her own business. They both raised their eyebrows.

* ** ** ** *

He sat staring at the tin box for a long time. Everyone else just waited. They knew how difficult this was.

Margaret thought back. It had taken her six months of near constant badgering. It started, in earnest, on his birthday, his 33rd. She had been thinking about it since Faye was born. Margaret suggested that it would be an ideal time to look inside. She used all her persuasion, both stick and carrot. She had enlisted the help of everyone, and finally Peter agreed. It was Christmas, and Aaron, Esme and Phoebe were visiting. Charles and Susan had come over for lunch and the box was now on the coffee table in the lounge.

Peter was remembering the worst time of his life. He had been happy in the flat with his parents. It was a bit cramped, but he didn't mind. Then, when he was five, they announced that they were moving, and that he would get a room of his own. They took him to the house they were going to buy. It was close to the river. Out of one of the bedroom windows, he could just catch a glimpse of it. He chose that room. But they never moved in. His father had disappeared in the January of 1940, and the nightmare began. His mother was distraught, and gradually things disappeared from the flat. He had to stop going to school and then they moved to the

East End. When they moved, his mother had told him that if anything ever happened to her, he must look after the tin box and take it with him everywhere. He must never let it out of his sight. She had been so insistent and made him promise. When the bombs fell, that was his first thought, to get the box. He had run home and grabbed the tin. It was almost time for his mother to arrive, so he waited. Eventually he saw her coming down the road, but then the bomb came.

He had allowed Constance to open the tin when he was in hospital to get out his birth certificate but after that refused to allow anyone else to open it. It was all he had of his mother.

It had come with him to Devon, residing in his cupboard at his home in Bishop's Tawton, then in the wardrobe of Veronica Cottage when he married Margaret, and now it was on the table.

He did not know what was in there. His mother had never told him. Just that he was to look after it. When he asked, all she said was just papers, certificates and things. He did not want to ask Constance what she had found when she got out his birth certificate. At the time it didn't occur to him; he was too young. Later it evoked too many painful memories.

He moved the tin box round and round, staring at the picture. He couldn't remember what biscuits it contained. They had always had biscuits before the war.

Finally, his hands rested on the lid. He felt the ridge to open the box. He slowly pulled the lid off.

CHAPTER 18

There, the box was open. Peter did not know what to expect. Nothing happened. He was half expecting a jack-in-the-box to pop out and say, 'fooled you'. Everyone just sat there looking at it.

"I remember when your mother bought that tin. It was the first Christmas we were married. She loved the fairy tale pictures. She didn't want to throw it away and kept filling it with biscuits."

"I remember, when I came home from school, she would give me one from the tin to keep me going until you came home for supper."

Peter and Aaron looked at each other, sharing the memory.

"No one has looked in it since. When we left the flat, she told me if anything happened, to make sure I had the tin. Possessions can be replaced; the memories will be in your head, but some things are harder than others to remember or forget. Only Constance has opened it. That was 25 years ago, and it was only for a few seconds, so my birth certificate must have been on top."

Xavier came into the lounge and peered over his mother's shoulders.

"Nothing exciting then," he said when he saw the tin. He had been expecting treasure. "Can I watch TV?"

"Yes, but turn it down. I don't want music from *Top of the Pops* disturbing us."

Xavier had broken the spell. Phoebe joined him. She had been expecting something more as well and was disappointed it was just papers. Peter started to lift out the documents. There was an official-looking document, folded over. Peter opened it and handed it to his father.

"Your marriage certificate." Aaron took it gingerly and stared at it.

"I thought this was lost. Thank you." He passed it to Esme, who passed it to Margaret. She gave it to Charles and Susan.

Next was a photograph of their wedding, similar to the one that Ruth had. Some more photos in a case of Peter. Then a wallet.

"That's strange," said Peter, turning it over in his hands.

Aaron looked up from the photographs and gasped.

"My old wallet. How did it end up in the tin?"

"I assume Mother put it there."

"Yes, but how? That was part of the problem. I had left it at the enlisting station with all the papers. In my fevered state, I left everything behind. That was why no one knew who I was."

Peter looked in the tin again and pulled out more folded-over papers. He handed them to Aaron.

"Some men in army uniform turned up and wanted to speak to you. They had these. They searched the flat. They thought we were hiding you. The men threatened Mother to tell them where you were. I don't think they believed her when she said she didn't know. They thrust these documents into her hands and left."

"I'm sorry," was all Aaron could say. Peter studied him for a moment, then returned to the tin. He pulled out a bank book.

"Yours, I think." Aaron took it and opened it, then gasped.

"Didn't your mother take any money out? There is a lot in here. I thought she would have used it. It was some money for the house." Peter thought.

"I remember her coming in and throwing the book on the floor. They wouldn't let her access the money; it was in your name only."

Aaron groaned and held his head in his hands.

"I was going to change it to both our names, but I didn't get round to it." He sat up. "This has been sitting in the tin all the time. Why didn't she ask Derek to help?"

"From what I have heard about her, she was very independent and would not have liked to ask for help. Especially as Derek was so busy," Esme interjected.

Both Peter and Aaron nodded. Peter turned his attention back to the tin. There wasn't much left. Some more photos – he did not recognise the people. He passed them to Aaron. Aaron did not know who they were either. Suddenly he stopped passing them round and stared at them.

"That is your mother. I'm sure of it."

Peter studied the one he was holding.

"I'm not sure." He passed the photograph to Margaret. She studied it.

"It may be. Let me look at the pictures of you and your mother." Everyone started comparing the pictures of the older Veronica with the young girl. Finally everyone agreed. It was her, but who were the boy and the older people?

"It must be her family," said Aaron. "She never said much about them. I think there had been a disagreement. I didn't like to press her, as she always got very upset."

Peter pulled out the final two items. One was his mother's birth certificate. His father's was in the documents he passed to Aaron earlier. The other was an envelope.

Peter held it up to his father and looked quizzically at him. Aaron read the front of the envelope. *Darling Nicky.* Aaron shook his head. Peter turned it over. There was a faint mark. He held it up to look closer.

Suddenly the Beach Boys could be heard singing loudly.

"Sorry, I asked him to turn it up. I didn't mean quite so loudly."

"That's alright. It just made us jump. Xavier, turn it down a little. Look at the time! I need to make some tea for the Queen's speech."

"I'll help you, Margaret," said Esme. They put down the photos they were holding and went into the kitchen.

Peter picked up all the documents, except the ones Aaron had, and put them back in the tin. He put the tin in a cupboard in the display unit.

* * * * * * * *

"Thank you for helping me," said Susan to Margaret.

Margaret shrugged her shoulders.

"It is the least I can do."

161

"I think that is the last box." Susan carried the box down the stairs to the large wooden-floored hall. She sighed.

"Let me take the box to the car. You check we have left nothing behind. The furniture is staying?" Susan gave the box to Margaret and nodded. At the moment, she was going to let the house furnished.

She wandered upstairs. The staircase split in two, the left going to her parents' wing and the right to where she and Angela had rooms. She wandered down again, pausing in the hall, which had doubled as a dance floor at her parties. They seemed a long time ago. She moved to the small reception room and paused again in the doorway.

"This is where I first saw your father," she said to Margaret, who was coming back in. "I fell in love with him as soon as I saw him. If Arnold had not died that night, I don't know what I would have done. I could not have continued being married to him." She sighed and turned to Margaret. "But I thought I loved Arnold, so I am not a good judge."

Margaret boldly put her arm through Susan's.

"But you were very young when you met Arnold. He cleverly seduced you."

"Thank you, dear." Susan patted Margaret's hand. "Your father would not have behaved in that way. If only I had not got pregnant. Father had to go and plead with Arnold to marry me. Poor Father. I have never forgiven Arnold for that. If only we had known of a refuge like yours, it would have been different. It was so awful to be pregnant at 18."

"Sixteen is even worse," muttered Margaret under her breath.

"Sorry, what did you say?"

"Nothing. I was thinking of the girls at the refuge. Some of them are younger than that."

They went outside. Susan locked the door of Eastwood House. She looked back at it, with the spring sun shining on it. She was only next door but felt a million miles away.

"I hope whoever rents it will be happy here. It is only let until Angela and Vince move back. Vince is leaving the army in about 18 months. It will be nice to have my grandchildren next door."

"I'm sure they will. I will take you home now."

"Thank you. I didn't expect it to end like this. I mean, I knew Mum and Dad wouldn't live forever, but to lose them both so quick…" She trailed off.

"After your mother died, I don't think your father could go on."

Susan nodded. "He was lost without her. While she was in hospital, after her fall, I could sense he was more with her than us. Then when she died, well, he just gave up."

Margaret drove the short distance to The Firs.

"You go in. I will get Ross to unload the car." Susan nodded. She wanted to see Charles.

"I got Ross to put the boxes in the drawing room," Margaret said, walking into lounge. She accepted a cup of tea from Susan. Charles was so happy to see his wife and daughter getting on so well. He never thought it would happen. After Constance passed away, and even before then, since she became ill, Susan had been there for him. He remembered his meeting with her. He certainly admired her right from the start. It was so hard not to succumb to their desires, but he could never be unfaithful to Constance. He knew it was hard on Susan. They used to meet at the connecting gate between their two properties and walk round the garden and fields. Luckily, she was there to help when he fell over a tree root and hurt his leg. He still had the limp.

He and Constance would have been married 50 years this year. Susan had tactfully arranged a small party to celebrate. He knew it had been hard for her, but they both wanted to keep her memory alive for Margaret.

"I must go," said Margaret, standing up. "I need to finish packing for our holiday."

"Thank you for all your help, Margaret," said Susan. "Please give our love to Aaron and Esme." Margaret hugged Susan and Charles.

* * * * * * * *

"That cat is always in the drive when we arrive. I'm sure it knows we are coming. I've a good mind to run over him." Xavier laughed as he got out the car and picked up the ginger cat.

"Don't worry, Watson. Papa doesn't mean it."

"Doesn't he?" said Peter, getting out the car. "One day." His smile showed he was not serious.

"Oh, good, you've arrived," said Ruth. "Come in. I don't know why Eric is bothering with this party. There is so much work."

"Because you deserve it. The family has missed out on so many birthday parties over the years." He patted her shoulder. He knew she was pleased, even though she never stopped moaning. He knew her 60th birthday was a good opportunity to get everyone together. "Come on in! Aaron, Esme and Phoebe have already arrived."

Eric had arranged a party for Ruth for the Saturday night, but everyone would be staying until the Monday. On the Monday all the guests set off for Royston House. Aaron, Esme and Phoebe were staying there one night, leaving for London after breakfast the next day, but everyone else was staying until Thursday. Xavier had moved into Hugh's old room permanently. Marcus and Faye were in the nursery with Ivy, and Aaron, Esme and Phoebe had the two guest rooms in the middle of the house.

Margaret and Phoebe went riding in the afternoon. Xavier wanted to go but was told that he was too young to ride the horses. Margaret realised she would have to get a pony for him to ride when they stayed there.

* * * * * * * *

It was nice to have Phoebe to stay, but she had brought her friends with her. Originally all three of her ABC friends were coming, but Mirabelle could not come as her parents also booked a holiday at the same time.

Phoebe was given the bedroom with the Jack and Jill bathroom, sharing with Xavier. She was sharing the room with Adele. Mirabelle and Camilla had the other guest bedroom with its private bathroom, but now Camilla had it to herself. Peter found it uncomfortable to have Adele and Camilla in the house. He moaned to Margaret, but she reassured him.

"It is only for a few days. Anyway, it's nice for Phoebe." Peter grunted. He wasn't sure.

Margaret, Phoebe and Xavier were going to spend the afternoon with the horses. Adele and Camilla decided to go to the cinema. After lunch Peter ran them into town, dropped them off at the cinema and watched them go in. He drove away and glanced in the rear view mirror, then noticed them come back out and furtively run the other way. He shrugged. They were 19 and 20, after all.

He had mixed feelings as he dropped them off at the station. He was sad to see his sister leave but was glad that her friends were leaving.

Ten days later the telephone rang. It was a frantic Esme, after minimal pleasantries. She explained why she was ringing.

"Cam has gone missing. Apparently, she did not get on the train with Phoebe and Adele."

"But I left them at the station," said Peter.

"Yes," agreed Esme. "But after you left, Cam told Phoebe and Adele that she was going to spend more time in Barnstaple. She rang her parents and said that she was going to stay with Adele for the rest of the summer. They thought it was a bit strange, but they were at different universities, so just accepted they wanted to spend time together. Anyway, Cam's father ran into Adele's mother by chance, walking the dogs in Hyde Park. They chatted and discovered that Cam was not at Adele's. They confronted Adele, who explained what happened and Phoebe confirmed it. She wanted to stay in Devon with someone called Alan, who she had met in a pub." Esme paused for breath.

"But she is 19," said Peter, suddenly feeling guilty.

"Yes, this is why her parents are reluctant to call the police. But they don't know where she is. They were hoping you could help. I know Alan is a common name, but after questioning Phoebe and Adele exhaustively..." Peter could sense the weariness in her voice and knew they had been grilled very vigorously.

"All they could tell us was he was about 10 years or so older than her, nearly 6ft with dark hair. I know that description applies to a lot of men in Barnstaple. But Adele said she had met him briefly before they disappeared together. She was a bit put out and had to kill a lot of time by herself. She also said that he was at the station, wearing some sort of uniform. It all happened so quickly they didn't have a chance to catch their breath and then they were gone." She paused again. Peter sensed that more was coming, finally getting to the point. "Phoebe says that she vaguely remembers seeing him around before, but she can't remember where, in a car or something. What we are hoping you will, can do, maybe, is, I don't know...It is like looking for a needle in a haystack, but I promised, and they are frantic."

Peter understood.

"I will talk to everyone and see what I can find out. As you say, Alan is a common name, but I will do my best. I will start with the Alans I know. Maybe Phoebe saw him come in his car to the garage."

"Thank you, Peter."

* * * * * * *

"How are all the other arrangements going?" Margaret knew what Elizabeth meant.

"It is a bit hectic. Everyone is moving around. Xavier has declared that, now he is 10 and nearly a half, he wants the nursery rooms. So, with Ivy moving out, we have put Marcus in Xavier's old corner room, and Faye is having the room next to us. We are making the bedroom over the kitchen the main guest room."

"Have Ivy and Mark found a house?"

"Yes, they are buying one in Landkey, not far from Ross and Lucy. Ivy is moving out after her wedding in three weeks. I don't know how I will cope without her."

"Where are they going on honeymoon?"

"They are taking Mark's mother to Blackpool, a bit later than July as usual, August this year, then they are going to Scotland for a week, picking his mother up on the way back."

"How are you managing without Sally? How is Emma coping?"

"So far it is going well. When Sally said she was leaving, after Jeremy and Doris's wedding, I didn't know how we were going to cope, but Susan stepped in and offered Emma. It was decided that Jeremy would manage the Exeter garage, Doris would open a new salon in Exeter, and Irene would run the one in Barnstaple for her. I asked Sally if she wanted to come back, but she said she was happy working at the lace factory. Susan had always felt a bit uneasy about having a full-time maid for just the two of them. She said she didn't mind having Norman and Kathleen Grayson at Eastwood House because her mother needed help with the four of them. Emma started helping the Graysons about 18 months ago, when they first mentioned they wanted to retire. Rose had been helping but not getting paid. When she started to work for you, she had less time. But with Susan's parents passing, Emma was no longer needed, so she suggested we share Emma. Emma comes to us Mondays, Wednesdays and Fridays to help. The Graysons stayed on after Susan's parents passed away, but now the house is rented, they have moved in with Rose and Oscar."

Elizabeth smiled. She had heard from Peter about Margaret's first and only attempt at housework. She nearly broke the Hoover trying to get it to work. She coped with the floor, after finally managing to plug in and switch on, but when she got the hose out, she nearly sucked up everything. A cloth from the hall table got stuck in the tube, and Margaret had thrown it down in disgust.

She changed the subject.

"Has Angela had her baby yet?"

"No, Susan has gone to see her in readiness. It is due any day now. It is lovely not having her around while Vince is in the army. I hope she will be busy with their family when they return in a few weeks and keep out of my way."

Margaret looked at Elizabeth from under her eyebrows. She smiled.

"I have news that you don't know."

Elizabeth looked surprised. Margaret never had news. Margaret nodded.

"You know Phoebe's friend, Camilla, disappeared last year." Elizabeth smiled and nodded but kept her silence. She had a feeling she already knew. Margaret continued. "Well, at Christmas she turned up. We got told by Esme. She rang her parents. She was pregnant. I am not judging her," she added quickly. "It was a relief to hear from her, but guess who the father was?" She sat back expectantly. Elizabeth looked at her, debating within herself. Margaret was watching her, waiting for her to speak.

Suddenly she threw her hands in the air.

"You know, don't you?" she said accusingly. Elizabeth nodded.

"But you were so excited, and I didn't want to disappoint you. I wanted you to tell me. It was Alan Taylor." Margaret nodded, slightly deflated now. Elizabeth tried to reassure her.

"Sorry, but you know how small the village is and everyone knows everything – well, almost. But they got married here in... February."

They both burst out laughing.

CHAPTER 19

"Oh, Beth, how will I cope with Xavier away?" Margaret was at Elizabeth's house for the last time before the summer holidays began and they had to postpone their meetings. "He starts in September. He seems so young." Elizabeth smiled to herself. She knew Xavier would be able to cope. He always seemed older than his years.

"You will manage, Maggie. You know it is the right thing to do. Why did you arrange it if you weren't happy?"

"I didn't. Hugh did."

"But Hugh has been dead 10 years. How did he arrange it?"

"Peter said..." She trailed off.

"Come on, what did Peter say? You don't have any secrets from me. Tell me." Margaret sighed.

"We were discussing the arrangements last week. I was not happy with them and wanted Xavier to stay at his current school. It got a bit heated, and Peter let slip about the conversation he had had with Howard." Margaret repeated Peter's conversation to Elizabeth. "I don't think Hugh ever loved me. He was going to divorce me and live with... in Italy." Elizabeth went over to her and took her hands. "Why did I marry him?" Margaret asked.

"He did love you, and you loved him. Maybe not with the same love you have for Peter, but you were not ready for Peter then, after everything that happened. You needed Hugh, and Hugh needed you. But Hugh must have realised that his happiness lay with Howard and yours with Peter."

"But... Howard," she whispered. She could hardly say his name. "I had not realised that Hugh was... like that."

"I had heard some comments, but I had to ask Bill to explain them. I didn't understand at first, but I believe it to be true." Elizabeth took a deep breath. "Think about how we found

Stanton, Hugh's valet. That was why we had to move him." The women recalled how they had taken Stanton from Hugh's room to his own and found the secret door. Margaret spoke.

"You mean he was in love with Hugh as well."

"Yes, I'm not sure if Hugh loved Stanton the same way, but I am sure they were…" She couldn't say any more. Margaret nodded and remembered the one and only time she had opened the bedrooms' connecting door. She just thought Hugh didn't like being interrupted while dressing, but now she could see things differently.

"What you need is a distraction after you have taken Xavier to Eton. You know I am on the parents committee at both Duncan's and Chloe's schools; well, I am thinking of standing for governor at Chloe's school, my old school. Why don't you do the same at the boys' school?"

Margaret shook her head.

"No, I don't want to draw attention to myself." Elizabeth understood. Margaret's experience of appearing in the glossy society magazines still hurt. "But you are right. I do need a distraction and I have a plan." Elizabeth looked at her enquiringly. "When we have returned from dropping Xavier at school, I intend to try and track down Peter's mother's family." Elizabeth's mouth dropped open.

"What does Peter say?"

"Peter doesn't actually know yet. I have raised it a couple of times since we opened his tin, but he has brushed the suggestion aside. The tin is still in the cupboard in the lounge, where we left it three years ago, so I will bring it out when we return. I could look at it anytime, I know, but I don't want to go behind his back. It was so hard when his father contacted us. I don't want to go through that again." Elizabeth understood.

"When do you travel to Royston House?"

"We are going on 1 August. Peter is returning on the Tuesday but then will spend the last two weeks with us before we take Xavier to school. Ivy and Mark are going to pick Marcus and Faye up on 30 August and bring them back here. They will visit her family in London first. She and Mark will stay in the guest room at The Firs until we get back."

"You will enjoy looking for a larger pony for Xavier to ride at the weekends he spends at Royston House." Margaret nodded. That was the only good thing; she would enjoy looking for the pony.

* * * * * * *

The tin was, once again, on the coffee table in front of them. Margaret had put Faye and Marcus to bed; it was something she liked to do. Since Ivy had left, that had been her role. She regretted missing out with Xavier. She liked the last hug before they went to sleep and reading to them. Faye liked Beatrix Potter stories. Marcus had liked the Noddy stories but had now moved on to adventure stories, and she was reading *Treasure Island*. Peter had made some coffee, and they were sitting on the sofa in the lounge. They both had a feeling of déjà vu.

"Let's just put it away," said Peter.

"No, we need to know. I need something to do." Peter took her hand. He could not understand her desire to find his mother's family. He had never known them, but he could feel her need to keep busy.

"As if you are not busy enough with Marcus, Faye, the horses and the house," he said, smiling.

"I know, but I need something different to distract me. Especially now Xavier is at Eton. Anyway, we know I am useless at housework." They laughed, remembering Margaret's disastrous attempts at domestication.

"Alright, let's do it." Peter lifted the lid for the second time, nearly three years after the first. He carefully picked up the photographs and spread them carefully on the table. Then he got out his mother's birth certificate; this he handed to Margaret. Margaret looked at it and read out.

"It says *26 June 1910, Meadow Court, Henley-upon-Thames.*" Margaret glanced at Peter. He was listening intently. She continued, "*Veronica Harriet, girl. Father – Rufus William Cross. Mother – Stella May formerly Pattinson.*" Margaret stopped reading and looked at Peter. They were silent for a few minutes.

"Your grandparents," Margaret finally said. "I wonder if they are still alive." Peter couldn't speak. He had never thought about any grandparents. When Aaron had contacted them, he thought then he might have some, but both his paternal grandparents were dead, and he didn't think about his mother's family. It had never been mentioned by her or Aaron, therefore it never entered his head. "You might have more aunts and uncles, like Aunt Ruth, and cousins." Margaret picked up the photos of his young mother. "If these pictures are anything to go by, it seems you at least have an uncle."

"If they are still alive," Peter said with emotion. Margaret moved closer on the sofa.

"We will find out. We have nothing to lose. If they are dead, we are no worse off, but if they are alive..." She trailed off.

Peter studied the photos. He shrugged and was about to put them back in the tin when he noticed the envelope at the bottom. He slowly took it out.

"Who is Nicky?" he said, passing the envelope to Margaret.

"Someone your mother knew before she met your father, an old boyfriend, or maybe it's her brother in the photos. Shall I open it?" Peter shrugged indifference, but he was getting intrigued. Margaret slowly lifted the flap; the glue had perished. She pulled out a photo and a piece of folded paper. She handed the photo to Peter; it was a picture of a baby. She opened the paper. She gasped and started to read again.

"It reads, *19 October 1929. City of London Maternity Hospital. Nicola Harriet, girl. Father – Thomas Rory Winters. Mother – Veronica Harriet Cross.*" Margaret stopped reading and looked at Peter. "You have a sister."

Peter stared at her.

"But Mother never mentioned her." Margaret was thoughtful. She looked at the certificate again.

"Peter," she said slowly, and she waited until he looked at her. "Peter," she repeated. "I don't know how to say this, but I think your mother... I don't think she was married." Peter stiffened. "Sorry, but look at the certificate. On your birth certificate, your mother's and the children's, under 'mother name' are the words 'formerly' then a name, but there is nothing on Nicola's certificate." Peter took the certificate, his hands shaking.

"But…" he was thinking, "at least she knew the father. She kept this secret all those years. She never said a word. I wonder if Dad knows." Margaret shrugged.

"What happened to Nicola?" Peter asked. "Perhaps she was adopted. Mum met Dad shortly afterwards." Margaret was shaking her head. She picked up the photograph. She stared at the baby in her pram; she looked very small. Margaret turned it over. There was writing on the back. It was faded and hard to read. Margaret read it out loud.

"*Nicola… Christmas 1929.* I can hardly read it. Something then a date. It looks like a 2, then another 2, then a 30. You have a look." She passed the photo to Peter. He took it slowly and peered at the writing.

"Yes, it is a date. The word is… died." He put the photo down quickly. "She died. She was only three and a half months."

* * * * * * *

They left the hotel in Oxford deep in thought. They slowly walked to the record office and the library. They agreed to divide into two parties and to limit the time spent to two hours, then come back to the hotel for lunch and compare notes, though they were not hopeful there would be any notes. The expectations of finding anything in the records or papers were very low. Then they would visit Henley-on-Thames in the afternoon.

It was the summer following the discovery of Peter's half-sister. It had taken many months of indecision before deciding to have a go at finding Peter's mother's relatives. It was agreed that they must wonder what happened to her. They would not know she had been killed during the war.

Finally, everyone agreed to visit Oxford and Henley a few days before Margaret and Peter had to collect Xavier from Eton at the end of his first year at the school. Aaron and Esme met them at the hotel the previous evening.

Peter and Aaron were going to look at the national census. They knew they would not find any mention of Veronica or her parents, as the latest record they could look at was 1861, but they might find Peter's great-grandparents. They knew it was a long shot, but they would note any references to Pattinsons or Crosses. Margaret and Esme were going to look at the pre-war local papers in the birth, marriage and death sections. Again they had little hope but expected more luck there.

When they met up, it was as they thought: there was little information. Peter and Aaron had found lots of Pattinsons and Crosses but too many to make notes of. Margaret and Esme had only gone through a few years' papers. They not only looked at births, deaths and marriages but at other pages in case any Pattinsons or Crosses had made a mention, but there was nothing.

After lunch they set off for Henley, not anticipating finding any information but determined to have a nice afternoon by the river.

First, they visited the library to look through old newspapers. They agreed to limit the search to 10 years – five either side of Veronica's birth date – looking for any information at all. They took the *Henley and South Oxfordshire Standard* newspapers to a large table under the watchful eye of the librarian– she would only let them take a few at a time. Aaron and Esme were going to work backwards from Veronica's birth, and Peter and Margaret forwards. They got the issue that covered Veronica's birth, nothing. But in the following week's paper, there, in black and white, was Veronica's name and birth details. They all looked at each other.

Esme broke the silence.

"Yes, this is all well and good, but there is no more information here than we already knew."

"There are a couple of things," Aaron corrected her. "We know we are on the right track, and she did not have any older siblings. So, she was either an only child or had younger siblings. Peter, Margaret, concentrate on marriages, and look for Rufus and Stella. I would say start nine months before and..." He trailed off, shrugging his shoulders.

"You are right," agreed Esme. "We will go forward, looking for any brothers or sisters." Everyone nodded and got to work.

Margaret excitedly broke the silence and pointed out an announcement to Peter. He looked at it, then got Aaron and Esme's attention. They looked at the announcement and sat back.

Aaron spoke first.

"I don't want to rain on the parade, but there is not a lot more detail in the article. But let's note the new information." He got out the note book and picked up a pen. He opened it at the page and started to write. He noted the church where the bride and groom got married, and that the bride was attended by her sister. Nothing else seemed relevant. After a hopeful start, everyone was deflated.

"I will see if there is anywhere we can get a cup of tea. We need a break, then we will resume going forwards." Esme stood up and went over to speak to the librarian. Everyone stood up and got their belongings. Esme returned.

"The librarian will bring us some tea." Everyone sat down again. Esme continued. "She was intrigued by our search and said that the name Cross rang a bell. I pointed out it was a common name. She agreed but still said there was something."

The librarian brought the tea and some biscuits. Aaron got out his wallet to pay for it, but the librarian waved away his money. She was captivated by their search. Again she said that there was something at the back of her mind, not recent. A few years ago it had come to her attention. She remembered feeling sad.

Everyone continued their search. This time it was Peter who broke the silence. He was pointing to a birth announcement.

"Look, there is an announcement of the birth of Peter Raymond Cross, brother for Veronica. That must be her." Everyone nodded, and Aaron noted down the name and date in his book. Margaret took out the photographs from her bag.

"This must be Peter." She pointed to the picture of the boy playing with Veronica.

"I always wondered why she was so adamant that she wanted to call you Peter. Now I know it was after her brother," said Aaron.

"I have an uncle now," said Peter. "Uncle Peter, as well as Aunt Ruth." He smiled. He was glad now they had come on the search. He had had his doubts, but now he had two bona fide relations. Peter's joy infused everyone. They agreed that there was no point looking at the next nine months' worth of papers. So they moved onto 1914 and agreed to stop in 1920. They decided to stop there, as they were all getting tired. They were tidying up when the librarian appeared, looking very excited.

"I knew that it rang a bell. I remember because it was my grandparents' golden wedding anniversary at the same time." They looked at her expectantly. She opened her newspaper from a couple of years back and showed them. She was pointing to a photograph of an elderly couple; *60 Years of Harmony*, said the headline.

"I hadn't thought much about anniversaries until my grandparents' golden wedding anniversary, then they seemed to be everywhere, I can't remember them all but this one stuck in my mind." She pointed to the next photograph. Everyone glanced at it politely and returned to the photo of Rufus and Stella.

"There is not much new information here," said Aaron, reading the article. "It says they celebrated with their son, two grandchildren and one great-grandson. No other names." Aaron folded the paper and gave it back to the librarian. She took it and unfolded it. She turned to another page nearer the front and pointed. Everyone looked with interest. It was about Rufus and Stella, and their diamond wedding, and how it was tinged with sadness that their only daughter could not be there with them. The whole party sat down to read the article. It was difficult, and the librarian was worried the paper would be torn, so she picked it up and read the article to them. When she finished, she looked at them and said,

"That is why I remember. It is so sad. I wonder what happened to their daughter." No one said anything. Aaron took the paper and silently made more notes. When he had finished, he handed the paper back to the librarian. They thanked her politely and left as quickly as they could.

They made their way to the river and walked slowly along its bank. They had walked in silence to Marsh Lock. When they arrived, they stopped and leant on the fence, watching the Thames flow past.

"Well," said Aaron, "that was a revelation."

"Your poor grandparents, Peter," said Esme, "wondering what had happened to their daughter all these years. If Phoebe vanished like that, I don't know how I would bear it." Aaron took her hand.

"We need to tell them she was killed in the war, and that they have a third grandchild." Peter looked startled. He hadn't thought about them like that. This was his family.

"But how? It might upset them more."

"I don't think so," replied Esme. "It might, but I think they would like to know. Like you with your father. You thought he had abandoned you and your mother, but in reality, he had been ill, and it was an unfortunate set of circumstances that kept you apart. Now you know the truth, is it easier to bear?" Peter nodded.

"But I just wish Mother had known the truth. She went to her grave thinking that she... we had been deserted. Yes, I agree, I think it will help them to know what happened. They are probably expecting her to walk in at any moment, and that is not a good feeling." Everyone could feel his pain. He was remembering how he kept looking at the door hoping his father would walk back through.

"Right, that is decided. Tomorrow, we start the search for your mother's family," said Aaron decisively in an emotional voice. "But we need a plan. We can't just drive around Oxfordshire."

They discussed everything over dinner and came up with a plan.

* * * * * * *

Esme paused at the door, looked back at the expectant faces in the car and sighed. She knew it was the right thing to do, but she was still very nervous. She rang the bell and stepped back. She studied the house. It was a well-built red brick house, with the wooden door in the middle and two large windows each side and matching windows above. She smiled at the party in the car, parked at the end of the drive. She heard a noise at the door and took a deep breath.

The door was opened by a woman aged about 50.

"Yes?" said the woman. Suddenly Esme was overcome with the enormity of the task. She stumbled on her words.

"I... Veronica..."

"You are not Veronica," interrupted the woman. "Now go away." She started to shut the door. Esme put out her hand.

"No, I am not Veronica, but I... have news." The woman stopped shutting the door. She noticed the others getting out the car.

"You are a reporter. We have had enough of your sort. Take your colleagues and leave." She resumed shutting the door.

"No," said Esme anxiously, "we are not reporters and we do have news." The woman studied her and looked at everyone else. They had worried expressions. She sighed and released her grip on the door.

"We have had so many crackpots and reporters round since the story about Veronica appeared in the paper. What is it you want?" Esme looked at Peter and shook his head. He didn't know what to do. The woman looked at Peter and took in his appearance.

Esme continued.

"We really do have news for you. Can I ask who you are?"

"I am Miranda," she said absently, still staring at Peter.

"Can we come in?" asked Esme. This brought Miranda back to her. She was thinking, maybe this time they did have some news, but she didn't want them to come in now; she needed time to think.

"No. Not now." She saw their shocked faces. "I need to speak to the family first." They nodded in agreement.

"We are staying in Oxford," Esme said. "We are leaving tomorrow." Miranda was thinking.

"Come back tomorrow morning – that should be acceptable. Which hotel are you staying in? In case tomorrow is not possible." Esme quickly told her and hurried everyone back to the car.

Miranda watched them leave and then turned to the man who had come up behind her.

"Don't get your hopes up, Uncle, this is probably just another elaborate hoax." She saw the tears in his eyes and took his hand. There had been so many false alarms over the years. Each had taken its toll, but this time it did feel different. She shook herself and led her uncle into the sitting room.

"Come on, let's have a cup of tea and ring Pete." She closed the door firmly.

CHAPTER 20

The following morning they arrived at the house again. This time they pulled onto the drive in their separate cars. As they got out the cars, the door was opened immediately by a man. He watched them walk up the path. Miranda was right; there was something different. They had a confidence and something else. They stopped in front of him. He held out his hand and introduced himself.

"I am Peter Cross – Pete." Aaron took his hand.

"Aaron Eastman." He shook Peter's hand, then introduced Esme, Margaret and Peter. Peter raised his eyebrows at Peter's name but said nothing. He led them into the sitting room.

"This is my wife Lavender and my cousin Miranda."

They all shook hands again, recognising Miranda from the previous day.

"As it is a nice morning, why don't we go into the garden to have tea," said Miranda. "I will put the kettle on."

Pete showed them to the seating area in the well-tended large garden. Aaron looked up at the back of the house. He could see someone in the upstairs window. They waited for Miranda to bring the tea.

"So, you think you have information about my sister?" said Pete. They looked at Aaron. They had agreed that Aaron should take the lead.

"Yes. I don't know where to begin." He wiped his forehead with his hand. "This is very difficult. We only decided last year to... We only found out about you two days ago. Oh dear, this is so difficult. I was married to your sister." He looked at Esme for reassurance, and she smiled.

"Mr Cross, tell us about your sister. We got a few details from the article, but you tell us about her."

"We were close. We didn't fight, like usual brothers and sisters. We liked to be in each other's company. Besides which, there were not many other children to play with around here." He stretched out his arm to indicate the area. There were no other houses for a couple of miles. "When I was 15, I got scarlet fever. It was touch and go. Veronica nursed me through it. Mum tried her best, but she was...It was difficult for her. This brought us even closer. Then the following year she disappeared." He was surprised how it still upset him after all these years. "She set off to go to her friend's house. She planned to cycle the five miles. We did not know she was missing until she did not return a few days later. We rang her friend, but she did not know anything; she had not been expecting Veronica. Her bicycle was found a few weeks later in Oxford. Somebody wondered why it hadn't moved and contacted the police, who contacted us. And that's it. We haven't seen her since."

No one spoke. Margaret looked around. She nudged Peter excitedly.

"Look!" She pointed to a far corner. There was a large tree with a swing and white bench. She fished in her bag and brought out a photograph. "It's the same, well, without the children and woman on the bench with the white dog on her lap." Peter took it and looked. He nodded and gave it to his uncle. Pete took it with a shaking hand.

"Where did you get this?"

"From Mum's tin," replied Peter. Pete looked at Esme, and she saw the confusion in his eyes. She said quickly,

"Aaron, why don't you tell Mr Cross how you met Veronica."

"Please call me Pete."

"I fell in love with her the moment I saw her. I was taking a circuitous route back to the office after lunch at the flat. I needed to think about a case. So, I was walking down a different road than usual. Roni was looking in the corner shop window. I went up to her and startled her. She told me off. I asked what she was looking at. She said she needed a job. I introduced myself and said we needed another receptionist. I arranged for her to come for an interview that afternoon. I persuaded everyone that she was perfect for the job, so she got it. That was the autumn of 1930. I proposed the following spring, and we married a year later. Peter was born two years after we married."

"Why didn't she invite us to the wedding? Why didn't she come home?"

"I don't know. I asked her a few times about her family, your family, but she always got upset, so I stopped asking. But..." He trailed off. He looked at Esme, and she shrugged. Pete noticed the communication.

"Is there something else?"

"We are not sure." Aaron took a deep breath. "We did find something. She had put important papers in a tin and instructed Peter to always take the tin if there was an air raid and she wasn't home. For a long time, the tin was not opened. Too many memories. Anyway, the tin was opened about five years ago and some documents were retrieved, but some got put back in the tin. These were re-examined last year. This is when we started the search for you. In these documents, we found this photograph," he indicated the one Margaret got out earlier, "and another photograph."

Aaron looked at Margaret, who slowly got out the other photograph. She handed it to Pete, her hand shaking this time. Pete looked at the picture of the baby and turned it over. His hand flew to his throat. He passed it to Miranda. She nodded in agreement.

"We also found a birth certificate. Well, two actually. Roni's, which helped us find you, and Nicola's." Margaret went to her bag again and took out the documents. Pete opened them slowly.

"No," he said in anguish as he unfolded Nicola's certificate. "No, not him." He slumped in his chair.

"You know him?" asked Aaron. Pete nodded.

"He was my tutor. I missed a lot of school while I was ill, and Mum and Dad hired him to help me catch up. I had no idea he and Veronica were..."

Everyone waited for Pete to recover from the shock.

"Why did she not tell me?" he said quietly. "Why did she keep it secret? I could have helped." He wiped his eyes. "I don't know how to tell Mum and Dad." All doubts from both parties that they had found each other were gone and acceptance had taken over. Miranda answered.

"I think you will find they are stronger than you think. We need to tell them now we know that these people are genuine, and this is not a hoax." Pete nodded. Miranda stood up.

"I will fetch them and start to get lunch. You will stay, won't you?" She looked at the Eastmans. They glanced at each other and nodded.

"If it's not too much trouble."

"We can go somewhere else."

"No trouble. We have much more to catch up on," insisted Miranda. She was gone about 10 minutes. During that time Peter and his uncle established their relationship. Miranda returned with Rufus and Stella, and another woman.

Introductions were made with floods of tears. Eventually everyone settled down and went to the dining room for lunch.

"There are still some gaps to be filled in. The biggest secret of all has been revealed: why Veronica left. But I still don't understand why she didn't tell us. We could have helped arrange the wedding or something," said Pete.

"But, dear, Thomas was already married," said Stella.

Pete looked at his mother. "Now don't look at me like that. I can always tell when you do." She turned to where the Eastmans were sitting. "I may be blind, but I can still sense things." She had asked where everyone was sitting when they went into the dining room. "That was obviously why she kept it secret. Thomas had not been forthcoming about his wife. He was also 12 years older than Veronica. When he applied for the job, he said he had one but did not mention her again. When he left, the day that Veronica said she was going to her friend's, he said that he and his wife were returning to London as his wife's parents were ill. We never suspected that he was leaving his wife and running away with Veronica." Rufus and Stella clasped hands. "He obviously never married her. Poor Veronica and little Nicola. I wish Veronica had come back home. She could have lied and said she just wanted to see London or something." Rufus hugged his wife.

"So we now know why she left," said Rufus, "and maybe why she didn't return when Nicola died. But why didn't she return when she married you?" He looked at Aaron. Aaron shook his head.

"I don't know. I wish she had. Then you could have met Peter earlier. But when I knew her, she was so independent." He sighed.

Rufus continued and squeezed Stella's hand.

"We assume she has died, as you are now married to Esme. You did not divorce?" Aaron nodded.

"I was away for a time. She thought that I wasn't coming back, so moved out of the Knightsbridge flat to the East End. She was killed in an air raid. Peter was nearly killed but was rescued by Margaret's mother." He didn't want to go into too many details. He still felt guilty.

Rufus and Stella hugged each other again.

"We have always thought she was dead but were hoping... Where is she buried?"

"In London."

"We must put up a plaque in the church yard here, for her and Nicola. I wish she had come home," said Stella.

"You want to put Nicola on the stone as well?" asked Margaret.

"Yes," replied Stella. "She is still my granddaughter, even if Veronica and... that man," she could not bring herself to say his name, "were not married. I... We would have cared for them."

Margaret stared at her. Peter noticed her strange expression and was about to speak but was interrupted.

"How did you find us eventually?" asked Miranda. "You said you only found the information last year."

"I could not bring myself to open the tin," Peter explained. Everyone nodded. "But Margaret persuaded me to. I am so glad I did. I did not realise how much it would mean to me finding my mother's relations. It is only just now that I felt I could do it. This was the most convenient time for us all meet up and start the search." He explained about checking records, newspapers and libraries, and about the librarian.

"We decided that we needed to do a physical search. We realised it was like looking for a needle in a haystack, but we had to try. We thought we might have to come back a few times. Yesterday, we left the hotel and pretty much drove straight to Marlow. We had lunch there and then decided on a more indirect route back. Esme had the Ordnance Survey Map, Dad drove, and Maggie and I looked for the house. We agreed to stay within 10 miles of the A40, if possible, zigzagging back to Oxford. We would do another area another time. But it was pure chance we found you. Esme wanted Dad to go right, but he turned left. We were trying to turn round when we saw your gateway."

"Peter, we must leave soon to get Xavier from school," Margaret said, looking at the clock. Peter agreed. Miranda was puzzled.

"Where do you live? I thought you were staying at a hotel."

"We live in Devon," Peter replied.

"But you can't get to Devon to pick him up in time."

"No, he is at Eton. As it is the end of term, we are collecting him and spending the weekend at his grandparents' in Sussex."

"Can I ask a few questions before we leave?" said Esme. "You don't have to answer them. When did you go blind, Mrs Cross?"

"It was shortly after Pete was born. I had always had trouble with my eyesight. It kept deteriorating but went completely soon after Pete's birth. No, it is not your fault, Pete."

"How do you do that, Mum? She always knows what I am doing."

"Miranda, you call Mr Cross 'Uncle', therefore Mrs Cross is your aunt, but how?"

"My mother was Aunt Stella's younger sister. We moved in after the war, when Dad was killed. She is here now but did not want to join us for lunch. Apparently, she knew about Thomas and Veronica, not that they had run away together, but that they were carrying on while he was here. They used to meet at our house. So she feels guilty for not mentioning before."

"But if she didn't know they planned to runaway, she should not feel guilty," said Esme.

"I know. I have tried to tell her. Maybe you could meet her next time." Everyone said that they would look forward to meeting again.

* * * * * * * *

"Your mother's face was a picture when she saw Chris and Jessie's outfits."

Peter accepted a cup of tea from Elizabeth then continued.

"The girls were waiting for us when we arrived. They were sitting on the bonnet of the car in their brightly coloured hot pants." Elizabeth smiled. Her mother was adaptable to most of the changes of the sixties, but the arrival of hot pants left her cold.

"Thank you for taking them to Bristol. I wasn't happy that Dad wanted to drive all the way to Liverpool."

"No, neither was I," agreed Peter. David was getting slow at driving, and Peter realised he would soon have to be firm and stop him. He knew he would have Elizabeth and Edith's backing. Also, David's car was on its last legs, but David insisted Peter repair it. Peter would have to explain that he would not be able to repair it next time. Edith looked very relieved when they all agreed that David could not drive to Liverpool and that someone would drive them to a meeting point at Bristol, then someone from Liverpool would meet them and take them the rest of the way. Initially, Elizabeth was going to drive, but Peter volunteered. One of Michael's daughters would meet them and take David and Edith to the party in Liverpool. It was arranged that Edith and David would arrive and depart on Wednesday, before and after Christine's 21st birthday party on the Saturday. Peter wanted to see Christine as he would not be able to go to the party. Peter and his family were going to his grandparents' for their own party. His cousin was getting married, and he felt it would be a good way of getting to know his family.

Peter was pleased that Jessica had turned up as well. He tucked Edith and David into Christine's car and waved them off. He could report to Elizabeth that he had delivered them safely.

186

Elizabeth and her family were driving up on the Friday, and they did not have room in the car for David and Edith as well.

Elizabeth and William arrived late on the Friday afternoon. Edith and David were staying with Michael and Louisa, but there was no room for Elizabeth and William and their family, so Michael had asked his neighbour if they could stay there.

The party was in full swing when Michael signalled for silence.

"I don't want to make a long speech but…"

"Hurray!" someone shouted.

"But I do want to say a few words," continued Michael. "We were thrilled when Chris came into our lives. We can't thank Louisa's brother, Clayton enough for finding her for us. It is a shame he can't be here today, but Chris will be meeting up with him when she arrives in America. Then Jessie arrived, and Stephen. Our family was complete."

"Good, let's party!" He was interrupted again but continued.

"I just wanted to say how happy you have made us, Chris. Enjoy your time in America, but don't forget about us when you find your parents. To Chris." He raised his glass with tears in his eyes. He felt Louisa take his arm.

"She will come back. She just needs to find out where she came from."

"I know but…" He trailed off, unable to continue.

* * * * * * * *

David awoke with a start and momentarily panicked that he was late for work. Then everything cleared and he realised that someone was knocking on the door. He rose from the armchair and went to answer the door. He opened it to a very tired-looking niece.

"Jessie!" he exclaimed. "Come in." He opened the door wide and took her suitcase. "This is a pleasant surprise." He put her case at the bottom of the stairs and showed her into the lounge. She sat down on the sofa, her head in her hands. David was perplexed. He hated it when people were upset; he did not know how to deal with them. *A cup of tea*, he thought, *that always puts everything right* – well, that's what Edith did.

"I will make the tea," he said to Jessica. She nodded. He walked slowly to the kitchen. What to do? he thought. He wished Edith was there. While he waited for the kettle, he went into the hall and rang Edith. He returned to the lounge with tea on a tray.

"Edith is not here," he said as he poured out the tea. Jessica smiled at the obvious statement. David was pleased to see her smiling. Maybe everything wasn't so bad. He relaxed a little. "Edith is at Beth's. She is waiting for Duncan and Chloe to arrive home from school. She will be back about seven, when Bill will finish at the hotel." He offered Jessica one of Edith's biscuits and saw her puzzled face. "Fabian was rushed to Plymouth Hospital a few days ago with a burst appendix – there were complications. Both Beth and Bill went with him and stayed a couple of nights. Bill, reluctantly, had to return as he had a coach party arriving for the first time and wanted to make sure everything went smoothly. Beth is still with Fabian; they hope to be home the day after tomorrow. Edith stayed with Duncan and Chloe while they were away, but now Bill is back, she comes home." Jessica smiled. She could see David was relieved to have Edith back. He did not like being without her. "Anyway, what brings you here? Michael did not say you were coming."

"No, he wouldn't. He didn't know I was coming." David looked confused again. He really wished Edith was here. Jessica continued. "I will tell everything when Aunt Edith arrives to save explaining it twice." David nodded in agreement. "Maybe I could go and meet her?"

Jessica was looking forward to the walk to see William. She had daydreamed about him for years. It was at her 18th party that she tried to act on her feelings. She was visiting Devon with her family, and they decided to have a small party at Taw Lodge Hotel. She remembered trying to sit next to William at the dinner and constantly 'accidently' bumping his knee or touching his hand. After dinner, there was dance with the resident band. She enjoyed her dances with him and tried to get him to dance with her for the slow songs, but he always chose Elizabeth. She danced with Stephen and that was when their romance started.

Edith was greeted at the door by an anxious David. He helped her out of her coat and quickly directed her to the lounge, then left, saying he would put the kettle on. Edith greeted a sleepy Jessica, and they sat down on the sofa and waited for David to bring the tea. Jessica was annoyed. She had fallen asleep and not woken until Edith arrived, so missed seeing William.

"Well, this is a lovely surprise," said Edith. "It is nice to see you again – last time was at Chris's party last year. How is university going? Are you still on course to become a doctor? How long are you staying?"

Jessica laughed at the rapid-fire questions.

"Just tonight," she said. "I will explain when Uncle David comes back." David soon came back with the tea, interrupting Edith and Jessica's small talk.

"I know you are wondering why I have just turned up. I wanted to ring but did not have your number." Edith looked at her quizzically. Jessica continued. "The past couple of days have been strange." Jessica ran her hand through her long brown hair. "As you know, Chris went to America to try and find her natural mother and family." Edith and David nodded. "Well, she did find them. So, I thought I would find mine. So, I applied for a copy of my birth certificate. I received it two days ago. It was the worst moment of my life." She slumped back on the sofa, tears in her eyes. She looked at Edith and David and said in a low voice,

"I found out that my lover was actually my brother."

CHAPTER 21

Jessica looked at their shocked faces and realised that she needed to do something. She started to explain how Christine found her family.

"Uncle Clayton was helping her. He could provide a lot of background information and the fact that she has three brothers. Chris has made contact with them, all the brothers. It was shortly after Uncle Clayton arrived at his new village parish, between Providence and Boston, a woman, Chris's mother, came to him and left Chris with him. She approached him after one of his services and said that now her husband was dead, she could not cope with four children. She had found a home for the three boys on a farm. The farmer and his wife could not have children, so they took them to help on the farm but did not want Chris. Uncle Clayton left to go to the office to get some papers, but when he came back, only Chris was there. Her mother and brothers had left. He didn't know what to do, then thought of his older sister, Mum, who was devasted that she could not have children. Mum and Dad had arrived for an extended work and Christmas holiday. They were very happy to accept Chris, formerly adopted her and brought her back to Liverpool." Jessica took a breath, and Edith and David looked at each other. They had known most of that but did not interrupt her. "So, Chris and Uncle Clayton took a visit to his parish. The village had grown since he was there last. It was now a small town. He looked through the parish records and found a record of Chris being baptised. The note also mentioned her parents' names and brothers' names. They asked around, and finally an elderly man remembered them – he had lived next door to them – but not that Chris's father had died, only that he had just abandoned his family to start a new life in New York. He vaguely recalled the farm that the boys were sent to – it was just outside Blackstone. He gave directions and they set off. They stopped when they saw the ranch sign. There was a lorry coming down the drive, so they waited until it left then slowly drove up. A dog started barking and ran up to greet them. A man came round from behind the barn to see who it was. Both Uncle Clayton and Chris drew a breath. The man stopped instantly as he saw Chris get out of the car. Chris introduced herself. He dropped his pitchfork and hugged her. This was her oldest brother. He took them into the house to meet his wife and adopted parents. He explained that their other two brothers had left. One was living in Florida – he was a baseball player – and the younger one lived in New York. Their mother had passed away, but before she died, she said that their father was not dead but living in New York, so her youngest brother set off to find him. Clayton and Chris were shocked; they had just come from New York. Chris got his address, and they met up for Thanksgiving. I don't know how they got on." She paused and drank some tea. Edith and David realised she was getting to the reason for her visit. "With Chris going to America to find her family, I thought I might like to find mine. So, I spoke to Mum and Dad, but they were not enthusiastic to say the least. I realised that they were probably upset about Chris, so I didn't push it. But with Chris managing to locate her brothers, I really wanted to try and find my family. I thought I would go over in the summer break and made the arrangements. I asked Mum and Dad again, determined not to be fobbed off. Steve backed me up, but they were adamant they knew nothing and would not help. I spoke to Chris and Uncle Clayton, but he could not help, as he had not been involved in my adoption. Well, I insisted and had a big row with Dad. I decided to get a copy of my UK birth certificate. Dad let slip that I had a UK birth certificate when I demanded to see my papers. He had always kept them in a safe in his office. He never let us see them; we just signed any forms that he completed without question." She yawned. She was so tired. It had all been so emotional. She went straight to sleep when her head hit the pillow.

* * * * * * *

"Thank you for everything, Aunt Edith," said Jessica as they waited for the train. She felt much better now she had talked to someone.

"Look after yourself. I'm sure you will find the answers you want." They waited in silence. Edith was thinking about Jessica's short visit. Last night, after Jessica's revelation, she broke down completely. Edith let her sob in her arms. When finally the tirade of emotions subsided, they gently questioned her more.

"I don't believe it," said David. "Michael would never betray Louisa."

"Are you sure that your father's name is on your birth certificate?" asked Edith.

"Oh yes, quite sure. It is there in black and white. I don't understand. Why did he pretend I was adopted? Why did he let me and Steve fall in love? I HATE him. He has ruined my life." She started crying again, not so intently, but Edith and David didn't like to question her too much.

"What about university?" asked Edith. "You were so looking forward to becoming a doctor."

"I was. I am. I had already spoken to them and arranged to take a year out. I have done well in my exams and everything, so they agreed. Also, if I wanted to return sooner, then I could and resume my studies. I don't think I will ever go back. I just want to get to Chris and find my true family." She paused. "That is why I came here. I know you are my 'real' aunt and uncle and Beth my cousin. So, I wanted to say goodbye properly. I don't know when I will be back. I am sorry to have missed Beth. I am so tired. I think I will go to bed now." She stood up, kissed Edith and David, retrieved her case and went upstairs. As soon as she shut the door, David turned to Edith.

"I do not believe it," he said emphatically. Edith nodded.

"But Jess is adamant that his name is on the certificate. Could they have sent her the wrong certificate?" David shook his head.

"I think that is unlikely. Also to send the wrong one with Michael Harrison named as the father. No."

"It is very puzzling. It must be that there is another Michael Harrison in America. It is not a very unusual name, quite common, really."

"Oh," said David. "Are you saying we are common?"

"No, I didn't mean it that way." Edith laughed as they locked up and went to bed.

The next morning Jessica didn't wake up until late. They didn't like to disturb her. David had a council meeting but did not want to leave until he had spoken to Jessica. He had rung to say he would be late. As soon as Jessica rose for breakfast, he bid his farewell and rushed off.

Edith rang for a taxi to take them to the station.

At last the train arrived. They waited for everyone to alight. Jessica boarded the train and put her case down.

"Thank you for everything, Aunt Edith. I feel much better now."

"Everything will be fine. Please ring your parents soon – they must be worried sick." Jessica nodded.

"But they are not my parents, despite what the certificate says."

Jessica got on the train and opened a window. She leant out. Edith was thinking when the guard came past making sure the doors were shut. He blew his whistle and waved his flag.

"Just one thing," said Edith suddenly. "What was your mother's name on the certificate?"

"Margaret Sutherland."

* * * * * *

Jessica was startled by the expression on Edith's face. She stepped back without thinking and almost fell over her case. She felt someone grab her arm and steady her. She looked up at the stranger, and he smiled at her and guided her to her seat. He put her case in the rack and sat next to her.

"Well, that was an introduction," he said, still smiling at her. "Do you always make entrances like that?" She shook her head. "I'm Tim Anscott. Pleased to meet you." He held out his hand.

She slowly shook it. "It is usual to respond with your name when someone introduces themselves," he continued. She nodded.

"Sorry," she said and shook her head, making the curls of her brown hair dance. She took a deep breath. "Sorry," she repeated, "it was just the shock. I'm Jessica Harrison." She smiled at him, looking at him properly for the first time.

"I thought that was Mrs Harrison I saw. She's your..." He trailed off. He thought Edith was her mother but then realised that her daughter was Elizabeth.

"My aunt," Jessica finished for him. "Uncle David and my father are brothers."

Tim nodded.

"Are you going all the way?" he asked. "To Exeter," he added when he saw Jessica's expression. She laughed, which broke the tension. She explained she was going to London, then to America. Time soon passed and they arrived at Exeter. Tim stayed with her while she waited for the London train. They agreed to meet up again when she next came to Bishop's Tawton. They both waved long after they couldn't see each other.

* * * * * * *

Edith did not know how long she stood on the platform watching the train disappear. She only realised it was some time when Alan Taylor, the porter, came up and asked if she needed help.

"What? Sorry, no, thank you, Alan, I'm... I'm just leaving." She turned and went out of the station. She slowly walked in the direction of Bishop's Tawton. David had told her to take a taxi home, but she needed to think. She was still confused as she walked through Rock Park. She sat on a bench.

What do I do? she kept repeating to herself. "What do I do?" she repeated, shouting it out loud. A couple of women who were on the next bench turned to stare at her. She did not notice.

She wanted to talk to Elizabeth and David but knew she couldn't. She could not reveal Margaret's secret, even though Elizabeth was a part of it. She let out a long sigh and resumed her walk. She walked past Taw Lodge Hotel and was tempted to go in and have a drink. She felt she needed one but then decided against it. She just wanted to get home.

She unlocked the door and was warmly greeted by Peanut and Smudge. She let them out into the garden and put the kettle on. She realised that there was nothing she could do. Perhaps the only person she could talk to would be Michael. He already knew the secret. Obviously, he had put his name on the birth certificate so he could adopt Jessica, but she could not tell anyone that. But why did he have to? That she could not understand. She recalled a conversation she had had with Elizabeth shortly after Duncan was born, when Margaret started her charity for unmarried mothers. She tried to remember exactly what was said. She recollected asking about the father and if they knew who it was. She had assumed that that name would be on the certificate. Elizabeth had replied that they did know who the father was. But obviously, that was not Michael. So, why did his name appear on the certificate? She was so confused.

* * * * * * *

She smoothed the bedcovers and checked the room was ready for Jessica's arrival. Last time she had arrived unannounced, and David and Jessica had quickly made up the bed.

She thought back to Jessica's last visit. After Jessica had left, she was in turmoil. She had spent the afternoon roaming around the house. She was glad when the time came for her to go to Elizabeth's to look after Duncan and Chloe. She had had a restless night, trying to decide what to do. She needed someone to talk to. She decided to talk to Elizabeth anyway, but she was busy with Fabian. She needed her best friend Constance, but that was impossible. She knew Constance would have told her to be discreet for Margaret's sake. Edith decided to ring Louisa, as she already knew the situation so would not be giving away any secrets.

Edith waited for David to take the dogs for a walk, then rang Louisa. She hoped that Michael would not answer. She really did not want to talk to him yet, just in case Jessica was right, and he had had an affair in America. Edith had convinced David that it might be a different Michael on the birth certificate and the same could apply to Margaret, but she did not think so.

She waited for the telephone to be answered. Thankfully, she heard a female voice. It was the maid. She asked to speak to Louisa, who quickly came to the phone.

"Hello, Edith, how are you? How are Beth and Fabian?"

"I'm well," she replied. "Fabian is doing well. They are moving him back to Barnstaple tomorrow. I'm ringing about Jessica."

"She has disappeared," said Louisa in tears. "We are at our wits' end. We don't know where she is."

"I do," said Edith. She explained how she had turned up and was now on her way to America. "I'm sure Chris will ring you when she arrives."

"Oh, thank you, Edith. That is a great relief. I will ring Chris."

There was a pause. Edith didn't know what to say.

"Louisa, when Jess turned up, she said some things that were a bit confusing." Now it was Louisa's turn to go quiet.

"What did she say?" Louisa asked in a strange voice.

"This is difficult," said Edith. "She explained that she had left because she had seen her birth certificate. That Michael's name was on there. She, and we, thought that she had been adopted from America like Chris."

"Yes, that is what we wanted people to think."

"I do not believe that Michael is her father."

"No, he is not." Louisa's voice was getting quieter.

"She mentioned her mother's name."

"Yes," Louisa was whispering.

"I am not going to tell anyone because it is not my secret and I do not want to embarrass anyone unnecessarily, but Jess might. She is very upset."

"I will get Chris to talk to her."

"About Jess's mother." Silence. "I will not say anything. But why is Michael's name on the certificate?"

Louisa sighed. In some ways it was a relief to talk.

"The girls did not know the name of the father. I think Margaret was indisposed when it happened, and someone took advantage of her state."

"She was raped."

"Yes."

"But why did she not go to the police?"

"The girls did not say much. But they only realised what had happened when Margaret found out she was pregnant. Margaret didn't want everyone to know what had happened. So," Louisa took a deep breath, "we decided to put Michael's name on the certificate to make the adoption easier."

"But…" Edith trailed off. She was still confused because Beth had said that they knew who the father was. Louisa continued.

"It seemed like a good idea at the time, but we did not think it through properly. As soon as Beth rang us, we decided to adopt the baby, so we put out the story that I was going to America. I had thought about going because Mum was ill, but she recovered. When the girls arrived, I went to a hotel and waited. Once we had done it, we couldn't go back. Not that we didn't love or want Jess; we did. But it was so stressful every time we visited. We were sure that someone would notice the likeness between Jess and Margaret. Luckily, they were not together much. But we did worry about Elizabeth. Jess did not take after Margaret. She must look more like her father." The two women made small talk for a few more minutes and agreed to keep each other informed of anything that happened.

Edith left the bedroom and went downstairs to await Jessica's arrival. Jessica had rung a few days ago, asking to come and stay. She had had no luck in tracking down her parents.

David had gone to the station to get her. Edith was at the door to greet her. David took her case upstairs, and Edith led her into the lounge.

"I want to hear all about America," said Edith, "but you must ring your mother, let her know you have arrived."

Jessica nodded, and said she would that evening. She had spoken to her mother a couple of times while she was in America but refused to speak to her father.

Jessica helped Edith get the meal ready. While they were eating, she explained that her search was totally fruitless.

"Chris and I checked the list of employees at Grandpapa and Father's shipping company. There were so many, but we only looked at the records for 1952 and 1953. We could not find anyone with those surnames. So, we decided it was someone that Dad had met socially. We discreetly asked Grandmamma about the parties and things at the time. Chris said not to mention why we were asking, as the thought that Dad had cheated on Mum would upset her." David flinched at Jessica's tone. "But she did not recall anyone of that name." Edith was hoping she would not mention her birth mother's name, so she changed the subject.

"We are pleased you decided to come and stay with us, especially over Christmas. It will be nice for you to go back to university in January and see all your friends again."

Jessica smiled.

"Thank you for having me. I wanted to come back to see Ti... you." Edith picked up on her change of words.

"So who is he?"

"Tim Anscott," replied Jessica carelessly, flushing when she realised she had been tricked.

"Oh," said Edith. "He is a nice young man, an architect I believe. How did you meet him?"

"I bumped into him on the train when I left last time. He was going to Exeter for a job interview." She paused. Then asked, as nonchalantly as she could, if they had Tim's telephone number. They said they did. She tried to ask casually if they knew if he had a girlfriend, and they replied that they did not know.

Edith smiled. As Jessica left the room to ring her mother, she knew that Jessica would be making two telephone calls.

* * * * * * * *

This time Jessica helped her to make the bed for Louisa's visit. Louisa had insisted on coming to see Jessica. Jessica was reluctant. She eventually relented but would countenance her father coming.

Edith smiled to herself as Jessica talked about how she had hated her parents and had not yet forgiven them for their deceit.

Jessica had gone out the previous evening with Tim and planned to do the same this evening, she said defiantly. She didn't care if her mother was coming.

When Louisa arrived, Jessica forgot all her words and immediately ran to hug her, tears streaming down her face.

"I'm sorry, Mummy," she said.

"No, I'm sorry," replied Louisa, her eyes full of tears as well. "We should have explained it to you." Edith wiped away her tears and ushered them into the lounge.

They spent a pleasant afternoon together. As soon as they finished tea, Jessica announced she was going to get ready to meet Tim in the pub. She looked at her mother, daring her to try and stop her, but Louisa nodded. She was tired. She had left early and driven all the way from Liverpool. She was glad the M5 was being built as that made the journey quicker, but it was still a long drive, and the emotional reunion with Jessica had left her drained. She wanted an early night.

Next morning Jessica agreed to go back with her. To get ready for university, she said. She said she still did not want anything to do with her father or Stephen, and Louisa and Edith smiled quietly to each other.

They had just loaded the car when they saw a young man sauntering towards them. Jessica ran up to him, and they greeted each other with a kiss. Jessica dragged him into the garden.

"This is Tim," she said to her mother, who held out her hand. Tim shook it. He wasn't sure if he was ready to meet Jessica's parents.

"Hello, Tim," said Louisa. "It is very nice to meet you. Jessica says you are an architect, and you are looking for a job." Tim nodded his head. That did not sound like the good impression he wanted to make. He was hoping to get a 'proper' job before meeting Jessica's parents. Currently he was a temporary clerk in an estate agent's and helped on his parents' farm. He and Jessica had discussed him trying to get a job in Liverpool, and he agreed that he had more chance there.

"So, you are coming to Liverpool," Louisa continued. Tim looked more uncomfortable.

"I think there are more jobs there than here," he said. Louisa agreed and said she would help Jessica find him a flat and send him details of some vacancies. Louisa and Jessica finally drove away. Tim nodded to Edith and David and returned to the farm.

Chapter 22

Elizabeth and William were in bed. Elizabeth wanted to discuss her mother's visit, but William was only half listening. He was thinking about the hotel. He wanted to expand the business. He had discussed it with his parents, but they were happy just running the hotel in Torquay. They were always busy on the English Riviera except February when they took their holiday, usually to the Algarve. This year they had gone to Malta for a change but were planning to return to the Algarve next year. He had the idea for coach parties from them, and it had proved very successful. Also, his wedding package had taken off and they were fully booked this year and almost fully booked for the next year. He had spoken to his sister and Elizabeth's cousin, when they visited earlier in the year to ask for David's help, about planning permissions. They were looking to buy the farm next to their hotel and turn it into a holiday complex, the biggest barn to an indoor swimming pool, the smaller barns to self-catering accommodation and make a golf course, a touring caravan field and events field. They were busy, and this is probably what made him restless.

"Mum was very strange today," Elizabeth said. "She was on about being ready to support people if they needed it. I don't know why she needs support. Why do you think she asked?" She nudged William.

"Um, sorry, what did you say?"

"Why do you think Mum would need support?"

"Well, they are getting on a bit."

"Yes, but... surely she would have said if something was wrong."

"Maybe she doesn't need it yet but is waiting for something. Then, if it is bad, she will need your support." Elizabeth thought.

"You are probably right. I will have to wait until she tells me. I hope that whatever is the matter with her, or Dad, it is not too serious." She paused, worried now. Then continued. "She also said that Jessie will be coming to stay in a couple of weeks, beginning of July. It will be nice to catch up. I missed her at Christmas, and her previous visit. I want to ask her about America. Maybe we can visit sometime in the future." She waited for an answer, and it came in the form of a gentle snore.

* * * * * * *

There was a knock on the door.

"I'll just see who that is," said Elizabeth, putting down the tea tray.

"You can pour if you like." Elizabeth left the room and went into the hallway. Margaret heard her greet the new arrival. They came into the room.

"I will get another cup," said Elizabeth, and she went to the kitchen.

"I'm glad she has left us alone." Margaret looked at Jessica, puzzled. "I really need to talk to you."

Elizabeth came back. She sensed something had happened.

"What about?" asked Margaret.

"Sorry, Beth, but I really need to talk to Mrs Eastman alone," said Jessica.

"You can talk in front of Beth. She knows all my secrets." Margaret laughed.

Jessica accepted a cup of tea but was looking doubtful. She didn't know what to do. She had decided to come to Elizabeth's on the spur of the moment, hearing Edith say that Margaret was going to Elizabeth's as usual during school term time, and it would be the last one for a while as Margaret and her family were off to Sussex. She panicked and rushed over to Elizabeth's. She wanted to speak to Margaret as she and Tim would be back in Liverpool by the time Margaret returned. She wasn't sure when they would be back next, and she might not have another opportunity. But now, she didn't know what to do.

"No, I really need to talk to you alone," insisted Jessica. It had been drummed into her by her mother and Christine that she must be discreet, and her training as a doctor had impressed the need for confidentiality.

"I'm sorry," said Margaret. "I don't understand. What on earth *do you* want to talk to me about?" Jessica sighed.

"I really need to talk to you alone. It is... It is very personal."

Margaret looked at Elizabeth, confused. Elizabeth shrugged her shoulders. She had no idea what Jessica wanted. Jessica sighed again.

"Alright. I did tell you I wanted to talk to you alone, but if you insist on Beth being here, so be it." She took a deep breath. "I believe, I know, that I am..." She stopped, not knowing how to continue. Margaret and Elizabeth were looking at her expectantly.

Jessica looked straight at Margaret.

"As you know, I've been looking for my parents, since Chris found her family," she started to explain gently. They nodded. "I couldn't find them in America, but before I went to America, I got hold of my birth certificate." She paused and took a deep breath. "I discovered my mother's name was Margaret Sutherland and my father was Michael Harrison." She looked at their ashen faces. Jessica continued, looking directly at Margaret.

"I am your daughter."

* * * * * * * *

Margaret and Peter were enjoying a quiet time after a noisy meal with Aaron and Esme. Phoebe had taken Marcus and Faye to the local park, with instructions not to get muddy, though most knew that was unlikely. Xavier had insisted that at 15, nearly 16, he was too old to go, so he was in his room reading.

"You must be pleased that Phoebe is following in your footsteps," said Margaret to Esme. Esme nodded.

"She has nearly finished her master's degree, but she wants to work with deprived children. There are so many in London. It was your charity that started her down that route. She was so shocked at the situations the girls found themselves in, through no fault of their own, that she wants to help."

Margaret looked pleased.

"I am so glad that my charity has helped so many people and, with Phoebe, will help so many more."

"Does Xavier have any idea what he wants to do in the future?" asked Aaron.

"No, at the moment it changes every time we see him."

"You have a very good bond with him, Peter. Every time I see you together, I forget he is not your natural son. It is only when he looks at me with his brown eyes that I am reminded," commented Esme.

"Yes, well, I have known him since birth," said Peter. "And I have practically brought him up."

"What do you mean, when you look in his eyes? How can you tell a person's parents by their eyes?"

"No, I can't tell a person's parents by their eyes, but I can tell who their parents aren't. While I was studying, I looked into heredity. I was curious about my sister, Glynis, as she has Down's Syndrome, and so does a cousin, so I was curious. In my research I found that eye colour is passed down. Blue is a recessive gene, and both you and Peter have blue eyes, well, ish. But Xavier has beautiful brown eyes. Your first husband must have had brown eyes, Margaret?"

"Yes, he did, exactly like Xavier's," Margaret replied. She was now a bit distracted.

There was a sudden kerfuffle in the hall. Bull had charged in from the garden, passed the Christmas tree, almost tipping it over, and was pawing at the door. As it opened, he leapt at Phoebe, almost pushing her over, but did knock over Faye, who thankfully started laughing and tried to push Bull away as he began licking her frantically.

It was sometime before order was restored and peace reigned.

* * * * * * * *

Margaret was beginning to get annoyed. She had wanted to speak to Esme alone for two days and they were leaving tomorrow for

Sussex, for the New Year. Finally she was alone with her in the kitchen. She managed to turn the conversation her way.

"The other day, we were discussing heredity. Can you really tell a person's parentage from the colour of their eyes?"

"No, but you can tell who isn't their parent. It is not fool proof, just a general rule."

"Are there other ways you can tell? Hair colour, maybe?"

"Hair colour can be a guide but is not as good as eye colour. There are always blood groups." Margaret asked her to explain. "Well, basically, someone with O blood group will pass it on to anyone. If both parents are A or B, then the child will also be A or B. If one parent is A and the other B, then the child will be AB."

"What if one parent is A and the child is A, but the other parent is B?"

"Then the parent with B is not the child's parent as the child should be AB. This is only a general rule; it is a bit more complicated than that. I am sure that there are exceptions." Esme stopped washing up to look at her. Margaret thought quickly.

"That is very interesting. It may help some of the girls at the charity to determine who the father of their child is." Luckily, they were interrupted by Marcus and Bull running in from the garden.

* * * * * * * *

Margaret rushed over to Elizabeth's as soon as she could after returning from Sussex. They had arranged to stay for four days with Xavier's grandparents. Usually Margaret loved being at Royston House, but this time she could not wait to return to Devon. She rode Savannah every day to pass the time. Xavier rode with her on his new horse. The pony they had bought when he started at Eton was now too small. Riding helped. She had taken him to the hunt, and he had enjoyed it enormously. She had enjoyed it but was careful with Savannah, taking the easier options because of Savannah's injury and the fact that she was now getting older. Bedford had been retired and Lord Julius declared he was retiring from the hunt as well. She had enjoyed finding his pony. When he started at Eton and went to his grandparents' at weekends, it was decided they would buy him a pony. They had found a small black pony called Otto, who was bigger than his pony in Devon, though Xavier had grown so quickly his long legs seemed to nearly touch the ground. She had got him a bigger horse, a bay hunter called Archer. Faye had taken to riding Chaos. She also wanted to ride Otto. Margaret was dubious at first, but after a few lessons in the arena, Margaret was happy for her to ride him. Faye had wanted to go on the hunt but had been told she was too young. When the time came to leave, Margaret did find it difficult to drag herself away from the horses. She had enjoyed riding out with her children. She needed to get another horse for Xavier when he was in Devon so they could all ride together.

Arriving back in Barnstaple, Margaret had been frantically yearning to go over to Elizabeth's, but she had to wait until the children had gone back to school. She parked at Elizabeth's house and ran to the door.

Elizabeth opened it and Margaret pushed past her.

"I need to talk to you, now."

Elizabeth shut the door.

"Would you like to come in?" she said sarcastically. Margaret looked at her despairingly.

"Sorry, but I need to speak to you."

"So I gather. Let's go into the kitchen and make some tea."

Margaret followed her through to the kitchen.

Elizabeth made the tea and led the way into the lounge.

Margaret sat down and sighed. They had talked almost every week since Jessica had turned up last year. They had been invited to Jessica's 21st birthday party and were happy when Jessica and Timothy announced their engagement.

"We need to talk." Elizabeth nodded. She had thought almost constantly of Jessica. She could not believe it. All these years and she never knew. She slowly sipped her tea and thought back to that day when Jessica arrived and made her announcement.

She and Margaret had just sat there, stunned, silent, staring at Jessica. She felt Margaret grip her hand.

"What did you say?" she asked in a very squeaky voice.

"I'm sorry, I know this is a shock," said Jessica. "As you know, I have been looking for my mother. My natural mother. I followed Chris to America because Mum and Dad were out there the Christmas before I was born, nine months before I was born." Margaret gripped Elizabeth's hand harder. "I need to tell you what happened. I thought I had been adopted from America like Chris. I… found my birth certificate, and it said my father's name was Michael Harrison." She opened her bag and brought out a piece of paper. Margaret and Elizabeth grasped each other's hands tightly. "I thought that Dad had had an affair while they were in America, adopting Chris. I was hurt that they had not told me my dad was my dad. Does that make sense?" She shook her brown curls and continued. "Anyway, I stormed out and went to my friend's for a couple of days while I made arrangements to bring my trip to America forward. Then I thought I should see Uncle David and Aunt Edith; after all, they are my real aunt and uncle now. So I turned up out of the blue and left the next day. I did not show them the certificate. I had no luck finding anyone of either name in America, so I returned."

Jessica took a sip of tea. She continued, Margaret and Elizabeth gripping each other's hands in silence. She opened up the paper and showed it to them.

They looked at it and then at each other. Margaret never thought she would see that bit of paper again.

"Beth," she whispered.

"I know," Elizabeth replied, and she looked at Jessica. "Who else have you told?"

"No one. I have not told anyone. I know this is not easy and it is a shock, me turning up like this, but I had to come. Once I knew who you were, I could not stay away."

"Samantha?" Margaret asked hoarsely. They both looked at her enquiringly. Margaret continued. "Is it really you?"

"Um, yes," said Jessica, a little confused. Elizabeth looked at Margaret, baffled. Margaret saw their expressions and explained.

"In my head I always called you Samantha. I think I just need a moment." She left the room, and they heard her go upstairs to the bathroom.

"Beth, I have lied a little. I have told someone." She explained what happened at the station, then continued. "But Aunt Edith has not said anything." Elizabeth shook her head.

"She wouldn't, but don't worry; that doesn't count. Just please do not tell anyone else," begged Elizabeth.

"I won't. I promise," said Jessica. "At least, not without speaking to you both first."

Margaret returned to the room, ready to greet her daughter.

"How did you find us?"

"After my fruitless search in America, I wanted to come back here because I had met someone."

"Tim Anscott," interrupted Elizabeth, emphasising the Anscott. She looked at Margaret, who recognised the name.

"Yes, when I came back here at Christmas, I made it up with Mum but did not want to speak to Dad or Stephen. As you know, Tim came to Liverpool with me. He is really flourishing. He has already had a promotion," she said proudly. "Well," she coughed embarrassingly, "as soon as I got home and saw Dad, my resolve crumbled. He looked so old and dejected. I immediately forgot everything and hugged him. With Stephen it took a bit longer. I don't know if you know, but we were dating. This is another reason I was so angry with Mum and Dad; they let me date my brother. I know now he wasn't, but at the time... Anyway, as soon as he discovered I was his sister, apparently he was with a different girl every week. We are friends again now. Tim helped." She drank her tea. She saw their appalled expressions and quickly reassured them. "I have not told Tim about you, just that I had a big row with Mum and Dad, not what it was about." The women were relieved.

"But how did you find out about me?" insisted Margaret.

"It was last week. One reason we came was to meet Tim's family. I have met his parents but no one else. Last week, we were invited to his step-grandmother Susan's for tea. I was formerly introduced to her husband, your father, Charles Sutherland. Well, you could have knocked me down with a feather. I nearly choked at the name. I had been to America and back, and here were the Sutherlands practically on my doorstep. I knew, of course, about you, but I never knew your maiden name or your father's surname. And I only knew you as Lady Margaret, or Mrs Eastman when you married Peter. But to walk in that house and discover Margaret Sutherland was amazing. I have been trying to get you alone ever since. It has not been easy."

Margaret smiled at her.

"I must remember to call you Jessica, not Samantha." They laughed.

"I will answer to either."

* * * * * * * *

Elizabeth turned back to Margaret.

"Yes, we do need to talk. How are you feeling now? It was a shock for both of us and I am still trying to get used to the idea."

"Yes," agreed Margaret. "I had no idea that Michael and Louisa had adopted my daughter. How did we not spot it over the years?"

"Well, you had very little to do with Michael and Louisa, and I just blocked everything out." She sighed. "She doesn't really look like you. When I look closely, I can see she has your nose and mouth, but that is it. She doesn't look like Bill either."

"No, she wouldn't," said Margaret, watching Elizabeth closely.

Elizabeth stared at her.

"What do you mean?"

"I mean, she is not Bill's."

Chapter 23

Elizabeth looked intently at her.

"What do you mean?"

"I mean, she is not Bill's."

Elizabeth just gazed at her with a strange expression and drank her tea. Margaret couldn't bear the silence any longer.

"Say something," she demanded.

Elizabeth's blue eyes were flashing angrily at Margaret. Margaret had never seen Elizabeth angry at her before.

"After all this time, you now say she isn't Bill's."

"No, yes." Margaret ran her hand through her hair. "I only found out at Christmas." She repeated the conversation she had with Esme. "So, just on eyes alone she is not Bill's, but as Esme said, it is not a fail-safe method. What blood group is Bill?"

Elizabeth got up and went to the bureau and looked through some papers.

"When Fabian had his appendix out, we both had our blood taken, in case he needed it." Her voice broke at remembering the traumatic time. "Here it is. I am O, Bill is A, Fabian is A."

"I am B. I have already looked it up. We just need to find out what Jess is."

"Let's give her a ring."

Elizabeth picked up the receiver and dialled. Margaret sat beside her listening. The phone was answered eventually. Elizabeth disguised her voice, trying to eliminate all of her West Country twang.

"Hello, can I speak to Jess, please?"

"Just a moment. Who's calling?"

"Samantha." Just a slight hesitation as Elizabeth said the code name. They had all known that the only other people who knew, for sure, that Jessica was Margaret's daughter were Michael and

Louisa. They weren't sure about Stephen or Christine – they might have some clue. Margaret was not ready to open up to Michael or Louisa yet. She was still coming to terms with the news, but she promised Jessica that it wouldn't be long. In the meantime, they needed to keep it quiet. Jessica nodded understandingly. She was still trying to understand herself. They agreed that if Margaret or, to a lesser degree, Elizabeth needed to talk to her without revealing themselves, they would use Margaret's name for her, Samantha.

"Hello, Samantha," said Jessica brightly. "Alright, you can go now. Buzz off." Stephen grinned at her and went to the kitchen. "Sorry, Stephen was being a pest."

"I will hand you over to Maggie," said Elizabeth. She passed the phone over.

"Hello, darling, how are you?" She had this very strange feeling talking to Jessica. When she and Jessica had parted a few months previously, she had accepted her completely and they sat holding hands and hugged for several minutes before they had to leave.

"I'm good. It is nice of you to ring."

"Oh, Jess, I miss you. I so want to get to know you properly, but it is not possible at the moment. I just need to sort a few things out."

"That's fine," said Jessica. She felt a lump in her throat. She had been afraid that she would be rejected a second time, but she had not really been rejected the first time. She knew it was just circumstances that forced Margaret to give her up.

"I really need to ask you something." Jessica made a noise. "Can you tell me your blood group?"

"Blood group?"

"Please, darling, it is important."

"Yes, I am Group B. We all had to take blood and see what group we were on my university course." There was a faint noise. "Are you still there?"

"Hello?"

"Hello, Beth, is... Samantha there? What happened?"

"Yes, she is here. I'm sorry, we need to go now. We will be in touch soon. Take care." Jessica stared at the phone as the line went dead. She shrugged and put it back. She went to join Stephen in the kitchen.

Elizabeth held Margaret in her arms at the bottom of the stairs. Margaret had collapsed at the news, and the stairs were the only place to sit. Margaret looked at Elizabeth, tears in her eyes.

"You know what that means. I WAS raped. But by whom?"

* * * * * * * *

They had gathered in Margaret and Peter's lounge. Margaret and Elizabeth were sitting on the lounge together, arms around each other.

After the phone call to Jessica, they had discussed what to do. Elizabeth was so thankful her faith in William, after all these years, had not been misplaced. She had known he would never have forced himself on anyone. She had assumed that Margaret had said yes, then immediately regretted it, but he had not done anything. She felt light-headed with relief.

Margaret felt sick. She had always known that she had been raped but suppressed her feelings when she found out that the man was Elizabeth's fiancé. For the only time in her life, she put someone else's feelings first, but only because Elizabeth had helped her when she was pregnant, and that was a way to repay her. But now, it wasn't William, who she did like and respect for the way he looked after Elizabeth, apart from that one time, that one lapse. Now, she finds out it wasn't William. She was glad for Elizabeth, but if it wasn't William, then who?

Elizabeth and Margaret had discussed it. Margaret wanted to have a quiet word with William, but Elizabeth refused to let her.

"I have kept quiet for over 20 years, at great cost. You made me believe things about Bill I didn't want to. Now, the time for secrecy is over. I need to tell Bill, and you need to tell Peter." Elizabeth spoke in a steely voice and tightened her grip on Margaret's hands. "Darling, you need to tell Peter. He will support you. You know you should." Margaret started to cry. She knew Elizabeth was right. "I will be there to support you, as I have always done."

"It is so hard. It hurts."

"I know, Maggie, but we must lance this wound, for both our sakes." Margaret nodded but was still not convinced.

"I don't know. Can't we just stay as we are?"

"No!" Elizabeth shouted at her. Margaret was shocked. Elizabeth never shouted at her. "No, we can't." Elizabeth glared at her. "I have not said anything because you said that it was Bill that... did it to you, but it was not. You put me through hell at my engagement party with your accusation. I am just so glad that I followed my instincts." Elizabeth glared at her again, daring her to say anything.

Margaret, for once, sat quiet. She waited for Elizabeth to continue. Elizabeth was just so relieved, and so angry. She was glad that she had followed her first feelings and intuition. She knew Bill was not like that. Now she had proof. After Doris had broken up with David Bowden just before Christmas 1953, she had gone over to Doris's house to console her. Elizabeth persuaded her to come to the New Year dance at Taw Lodge Hotel. Doris was reluctant at first but finally gave in. Elizabeth remembered how Doris's cousin Alan Taylor tried to take advantage of Doris in her fragile state, but William had stepped in and protected her. Elizabeth had been worried as Doris was drinking too much, so was very grateful to William. Elizabeth remembered their intimate meeting a few months later, and how he had not taken advantage of her. She KNEW he was a good man and said firmly to Margaret,

"For too long, Bill and I have hidden your secret about him. But you were wrong. I will be telling Bill, and you must tell Peter. Now is the time." Margaret sat, wide-eyed. She was at a loss. She knew Elizabeth was right. So, they made a decision.

The two women were sitting on the sofa in the lounge, holding each other tightly. They had told William and Peter that they needed to speak to them. Elizabeth had arranged for one of the hotel maids to sit with her children. She did not want to ask Edith, as she did not want to offer an explanation, not yet. Margaret's children, Marcus and Faye, were staying with Charles and Susan. Xavier was in Sussex where he stayed at the weekends.

Elizabeth took a deep breath.

"We have asked to speak to you because we have something we need to tell you. It is easier if you are both here." Peter and William looked at each other with raised eyebrows. Elizabeth and Margaret were holding each other, shaking. "It has taken us 21 years, but now we know, and are ready to tell you." Elizabeth turned to Margaret, who was shaking her head. "Darling, we must. We must stop living this lie and tell the truth." Elizabeth tenderly moved Margaret's hair off her face. "We can't keep this secret any longer." Elizabeth and Margaret started crying and wrapped their arms around each other. Peter and William had horrified expressions on their faces – they could see that the other was thinking the same. Peter got out of his armchair and strode around the room, and William put his head in his hands. The women did not notice. Elizabeth took a deep breath and, in a small voice, continued.

"We need to tell you, but this is difficult. It all began 20-odd years ago, on a New Year's Eve." Peter stopped pacing. William still had his head in his hands and groaned; he so regretted that evening. "Someone got themselves so drunk that they were unconscious for a few hours." This time it was Margaret groaning. "It will be fine. We just need to get this over with, darling. She was very lucky and helped by two very kind gentlemen. One who gave her a place to rest and tended her, and one who safely brought her home." Elizabeth emphasised the words and looked at William. She suddenly noticed his distress and wanted to go to him but stayed with Margaret. "A few months later she asked for my help." She took a gulp of air and looked steadily at William. "She was pregnant!"

William's head shot up and he stared at Elizabeth.

"You mean, I have another child." Elizabeth tried to smile reassuringly, but she couldn't. She just shook her head. William looked confused. Peter strode across the room. For the first time he felt that his fears were unfounded. He knelt down beside Margaret.

"Why did you not tell me? I could have helped."

Margaret shook her head. She tried to speak, but the words hardly came out.

"I couldn't. You hated me."

"Oh, Maggie, do you still not know? I have loved you since that moment I saw you in Church Cottage."

Margaret broke away from Elizabeth and grabbed Peter, sobbing her heart out. Elizabeth slowly moved away from them. William went over to her.

"Are you leaving me?" he asked hoarsely, not wanting to hear the answer. Elizabeth looked puzzled.

"No, of course not. Completely the opposite." William looked puzzled now, but Elizabeth just kissed him.

They waited for Margaret to calm down.

"What happened to the baby?" Peter asked.

"I had it adopted." Margaret burst into tears again.

"Why are you telling us now?" Peter continued. Margaret moved her lips, but nothing came out.

"Circumstances have changed," declared Elizabeth. "What we thought had happened didn't. We need to try and see if we can discover exactly who... what happened that night in the hotel. I know neither of you want to talk about it, but we must. We must, Maggie." Elizabeth looked at Margaret as she murmured something. Then she turned to William and said, gently, "I know this is painful, but please believe me; it will be worth it. You found Margaret in the reception area." William nodded. He didn't know where this was going, but if it meant Elizabeth was not going to leave him, then he would do as asked.

"Yes, I saw her standing in the doorway, completely soaked, and so drunk she could barely stand up. I knew I had to do something. I wasn't in the best of moods. I had just broken up with Angela." He felt Elizabeth wince in his arms. He hugged her and continued. "I took Maggie through to the private area but had to leave to sort out a fight or something. I had a few more drinks before returning to Maggie. When I returned, she was still sitting in her wet clothes. I helped her undress and get into the bed left for the night staff. The bed looked so inviting and I was so tired, so tired. I got in beside Maggie and we both went to sleep. I was woken by a knock on the door, so I disentangled myself from Maggie and answered it. There was trouble in the bar, and I had to go sort it out. When I returned Maggie was gone."

"When you were... in bed with Maggie..." This was hard to say, but Elizabeth continued. "Were you both... naked?"

William looked embarrassed but answered the question.

"I had undressed Maggie completely. As I said, she was soaked through, but I used a towel and dressing gown to cover her until she got in bed." He took a deep breath. "I took everything off, except my underpants and socks." He forced a laugh at the picture. Why had he left his socks on? Elizabeth saw Margaret and Peter listening intently.

"When you dressed to go sort out the trouble, were your underpants still on? Are you sure you had not woken previously and taken them off?" William thought hard.

"I am sure I had not woken before, and they were definitely still on." Elizabeth looked at Margaret. Peter caught the look.

"What you are saying is that Bill did not have sex with Maggie?"

Elizabeth and Margaret nodded in unison.

"But then, the baby, whose is it?" Margaret burst into tears again.

"I don't know."

Elizabeth turned to William.

"You behaved like the perfect gentleman I knew you to be. I love you so much, Bill." William still could not understand. He had been through the whole range of emotions and was not sure he was on the right one.

"So, you are not going to leave me?" he asked again, wanting more reassurance. Elizabeth shook her head, smiling at him. "And I didn't have... sex with Maggie?" Elizabeth shook her head again. He jumped up, grabbing Elizabeth, and danced round the room with her. When they sat down, he was suddenly serious.

"We came so close to splitting up at our engagement party, over nothing. Thank you so much for believing in me. The Sword of Damocles hanging over my head has gone. I have been so worried over the years that that incident would make you leave me."

Peter interrupted. "Again, I ask, if the baby isn't Bill's, whose is it? And why now?"

Margaret tried to talk, but it was impossible. Elizabeth spoke for her.

"We have discovered what happened to the baby and information shows that she is not Bill's."

"A girl?" interrupted Peter. "I wondered what it was."

"So, as she is not Bill's, someone else came into the room and... raped Maggie." There, she had used the word.

There was silence as everyone digested this information.

"Bill, who else was in the hotel when you left the room to sort out the trouble?" Elizabeth asked him. William thought back. He was happy to do so now. He rubbed his head as he thought.

"Well, there was the waitress who knocked on the door, but I think we can dismiss her and all the women. There were a dozen guests staying at the hotel; half were men. It could have been one of them."

"Were they wandering around the hotel?"

"No, they had all gone to their rooms. It was only staff left downstairs."

"The guests wouldn't have gone into the private area anyway. Which staff members were left?"

William listed the four staff members.

"But they were busy tidying up and were with each other or female staff." There was another silence.

"What was the trouble that you had to sort out?" Peter asked, curious.

"Someone was pestering one of the barmaids. He was insistent that she kiss him. He had torn her blouse." Everyone sat up.

"Who was that?"

"Larry. But I didn't see him; he must have gone home. I looked for him for ages but couldn't find him. I checked that the barmaid was okay and made sure someone took her home."

No one wanted to speak. The silence was broken by Margaret.

"Larry," she whispered. "Are we sure? I do not remember a thing. I did have bruises on my legs the next day, but if it hadn't been for Je... the baby, I would never have known." Peter noted the information.

"Well," said Elizabeth, "he does have brown eyes. But who knows what blood group he is? I don't know how to find out. I suppose we could ask your sister." She looked at William, who just shrugged.

"We can't do that tonight," said Peter. "That will have to be left to another day. But tonight, I think that we have established that Maggie was raped that night. I think we all knew that but were treading on eggshells out of deference to Beth and Bill. That is over now, and we can treat the matter the way it should have been treated. A very serious case of rape. We need to tell the police."

"No," cried out Margaret vehemently. "No, I can't, don't. Please don't, Peter," she begged, shaking violently.

Peter calmed her down and reassured her he would not.

"But tell me one thing. Why are you doing this now? What information do you have?"

CHAPTER 24

Elizabeth took William's hand and stood up.

"We will leave now."

"But — " protested William.

"I will tell you everything when we get home. Everything," she said again firmly, looking at Margaret, who nodded miserably. Peter saw them out and went back to Margaret.

"So, now, tell ME everything." He saw the expression on Margaret's face. "We have all night, and we did promise no more secrets." Margaret sighed.

"This is a very big secret but my only one. I did keep it secret that I was having a baby. Could you imagine what that would have done to Mother? I did not know anything had happened that night until I was pregnant and the only person I could remember was Bill, so I assumed it was him. Beth was brilliant; she arranged for us to stay with Michael and Louisa. After the baby was born, I went to America to recover. I never saw the baby again until…"

"Until now," continued Peter. "I remember you and Beth going away but was engrossed in my garage so didn't think much about it. I was unhappy when I heard you had gone to America. I was afraid I wouldn't see you again. It was a long time, then when I did see you, you were engaged to Hugh."

"I was so confused. Hugh helped me. He stabilised my life."

"I would have done that," said Peter.

"I know, but I wasn't ready for you. I needed more time." Peter understood now.

"So, how did you find out that Jessica was your daughter?"

Margaret looked sharply at him.

"You have known all this time. You have just been playing with me."

"No, I only found out this evening. You nearly said her name and I just put two and two together. Am I right?"

Margaret nodded.

"Why did you not say sooner? All these years and you never said anything."

"I only found out last year, when Jessica came down in the summer. I was still trying to cope with the news. When we visited Aaron and Esme at Christmas, she started talking about parentage. I had Jessica on my mind so thought about her and her brown eyes. That's when I started having doubts. I was getting more confused. Esme also told me about blood groups. A couple of days ago I contacted Jess, and she confirmed what I already guessed. So, Beth and I decided to get to the truth. We needed to find out what had happened." Peter pulled her to him. He kissed her head.

"This is a lot to take in. To think that Jess is your daughter. I thought that she went to America to find her parents. How did she find you?"

Margaret told him the whole story, filling in all the blanks.

"What do we do now?" she asked.

"Well, I'm going to bed. I'm tired. Are you coming?" he asked, standing up, smiling. Margaret scrambled up as well and took his hand.

* * * * * * *

"So now you know everything," said Elizabeth, sitting in Church Cottage's lounge drinking tea with her parents a few weeks later. Elizabeth and Margaret decided it was time they told everyone but slowly and discreetly, as Margaret was still anxious over people's reactions. "I am sorry I could not tell you before."

David could not say anything – he was still in a state of shock – but Edith spoke.

"So all those years ago, when I asked about the father..."

"You already knew?" interrupted David.

"Yes and no. I only knew that Maggie was having a baby; I did not know any other information. And I helped Beth and

Maggie go to Michael and Louisa's." She continued. "When I asked about the father and you said you knew, did you really?"

"Well, I thought I did. I was praying that you would not ask his name."

"It sounds as if Jess has had about four different fathers. Do we know the real one?"

"We are pretty certain it is Larry. But we are not 100 per cent sure. We know it is not Michael or…"

"I told you he would never betray Louisa," interrupted David again, a smug expression on his face.

"Yes, dear, you were right," said Edith, smiling at his satisfied expression. "No wonder you were so upset at your engagement party. To find out Bill and Maggie had… but then they hadn't. I am so glad that you followed your instincts. I'm not sure I would have been able to."

"Well, I knew Bill," she said purposely. "Anyway, you knew a couple of years ago." David turned to Edith.

"Did you know? When? You didn't say."

"No, I couldn't. When Jess left for America, I happened to ask the name of her mother, just as you do. I did not expect the answer I got. I saw then what had happened, but I really could not say anything."

"No," said Elizabeth, "none of us can. We must still be very discreet." Both Elizabeth and Edith turned to David and burst out laughing at his pained expression.

* * * * * * * *

Peter and Margaret knew they needed to tell Charles and Susan. Elizabeth had reassured Margaret after speaking to her parents. They decided to tell them before Xavier came home for the Easter holidays. Margaret was tense as they made the journey to The Firs.

"Well, this is unusual," said Susan. She had been wondering why Margaret and Peter had made a special trip to speak to them. She put the tea tray down and started to pour.

Charles noticed the tension in the air, and suddenly realised that this was out of the ordinary. He felt a chill go down his spine.

221

He hoped that it was not what he thought. Everyone sat in silence drinking their tea. Margaret could stand it no longer. She put down her cup and stood up.

"Dad, Susan, I have something to tell you." She started pacing. "I have..." She sat down again suddenly, her head in her hands. "I can't," she whispered.

"It's alright, love, I will tell them." Peter looked at Charles. "This is very difficult, as you can see. We have some very important information we want to tell you. We don't have to tell you, but we don't want any more secrets. It brings back painful memories and Margaret needs your support."

Susan spoke first.

"She certainly has my support. Whatever it is. I have been in a terrible situation, so will not judge." Margaret looked at her, and Susan gave her a reassuring smile. Margaret started again.

"Twenty-three years ago, I was ra... attacked." She could not bring herself to say the word. Susan's hand flew to her mouth. Charles looked murderous.

"Who is this fellow? I will kill him." He stood up, shaking his walking stick. Margaret tried to laugh at him, but tears started forming. She sighed. She thought she was all cried out.

"Sit down, Father, it will do no good. I do not have any proof."

"Just tell us what happened," said Susan, indicating to Charles to sit down.

Margaret started her story again. When she finished, she sat back, exhausted.

Charles got up and walked around. His leg pained him where he had injured it all those years ago. Now, several things were making sense.

"Thank you for not causing a scandal. Constance would not have liked that. I must thank Beth when I see her; she has been through much as well. I wish you had told me before."

"There wasn't much to tell before, and I had got the wrong man, so, far from thanking Beth, you would have made her a widow." This brought a smile to her father's face, as she had hoped.

"I still want to kill him," stated Charles defiantly. "I will next time I see him."

"You won't be able to do that for a long time. He is in prison."

"In prison!" exclaimed Margaret. "Really, I am so pleased. What for? How long?"

"He was arrested for rape. Yes, I know." Susan nodded to Margaret. "He raped Irene Grayson about 12...13 years ago, just before you married, and assaulted a few other young girls. One was able to identify him immediately, and then Irene came forward, and a few other women he had attacked. He was sentenced to about 20 years. I don't know exactly." Margaret sat back, relieved. Susan continued.

"Well, Jess seems a lovely young lady and I know Tim is smitten. You say it was visiting us that she discovered you were her mother. There you are, Charles, you were instrumental in bringing mother and daughter together."

"Only because I married you," he retorted. "I knew it was a good idea." Everyone laughed, not because it was funny, just to relieve the tension. Susan made to clear the tea things. Margaret helped and followed her to the kitchen.

"I am glad Father married you," said Margaret. She had lost all animosity towards her now. "You know how to handle Dad, and it was an integral part of bringing me and Jess together. We have finally managed to get to the truth." Susan gave her a hug.

"My life has not always been easy, but I do love your father. I know the pain of losing a child, but you are together now." Susan wiped away a tear and started to wash up. Margaret picked up a tea towel and they finished the task in companionable silence.

* * * * * * * *

"It is nearly like old times," said Edith to Louisa as they sat in front the fire, sherry in hand.

"Yes, almost. I am glad you suggested the party, not that I want to be reminded I am 60, but it is good to get the family together. It is easier for us to come here," replied Louisa.

"It was a lovely wedding," said Edith. "As you say, it is easier for you to come to Bishop's Tawton for events as all of Tim's family are here as well. Jessica looked so beautiful, and it was good of you to let Margaret be 'mother of the bride' as well. I know she really appreciated it and was worried that you would be upset. She did not want to upset you."

Louisa sighed. "It wasn't easy, but it was the right thing to do. We knew it would happen one day that Jessie would discover Margaret was her mother, so we had discussed it and were prepared. We didn't want to alienate her, so we agreed to do whatever she wanted. After she disappeared to America, we were very anxious not to cause her to disappear again. So, it was for the best. Also, that she had her sister, Faye, to be her bridesmaid. We are closer than ever."

Their conversation was interrupted by three men returning from the pub.

"I'm glad to see you made it back at a reasonable time," said Louisa to Michael.

"I had to drag him away," said Stephen, and he ducked as Michael playfully made to strike his head.

"It was very quiet," said David. He was glad to be home. He didn't really like going to the pub, but Stephen and Michael had wanted to go.

"Well, we can all have an early night. Tomorrow is going to be busy," said Edith. She sighed at the thought of the party the next day, Louisa's 60th. The family had got bigger and there was only one place to cater for them all, Taw Lodge Hotel. They planned a big party there. Everyone would be going back to Liverpool the next day.

* * * * * * * *

"Thank you for letting me have Jess to stay, and Tim, of course," said Margaret, laughing, as they were getting ready.

"Don't be silly; she is your daughter."

"Yes, but..."

"No buts, just enjoy her company before she returns to Liverpool." Margaret went to Peter. She kissed him on the cheek, and he pulled her closer. They broke apart when they heard the hall clock chiming six, and Jessica and Xavier going down, chatting noisily. Xavier was still unsure what was happening. All of a sudden, he had a sister. He wasn't sure he wanted another sister – one was bad enough – and now he had a brother-in-law as well. Peter had spoken to him about Jessica. He understood the situation but was still reeling from the news. He wished he was younger like Marcus and Faye; they did not really understand everything. He hated the thought of his mother being attacked, but Peter had reassured him that she didn't remember anything, and she was delighted to have Jessica here. He shrugged his shoulders and decided to make the best of the situation; after all, he was getting some time off school. It was harder studying for his A levels, but he felt he was treated better by the lecturers.

Tim and Jessica left together. Everyone else was going in Peter's car.

"It is so nice to have all my children under one roof, if only for a few days, with Jess returning to Liverpool after Louisa's party tomorrow." Peter agreed with her.

"Yes, it is nice to have all the children together, except there is one more I need to tell you about." Margaret sat up quickly and looked at him. He could not keep a straight face and started laughing. "Your expression was priceless." He had to stop as a cushion came his way, followed by another one and then Margaret.

* * * * * * * *

Elizabeth and Margaret were just having a quiet five minutes in the midst of the thriving party. They had chosen a semi-secluded spot in the corner of the room. Elizabeth drank the last bit of her wine.

"I am so glad you suggested this party. I wasn't sure I wanted to advertise the fact that I am 40, but it is nice to have all the families together. Now we are getting so big, it is difficult."

Margaret nodded. She was conscious of her expanding family, now with Jessica's family and Tim's family to include after their wedding.

"Yes, and everyone has been so nice to me. I was worried about telling people about Jessica. But no one blames me and is very sympathetic. I don't know why I worried so much."

"Because at the time you didn't want to upset your mother and later me." Elizabeth stood up. "Come on, let's go and have a dance." She pulled Margaret out of the chair, and she followed her, laughing. But as they approached the dance floor, Margaret stopped. Elizabeth stopped too, as she felt Margaret's tug. She turned to look at Margaret. Margaret was staring at the doorway. Elizabeth turned to look and gasped. She frantically searched the room for William and Peter. She spotted them and pulled Margaret towards them. William and Peter were at the bar with Vince and Malcolm Burrows. Peter caught sight of Elizabeth and Margaret frantically making their way over to them. He was nudged by William, who had just noticed the person in the doorway.

"Oh no," exclaimed Peter. "You look after Beth and Maggie," he ordered William. "I will deal with him." He started towards the door. William made his way to Elizabeth and Margaret. Vince and Malcolm both followed Peter. Peter arrived at the door and pushed the man back through.

"What are you doing here? You are supposed to be in prison," he demanded, trying to keep his voice down.

"Nothing, just visiting, enjoying the party. Got out early, good behaviour."

"You are not invited." Peter looked back at the ballroom. He saw that William had Elizabeth and Margaret. He had his arm around Margaret, comforting her. Elizabeth was looking at the door, a worried expression on her face. Suddenly, it turned to a horrified expression, and she rushed towards him. She was trying to make her way through the guests. Peter saw she was making her way slightly to the left of the door. He peered around. He pushed the man further back into the foyer. But it was too late. Elizabeth just caught up with Charles and Susan as they went through the door.

"You!" declared Charles. He stepped forward as quickly as he could and waved his stick at the man.

"Well, old man, what are you going to do?" came the taunt.

"You assaulted my daughter. I will make you pay." Larry took a step towards Charles, who was being pulled away by Susan. Charles tried to hit Larry, but Larry just pushed him away, laughing. Charles fell back, and Larry bent over him.

"Take this!" He punched him in the face. He was about to kick him when he felt his arm being pulled behind his back.

"I'm arresting you," said Malcolm Burrows. "I will take you to the station to formerly charge you with assaulting Charles. You are going back inside." He shrugged an apology at Margaret, who had arrived at the door. "Margaret."

"I have already rung the police," said Elizabeth. "They should be here shortly."

"You can't keep me here." He yanked his arm free.

"Yes, we can," said Peter. He stepped in front of him, and Malcolm re-grabbed his arm. Vince also stepped forward, as did William. They heard the sound of sirens. Larry looked round frantically, but there was no escape. Two police officers came in and took Larry to their car.

"I will go with them," said Malcolm. "Tell your mother I shouldn't be long," he added to Vince.

Everyone watched the police car leave.

Margaret was helping Susan get Charles back on his feet.

"I really wanted to hurt him for what he did to you," Charles said to Margaret.

"I know, but what you did was enough. He will now be arrested again, and we can forget all about him. Come on, let's party."

There were just the four of them left.

"Don't worry, Maggie, he won't hurt you again." Peter put his arm around her.

"I know, but what about all the publicity? The very thing I tried to avoid."

"We knew it would come out eventually, but we did our best. But if things get too bad here, you can go to Liverpool, London or Sussex until it blows over. We will always look after Marcus and Faye. You don't have to worry." Elizabeth tried to comfort her.

"Thank you. You have been wonderful."

CHAPTER 25

"I'm not sure I am old enough to be a grandmother," said Margaret. Margaret was sitting in Elizabeth's comfortable armchair. Elizabeth laughed.

"You will love being a grandmother. You will enjoy all the benefits without the responsibility because you can hand the baby back. Jess will act as a nanny like Ivy with your children." She laughed again at Margaret's indignant expression. She changed the subject.

"So, Xavier has decided what he wants to do after his A levels."

Margaret nodded.

"I am looking forward to seeing all the foals. We are supporting him, but he has to do a business course so that he knows how to run a business. We like Luke. We are happy that he is going to be his business partner. He will be able to guide him."

"Yes, he has had experience running the farm with Ronald. I know he loves horses, and with Xavier's connections from Eton, I think they will enjoy running the stud. Have they decided on a name?"

"I think they are just going to call it The Royston Stud. I will miss him when he moves permanently to Royston House."

"But he has been away at school." Elizabeth sighed. "I hope that he and Luke make a success of it. Where will Luke live?"

"First he will stay at Royston House. There is a cottage just down the road for sale that he is buying, for him and his fiancée."

"How did Simon get on doing his training?"

"He did well and is looking forward to managing the stud for them. And I am grateful to Duncan for keeping an eye on the books. He is so sensible and can keep Xavier's extravagance in check."

Elizabeth smiled at the praise for Duncan.

* * * * * * * *

"He is adorable, Jess," said Elizabeth, gently holding Jessica's son. "I think you are wise in your choice of godparents."

"We wanted to try and include all the family, so it seemed natural to ask Stephen and Faye, especially as she was my bridesmaid. Also Luke, Tim's brother."

"How are his wedding plans going?"

"They are going well. Anita's parents have everything in hand."

Someone called for Jessica. Elizabeth gave her back the baby and she wandered over to Margaret.

"Well, Grandma, it was a lovely christening." She smiled at Margaret.

"I can't get used to being called Grandma," she said, smiling back.

* * * * * * *

Margaret was sitting on the gate watching the foals playing in the field. Jason, Xavier's cross-breed setter, was by her side. She was glad they were visiting at the half term because Marcus and Faye could also visit. Faye was thrilled to see all the horses. Margaret felt strange not having Savannah to ride – she died the previous year. She jumped down, called Jason and wandered back into the stable yard. She saw Xavier and Anita were in the arena exercising a grey mare, Snow Blizzard. She watched as Anita brought the mare to a standstill, and Xavier helped Anita get down. He reluctantly let her go and took the mare's reins. They walked over to the gate and suddenly spotted Margaret, so Anita moved to the other side of the mare. Margaret got goose bumps. She hoped she was wrong.

Later that evening, when they were getting ready for dinner, she spoke to Peter.

"Peter."

"Yes," he replied. He knew something had been bothering her all afternoon.

"Peter," she said again, "what if you found out something, but you weren't sure. What would you do?" Peter looked at her, puzzled. She was obviously very upset. She knew something, but what?

"Well, Maggie, the first thing I would do is to take a rocket to the moon."

"Yes, but what would you do?" She turned to him. "What would you do?" She was getting agitated. Peter went over to her and held her.

"Sorry, tell me about it."

Margaret explained what she had seen.

"Tell me I am wrong," she pleaded. Peter hugged her. He had seen a couple of things as well since they arrived a couple of days ago, when they thought no one was looking. He was planning on having a quiet word with Xavier before they left tomorrow, but he had not had an opportunity.

They went downstairs with heavy hearts.

"It is lovely having Xavier with us. Thank you for letting him come," said Lady Agatha. She knew that Margaret missed him.

Margaret replied.

"He and Luke are doing well. Some more new mares are coming next week, he tells me."

"Yes, and the new training areas are nearly completed, so they will be able to offer their services for that as well." Margaret took a sip of elderflower juice. She loved the drink; it brought back so many comforting memories.

"How are Luke and Anita settling in?" She tried to keep her voice calm, but she felt it trembling.

"Luke is very busy. He is going all over the place trying to find out the best training facilities."

"Luke is away a lot?"

"Fairly often. They also have been renovating the cottage. I haven't seen it, but Xavier has been over several times and tells me about it." Margaret made a strange noise. Peter looked up

230

from trying to stop an argument between Marcus and Faye. He smiled reassuringly at her. She shrugged.

Xavier came rushing in, still doing up his tie.

"Sorry I'm late. I was just... settling in Snow Blizzard."

Margaret and Peter exchanged glances.

* * * * * * * *

Elizabeth could see Margaret was troubled. She had spoken to both her and Peter on the phone since they had returned from Sussex, and both sounded upset. Elizabeth broached the subject directly.

"Well, tell me what happened in Sussex. I know something has happened." Margaret looked at her with tears in her eyes.

"I don't know. I have no proof."

"Tell me!" Elizabeth ordered. "I presume Peter knows as well."

Margaret nodded and sighed.

"I don't understand why. I suppose she is fairly attractive, but it is going to cause so many problems." Elizabeth waited. She knew once Margaret started talking, she would tell her the whole story, eventually. "We are fairly sure what is happening but do not have proof and do not know what to do."

"I presume we are talking about Xavier." Elizabeth knew no one else except her children would upset her so much. Margaret nodded.

"He is... Anita. I know Luke is away a lot and she is probably lonely. Also they work the horses together." Elizabeth suddenly got it.

"So, Xavier is having an affair with Anita." Margaret nodded miserably. "Did you see them together?"

"Not really."

"What happens now?"

"We are just hoping that it is soon over. But what happens if she leaves Luke? This is Tim's brother. It is going to cause a big rift." Elizabeth didn't know what to say.

"Do you want me to speak to Duncan? He and Xavier are close. He may find out what they intend to do." Margaret nodded despondently. She had been so excited about Xavier's venture, and that he was starting well, but now it could all be ruined.

****

Elizabeth was putting the evening meal on the table. William always tried to get home from the hotel between five and seven, to be with his family. They were all sitting at the table. She spoke.

"Maggie was a bit perplexed about her visit to Xavier." She looked intently at Duncan. William was looking at her. Her voice was very measured. He spoke carefully.

"She loves seeing Xavier, especially now he has more horses. I would have thought that she would have been thrilled."

"Yes, initially she was, but something upset her." Elizabeth was still watching Duncan, who was concentrating on eating. William suddenly sensed something was happening. He was silent and looked at Elizabeth. Elizabeth shrugged at him and continued.

"Apparently, Xavier was distracted. So they really didn't get to spend much time together." Duncan was silent and just carried on eating. Elizabeth sighed. "Do you know why Xavier was distracted? Duncan!"

Duncan put down his knife and fork and stood up.

"I have finished. I have some studying to do. Thank you for the meal."

There was silence when he left the room. Chloe and Fabian realised something was amiss.

"What have Duncan and Xavier done?" asked Chloe.

"Nothing," said Elizabeth, starting to clear the plates. She grabbed Fabian's before he was completely finished. He was about to say something but decided against it.

William followed Elizabeth into the kitchen.

"What is going on?" he asked in a whisper.

"Maggie and Peter think that Xavier is having an affair with Anita, Luke's wife," she replied in a low voice.

"Oh," said William. He didn't know what else to say. He helped Elizabeth with the dishes then said he needed to get back to the hotel. He said he would return as soon as he could, and they kissed perfunctorily.

Meanwhile, as soon as her parents left the room, Chloe sped after Duncan. She went straight into his room without knocking and shut the door. Duncan was sitting at his desk, his accountancy books open, but he was not reading them.

"Well?" demanded Chloe.

"Well, what?"

"You know what Xavier is up to. Tell me."

Duncan shook his head. Chloe stood there, hands on hips, tapping her foot. Duncan shrugged. He suddenly didn't care; he didn't approve anyway. He pushed the books away and turned his chair.

"Xavier is carrying on with Anita."

Chloe sat down on his bed.

"Why? She is married." Chloe stood up and walked up and down, then sat down again. "Why?" she asked again.

Duncan shrugged. He didn't know what to say.

"Well, tell him to stop. He is your friend." Chloe glared at him and slammed the door as she left.

Duncan stared at the door. He had known that Xavier had lots of girlfriends. Xavier always boasted about it when he came to Devon. Duncan remembered a conversation he had had last year. Xavier was asking about Duncan's girlfriend. Duncan didn't have one at the time, so he asked about Xavier's. Xavier was more than happy to talk. He related his experiences of clubbing in London. Duncan asked what would happen if one of his 'girlfriends' ended up pregnant. Xavier laughingly reassured him that he took great care that would never happen and cited a case when he and some friends went out and met some girls. A few weeks later one of the girls turned up saying she was pregnant and that he was the father. Xavier denied it emphatically. They had slept together once and then she started to see his friend. She then found out that she was pregnant and insisted that Xavier was the father, knowing that he was a better prospect than his friend. But Xavier knew he was not the father and tried to talk to his friend, but he just laughed. Xavier stopped being his friend. Duncan was concerned and asked what happened to the girl. Xavier looked slightly embarrassed. After his boasting he did not want to tell Duncan that he had given her details of his mother's charity. He followed up to make sure she was taken care of.

Duncan sighed. He agreed with Chloe and did not approve of his relationship with Anita but could not do anything about it. He opened up his books and continued studying.

* * * * * * * *

Margaret was with Elizabeth in her lounge, looking over the garden and down to her horses.

"I wish that Luke had brought Anita back with him. I can't say I am very struck with her and don't like the idea that she and Xavier might get married." Elizabeth nodded in agreement. She had no grievance with Anita; she thought she was nice enough but did not think she was suitable for Xavier. She shrugged.

"Unfortunately, we cannot choose their partners; we can only hope that they make the right choice in the end." She reflected on the girls that Duncan had brought home. There had been only one she liked.

"I hope you are right. I hope that this... affair ends soon and he finds someone nice."

"I am glad Ron is out of hospital. It must be a relief for him to have Luke home to help at the farm."

"Yes, Susan says he is doing well."

* * * * * * *

"How did the wedding go?" asked Elizabeth. They were in her lounge this time.

"It was very nice, a small affair, but still very nice. It will be nice for Peter to have Phoebe around. Aaron and Esme are talking about moving down here now Aaron has retired. It was a shame that Ron and Colette couldn't go, but Ron was not well enough to travel to London."

"It all happened very quickly. How did they meet?"

"Yes, they got married as soon as Luke's divorce came through. Apparently Luke had already started divorce proceedings at Christmas, and it was granted quickly. It wasn't contested. Phoebe and Luke did not want to wait. Phoebe said she was getting too old to wait at 30. Phoebe and Luke had met casually over the years, when Phoebe came down. They had met at the field that Ron let me have for the horses. Sometimes he was with Tim and Ron, sometimes alone. They had always liked each other, so when he was free they decided to marry."

Elizabeth laughed and then was more serious.

"How is your father?"

"Not good. He is not responding like he should. I know that breaking a hip at his age is not good, but he doesn't seem to want to get better."

"I'm sure that's not true. Things take longer to get better when you are older. He is 80... something."

"I hope you are right."

CHAPTER 26

Chloe was anxiously looking at the door. Xavier had promised that he would come to Duncan's 21st birthday party. He had arrived back yesterday, and they had spent the morning riding at Veronica Cottage. She tried to talk to him about his break-up with Anita, but he would not say anything. When she got home, she set about questioning Duncan. He did not want to say anything at first, but under Chloe's relentless pressure, he explained.

"He broke up with Anita because she became too demanding."

"Yes…?" said Chloe encouragingly. Duncan gave in.

"Apparently, when she knew about the party, she demanded that Xavier bought her an expensive dress and matching jewellery. She said that it should only be fitting that they looked like the gentry that they were. Xavier was aghast and asked her to explain. She said that he was going to be the next Earl of Royston, and on his mother's side his great-grandfather had been the Duke of Cranley and that his cousin was now the Duke."

"Second cousin," he muttered under his breath. He was shocked. He knew one day he would be an earl but did not like to draw attention to it. It was something that everyone knew and just accepted. He was beginning to feel uncomfortable. Anita made arrangements to visit London, but when they were due to leave, he refused to go. They had an argument and that was the end of their relationship.

Chloe had bought a dress especially – usually she only wore trousers. Every time the doors of the ballroom opened, she looked up expectantly.

She missed his actual entrance. She suddenly heard his voice, looked around and spotted him by the bar. She made her way over to him.

"Ah, there you are, Chloe." She gave him a big beaming smile. He carried on talking. "Let me introduce you. This is... sorry, what is your name? We met while I was driving back from town this afternoon. She nearly ran into me. Lucky me. And I invited her to be my partner tonight."

Chloe gave a snort.

"You are an idiot," she said in a loud voice before walking away.

He did not know what to do. No one spoke to him like that except his mother. His friend was laughing at him.

"Well, I wouldn't stand for being spoken to like that." He looked at her. Suddenly he couldn't stand her. He wanted to shout her, but manners got the better of him and he just politely asked to be excused and went outside for some fresh air.

Duncan came up behind him.

"Don't worry, mate. She shouts at me like that all the time."

"She doesn't usually shout at me."

"No, you really must have upset her. What did you do?"

"I have no idea."

"Really," said his sister, who had come up behind him. "Sometimes you boys are really stupid." She flounced off. Duncan and Xavier looked at each other after watching Faye disappearing back into the hotel.

"Women," they both exclaimed together and burst out laughing.

* * * * * * *

Xavier told his mother he did not want a big party for his 21st, but he would like a dinner party with his family and the Harrisons at Royston House. He was planning a night out in London with his college friends the following week.

It was nice to have the house full, Lady Agatha said to her husband. He wasn't so sure. He liked peace and quiet, though, with all the coming and going from the stables, it was not as quiet as it used to be.

There was a big discussion over who should sleep in which room. Lady Agatha knew it would be a squeeze. Jessica and her family were given the two guest rooms in the middle of the house. In Xavier's wing, he had his room, and Margaret and Peter had their room. Marcus's room, Faye's room and the spare room in that end of the house would not accommodate them and Elizabeth and William, Duncan, Chloe and Fabian. Faye volunteered that she and Fabian have two of the three nursery rooms, then Chloe could have her room and Duncan could have the corner spare room. Marcus would give up his room to Elizabeth and William and would go to the nursery as well.

Lady Agatha had arranged for extra staff for the weekend of the party. Some were staying in the staff quarters in the house, and others were living out. Lady Agatha had not felt such excitement in the house since Hugh, Sebastian and Sonia were younger, before the war. She was enjoying herself.

Chloe was also enjoying herself. Xavier was taking her round the stables, introducing her to all the horses and the stable hands. They agreed that they would exercise some of the horses the next morning. Chloe was only slightly disappointed that Margaret and Faye appeared the next morning as well. She swiftly swung herself up in the saddle onto Princess Lavender and saw Xavier watching her. He went over to help her with her stirrups. She let him, though she did not really need help. He quickly mounted a young colt they had just broken in, Drake. Faye was mounted on Archer. Margaret mounted Misty Hill with Simon's help, and he swung himself onto his horse, Maroon Star. They led the way down the lane, followed by the other horses that needed exercise. When they returned Chloe helped rub the horses down and spent an enjoyable morning helping with the horses. She was surprised when the lunchtime gong sounded.

The afternoon was spent not so quietly at Sonia's house, with her family coming and going, her daughters and their boyfriends or husband and grandchildren.

Dinner that evening was fairly early as there was dancing later. Simon had a small band. He played guitar and sang, with a pianist and saxophonist accompanying him.

They all danced that evening. Towards the end of the evening, Simon played a slow song. The three couples, Margaret and Peter, Elizabeth and William, and Jessica and Tim were enjoying the music and moved rhythmically. Lady Agatha and Lord Julius were waltzing uneasily on unsteady feet. Chloe took a deep breath and pulled Xavier onto the makeshift dance floor. She was surprised he offered no resistance and put his arms around her, so she gently put her hands on his shoulders. The mood was broken a few minutes later by Faye and Fabian joining the dancers but in a rowdy way, pretending to dance. Simon ended the slow song and started a more lively number.

It was in the early hours of the morning that Chloe and Xavier were helping the staff clear up the last of the party. Xavier told the staff to leave, that they would clean everything else in the morning. Chloe felt strange walking up the stairs with Xavier. They opened the door to their wing and shut it behind them. Chloe was aware that her parents were sleeping in the room they crept past. She wondered why they were creeping along the passage – after all, she was legitimately going to her room – and she suddenly wanted to giggle. At her door, she paused.

"Goodnight," she said.

Xavier was suddenly aware of what was happening and became instantly self-conscious. Usually he happily kissed his girls goodnight and went away. He was not sure what do. This was a new sensation.

Chloe took charge. She quickly kissed his cheek, went into her room and firmly shut the door.

* * * * * * *

Chloe was taking care in getting ready for her party, though she wasn't even sure she wanted one. She was looking forward to it but only because one person was going to be there. All her college friends talked her into it, but she didn't really need too much persuasion. They wanted a party after studying for their degree-level certificates. She was happily welcoming guests and accepting presents, which she put to one side.

The DJ started playing music, and she was led onto the dance floor by one of her friend's brothers. They danced to a couple of songs, and then Chloe asked to be excused. He was reluctant to let her go and followed her to the bar. He bought her a drink and then followed her back to her friends. Chloe went round to thank her other guests, followed by her friend's brother. He took every opportunity to touch her as they went round the ballroom. She was beginning to get tired of him. She was also getting anxious that Xavier would not be coming.

About half 10 she began to despair that he wasn't coming. She went over to Margaret, followed by her 'lap dog'.

"Did Xavier say he was coming?" she asked.

"Yes, he was driving down today, but he hadn't arrived when we left."

"I think that is bad form, to say you are coming and then not turn up," her friend's brother said.

Chloe turned to him, her eyes flashing.

"I don't care what you think. And I am fed up with you following me around. I would like it if you left."

"No, I want to dance again with you." Beer had given him Dutch courage; usually he wouldn't argue with Chloe. He grabbed her arm, and she tried to shake it off. Suddenly they were interrupted.

"The lady does not want to dance with you. I suggest you leave as you were asked to do."

Chloe spun round, a big smile on her face and the altercation with her friend's brother forgotten.

"I was beginning to think you weren't coming." Xavier kissed his mother.

"I'm sorry I am late, but I had to wait until they finished my present for Chloe." He had rung his mother from the jewellers as he didn't want her to worry – he knew she would worry if he turned up late.

He brought out a box from his jacket. He had discussed what to get her with his mother. They decided on some earrings. Margaret offered a pair of her mother's. He specifically wanted some ruby ones and there was a small pair. He asked the jeweller in Petworth to make some changes. He wanted a diamond added.

Chloe was delighted with them and got her mother to help put them in. She enjoyed the rest of her 21st party.

* * * * * * *

Duncan and Chloe arrived at Royston Manor at the beginning of August. Chloe was going to spend the summer there to get work experience for after university. She was still undecided about what she was going to do.

Chloe was shown into the guest room at the top of the stairs. She was surprised. She thought she would be staying in the guest room in Xavier's wing. Duncan would be in the adjoining guest room for the two nights he was staying.

Xavier had first thought that Chloe would stay in the guest room in his side of the house, but Lady Agatha said that it would not be appropriate; she wanted to protect Chloe. Xavier protested that Anita had stayed in his wing after splitting from Luke. Lady Agatha agreed and said that that didn't matter, but Chloe was who mattered.

Xavier reluctantly agreed but later was fully behind the decision.

Summer passed too quickly for both of them.

* * * * * * * *

Chloe decided not to go to university as she had been offered a teaching job at the agricultural college where she had studied equine care. Holidays were spent with Xavier, Christmas he returned to Devon, but Easter and summer she went to Royston Manor.

At the end of the summer, Xavier proposed, and the wedding was arranged for the following spring.

* * * * * * *

Elizabeth and Margaret were taking a breather from the excitement of the wedding.

"They make a beautiful couple," said Elizabeth.

"They do," agreed Margaret. "So do Duncan and his fiancée."

Duncan had proposed to his girlfriend on Valentine's Day.

"Yes, we are very pleased, but it was a surprise. We did not know that they were seeing each other. They met at Xavier's 21st party. I think Athena is the prettiest of Sonia and Wolfe's daughters." Margaret nodded but wasn't sure. Yes, she was pretty, but she thought Guinevere, the youngest, was prettier. She remembered how disgruntled Duncan had been to have to go to Sonia's but had left in a better mood. Now she knew why.

They were sitting together later. Elizabeth nudged Margaret.

"We might have a love triangle to disentangle." Margaret looked where Elizabeth indicated. She saw Fabian, Faye and Olivia. She watched as Fabian basked in the adoration from Faye and Olivia, then as Faye stormed off. Margaret sighed and caught Peter's eye. He had seen the same and winked. She smiled at him then turned back to Elizabeth.

"Does Fabian know what he wants to do when he leaves school?"

"Not as such, but I think he will be running the hotel. He is so outgoing and loves to talk to people; he will be perfect. And Duncan can keep an eye on the accounts. What about Faye?"

"She still wants to be a vet."

"I hope Xavier and Chloe don't wait too long to start a family. I want to be a grandmother to the same grandchild as you. It will bring us closer."

"I don't think anything can bring us closer, but I agree,and it is nice to have no more secrets, only very special friends."

They embraced and watched their families entwining and enlarging. Elizabeth caught Peter's eye over Margaret's shoulder. He winked at her. Then her daughter caught her attention. She was laughing, trying to drag both William and Peter, one in each hand, onto the dance floor.

That is one secret I will take to the grave, she swore to herself.

Lightning Source UK Ltd.
Milton Keynes UK
UKHW010646221222
414324UK00001B/65

9 781803 813189